'Evocative in its characterisation, the SF elements of *Salt* are understated. It may be set in the future, but the reasons behind the exodus from Earth are never stated, and the time deliberately vague. The power of *Salt* quietly creeps up on you, making a convincing and powerful debut.' *SFX*

'Adam Roberts' confident debut as a science-fiction writer is a pleasure to read. The plot – planetary settlement in the far future, tech solutions to problems – unwinds with only a light dusting of clues to the bloody future just over the horizon. It's a future shaped by chloride chemistry (the title *Salt* fits like a glove), framed by politics.' *New Scientist*

'Roberts' evocation of Salt's bleak landscapes is elegant and evocative, and his narrative is knotty and sophisticated . . . neither side is blameless; the moral shading is subtler than blunt schematic didacticism; the tragedy all the deeper. *Salt* is a strong debut, and an affecting, effective novel.' *Interzone*

'*Salt,* both in its ambition and execution, invites comparison to other SF novels of high stature . . . Let there be no doubt, however, that *Salt* is a novel that succeeds on its own terms. Roberts' prose carries the weight of a serious theme, but never becomes bombastic or portentous itself. This is the work of a writer who has already found his voice, and has something meaningful to say. With *Salt*, Adam Roberts has produced the finest first novel to grace the field of science fiction in many years.' sfsite.com.

'Adam Roberts' brilliantly written tale of the colonisation of the planet Salt has all the hallmarks of a writer with many years experience. Where do these accomplished debut writers come from?' *Starlog*

'Salt is a compelling tale . . . this narrative describes one of the darkest human fates Science Fiction has yet produced.' *Starburst*

Also by Adam Roberts in Gollancz

ON

Salt

Adam Roberts

The right of Adam Roberts to be identified as the author
of this work has been asserted by him in accordance with the
Copyright, Designs and Patents Act 1988.

This edition published in Great Britain in 2001 by

Gollancz
An imprint of the Orion Publishing Group
Orion House, 5 Upper St Martin's Lane
London WC2H 9EA

A CIP catalogue record for this book
is available from the British Library

ISBN 1 85798 787 X

Printed in Great Britain by
Clays Ltd, St Ives plc

I would like to thank the following people: Steve Calcutt and the Anubis Agency; Simon Spanton; Malcolm Edwards; Tony Atkins; Katharine Scarfe-Beckett; Angela Bloor; Sara Salih; Oisin Murphy-Lawless

This book is for Sarah.

De Morgan

Salt Ice

Salt Ice

SEBESTYEN

Als

Arady's
(Parsa)

Convento

Smith

GREAT DESERT

Barlei Dyke

Senaar

Eleupolis

Yared

Galilee

New Florence

Lantern

Babulonis

1

Voyage

Petja

Salt is crystal compounded of Sodium and Chlorine; faceted and transparent. Simple and pure. What life could there be without salt? It is known as God's diamond, by which we should be aware of the infinite variability of scale for the divine perspective. This tiny fragment of halite, it is a dot, an atom; but to God it can never be lost, it can never be overlooked or unnumbered. Every grain is a landscape, a world. It is a great cliff, a diamond as big as a mountain, a massive cube of ice. In it are embedded woolly mammoths, grimacing men in hides and skins, buildings, cars, trees, all at angles to one another. The surface of the world is a sheet, smooth as polished plastic, plain as glass.

And salt combines the good and the evil, yin and yang, God and the Devil. Take sodium, which is the savour of life. Without corporeal sodium the body could not hold water in its tissues. Lack of sodium will lead to death. Our blood is a soup of sodium. And here is the metal, so soft you can deform it between your fingers like wax; it is white and pearl, like the moon on a pure night. Throw it in water, and it feeds greedily upon the waves; it gobbles the oxygen, and liberates the hydrogen with such force that it will flame up and burn. Sodium is what stars are made of. Sodium is the metal, curved into rococo forms, that caps the headpiece and arms of God's own throne.

1

But here is chlorine, green and gaseous and noxious as Hell's own fumes. It bleaches, burns, chokes, kills. It is heavier than air and sinks, bulging downwards towards the Hell it came from. And here are we, you and me, poised between Heaven and Hell. We are salty.

We had been travelling for thirty-seven years. Not counting the eighteen months it took us to assemble in Earth orbit, and accelerate slowly with displacement rockets on a capture orbit to grab our comet. Nor the two weeks we spent grappling with that steaming ice-world; to fix our tether (my primary area of expertise); to set up burners in a zodiacal circuit around the central cable, and then to settle our final orientation with thrust-explosives. Then, pointed in the right direction, we began to speed up. Our comet, fuel and buffer, building speed slowly. Us, strung out along the cable behind, eleven little homes like seashells on a child's necklace-string. Do you know how long it took us to reach travelling speed? At accelerations of over 1.1g, we accelerated for over a year. A year of gravity, when there could be no hibernation; a year awake, crammed in with our sisters and brothers, our children, our friends and enemies, our lovers and ex-lovers. A year of feeling trapped and heavy, of smelling sweat and shit; of eating recycled food. A year of games, and talk, and medita-tion, and nothing to do and nothing to be done but hope our comet would lead us on to the brave new world.

And worry, of course, because there are many things that can go wrong. The comet can fracture, break apart like a gemstone under a hammer. No matter how expertly the tether is fixed, there can be flaws that it irritates, and that eventually shake it loose under the pressure of acceleration. And if that happens (I have seen visuals) then the whole ice-worldling simply bursts, breaks up like a blizzard of paper, like a storm of – well, salt. Then, if the acceleration has not built up too great a speed, you must use your precious fuel to slow down, to turn about, and return home at the slow, slow pace of the displacement rockets; which can take years. Twelve years, one recorded case. And if the acceleration has gone too far, if you are travelling at too great a fraction of c, then there is nothing to be done.

You would burn all your fuel trying to slow; you are in the blackness, in the nothingness. No comets to grab, to fuel a homeward trip. The best thing is to settle down, go to sleep, let the ships trundle onwards, hope that you will last the fifty years, or the hundred years, or the thousand years it will take to reach your destination without full speed. You won't, of course. You will go mad. Or, without a comet buffer, you will be battered to shreds yourself by the detritus of deep space. The mites, the specks. Even a speck can kill at fractions of c. This is another reason why we hide behind big lumps of ice-rock on our journey, to clear a pathway.

Sometimes a comet meets too large an obstacle. That happens, we suppose, but if it does who will survive to tell the history? Ships get lost. Some ships may be lost that we, knowing no better, assume are well. We think they have arrived at their destination, and have beamed a message the twenty light-years backwards to say so. And for those twenty years we think hopefully, we assume the best. But when no message comes, and no message comes after twenty-five years, or thirty years, we begin to doubt. Are they still travelling, slowed by some calamity? Or did their passage bump, at .7 c, into a medium-sized lump? Some effective barrier that happened to be in the way? Cosmic mine, laid by God. Think of the impact, the hugeness of the force. Even with our ships strung out the best part of a kilometre behind the buffer, the results would be catastrophic.

We are so fragile. We dissolve in immensity like salt in water. Ah, but I mustn't strain the analogy.

Shall I tell you the intimacy of living during the year of acceleration? The constant presence of other people, the lack of privacy such that privacy became a distantly remembered concept. People shat whilst nearby other people chewed their mid-morning meal, too bored even to glance. Lovers would copulate and within spitting distance an old man and an old woman would be bitterly arguing, oblivious. The sickly artificial lighting clicked on at dawn with a brutal suddenness; clicked off at dusk like hope being snuffed out. The dark would be filled with grunts, farts, sniffles, coughs. The murmuring of people still talking, but without the energy of a normal nightlife, because we were in the darkest of nights, the night-time of the interstellar hollow. To speak loudly, to sing or dance, seemed somehow impertinent in that dark and all that could be heard was the muttering of people talking to themselves in madness or despair. Curious, how the murmuring of someone in conversation, even if the interlocutor is only silently listening, is so distinct from the mutter of the solitary person. Shall I tell you what struck me the most during the first months? How bad people's skin became. We took supplements, vitamin, mineral, but nonetheless people's complexions faded and became pustulous. Blotches and spots, all manner of carbuncles and rashes. A beautiful woman, my lover before embarkation, developed great cold sores all about her lips, the same lips I had used to kiss with such passionate pleasure. Like decaying constellations in the sky, a ring of red, angry-looking sores, all about her lips. Like a mockery of her beautiful, kissing mouth; like a satire on the human desire to kiss with the mouth. But she was not alone. We all got spotty, we all felt our skin grow dry, and sore, and we all broke out. I did not dare go near a mirror; I did not dare. I was too scared to see how my own elegant features had been disfigured. People have always said I am a fastidious man; a few have been bold enough to call me vain. Perhaps I am vain, and maybe that year was a mortification for my vanity. God's movement is mysterious, like the motion of a dance we do not understand.

We sweated, and our clothes stank. Nobody could be bothered with washing their clothes, for all that we spent all our time in bored yearning for something to do. We all shat in the communal vat, where the machines would process our waste and give us blocks for re-eating. Am I revolting you? Perhaps I am revolting you. But you must understand how life lost its savour. The vending restaurants added salt to everything, but the salt did not add savour to our living. The light hurt our eyes, and eventually our sight dulled under the fluorescence. Everything became faded. Friendships faded, love faded, memory faded. We woke with the clicking-on of the great lights, and went about our business yawning and scratching, working from habit and not from conviction. We could barely stay awake

4

during the day, so wearisome the routine seemed. And then at night, the lights would blink out, leaving only a dying afterglow in the panels; and then it would be black, the blackness of the spaces between the stars. Human beings need some comfort to remain in the darkness, some sense of faint luminescence, a skinny moon behind dark clouds; in the total dark we find it too hard to settle. We could not sleep; we would lie awake and mutter to one another.

The floor was strewn with rubbish. No matter how many cleaning details I was assigned, there always seemed to be more rubbish. We were infested with lice. Nobody knew where they came from. All passengers, objects and effects had supposedly been sterilised; all cargoes had been stored in the out-bins, and had therefore been awash with space radiation which, surely, should have sterilised the contents anew. But the lice eggs came from somewhere, and then we were all infested. Other ships avoided the plague, but that only made us bitterer, made us feel unfairly singled-out for suffering. But where had they come from? Some people said they had been left by the workmen who constructed the ship in orbit. Some said (this was more fanciful) that the lice eggs were frozen in the comet itself, because we ran a line from the comet to our ship for water. A stupid story, this, since the sludge coming down from the comet was decontaminated thoroughly before being released into the general ship reservoir. But for some reason the story stuck; rumour is more tenacious than common sense. I suppose people liked the idea that they had been infested with space-lice, some prehistoric alien species caught in the ice-tomb of the comet, to be thawed out to feed on our blood. We shaved our heads, and applied a hastily improvised antiseptic washing soda to our scalps: it was a white, flaky solid, that we had to rub over our bald skulls with the palms of our hands. I remember, on one cleaning rota, gathering up so much discarded human hair that the machine clogged.

Shall I tell you what the rate of suicide was during the year of acceleration? Three people killed themselves within a month, but that probably had more to do with anxiety and distress at the departure than cabin craziness. By the six month mark there had been seven suicides, and another twelve attempts. Most took poisonous amounts of standard ship's chemicals. In the seventh month somebody stole a shuttle. We only had twelve shuttles, and they were precious to us, for without them we could not service our ship. Have you ever watched birds? We had birds, of course, as part of our ark, but they were desperate creatures, hurling at the walls and shearing away with a blurring of wings, trapped in the cage that was our ship. They were not the angels we had hoped, they were machines for producing slimy shit and messing our home. But when you watched them, you saw how fastidious they were, how they carefully preened themselves. How they would caress each feather in turn with their beaks, paying the closest attention to their plumage, because unless it stays in the best condition they cannot fly. And so it was with us, for we too were flying creatures, flying onwards without air. The most popular work detail was the shuttle detail, because it gave the illusion of escape. To leave the ship, even if only to travel a few metres. And then to preen, to check the surface of the ship, to test the cable, to travel with news and trading supplies up the cable or down the cable to the neighbouring ships. How we prized the shuttle detail! I do believe there was corrupt practice to obtain the postings, that there was bribery and illicit sexual compacts. The detail became like a currency with us, like money. And why? I had travelled through each of the eleven ships, travelled extensively through them as they were constructed and augmented in orbit. We all had. The ship above us, the *Senaar*, was in most respects exactly the same as ours; the ship down the cable, the *Babulonis*, was the same again. The people were the same people, the people we had sought to avoid before the journey. But how small becomes the human mind; we reached that stage where a trip up the cable to drink tepid vodjaa with some Senaarians seemed to be almost a journey to Mount Zion to glimpse the Promised Land.

But this one woman, and I remember her name was Katarinya, she obtained the shuttle detail. And at the air lock she disabled her partner for the detail with a knife (it was quite a deep cut, I remember, and of course it did not heal for many many months; in

6

that air, cuts refused to heal). So she took out the shuttle, and burnt out the engines flying downcable. Watch the visual of the escapade, and you'll see the engines flare, and flare too brightly, and then suddenly burst with light and die. Overplayed the engines, but she did it deliberately. She swept down the cable, and overshot the two ships dangling there, and then she clipped the ore-anchor at the cable-end. A silent collision, a crumpling of the craft, and a glitter as the innards spilt. Now, some said she had not intended to crash into the ore-anchor and die so spectacularly; they said she had gone crazy for a child left behind, that she had been making a nuisance of herself with calls to the captains of the other ships in an attempt to have the mission reversed. But there was no reverse, and (they say) she went cabin crazy and stole the shuttle to fly back home, but she overworked the engines and they blew and so she crashed. She would have needed craziness, because the trip would have been death, even without the ore-anchor getting in the way. We were seven months away, at an average of .36 c. You work out the distance. And how much air and water is there in a shuttle?

But she was merely the most spectacular of the suicides. How hungry we were for news! And yet how quickly we tired of this, the most markworthy thing to happen all voyage. How tired we were of the news, and yet how we carried on talking it through. Going through the woman's history, her family, her motives. And me? Shall I tell you (but you must not think me cold-hearted) that my worst fears were for the ore-anchor? But I had tethered that ore, I had worked for weeks to balance out the separate components of ore so that no part of it was more massy than another; the melding of minerals rare in the destination system; plus a mass of prefab bucky. And then, behind it, we hung the oxygen: 750,000 tonnes of frozen oxygen, mined from the Jovian system, and held in place with a network of architectonic cables. She could have broken everything clean away. What an inconvenience that would have been! But the ore-anchor held firm.

Whatever others say, I know Katarinya intended to collide with the ore-anchor. That was her way. She could not abide the slowness and the waiting; she had to have fireworks. We should be grateful, and I am, that she decided not to fly upcable, and to bash into the much more friable comet. That way, we could all have joined her in death.

After that there was a craze for suicides; the topic was hot, and with everybody talking about it and there being nothing else to talk about, it rose to the status of obsession with some. And if you think of nothing but one thing for days and for nights, there will come the time when you must try that thing. People stabbed, and swallowed, and tried to climb to use the 1.1g to pull them from tower-tops to their death. A dozen died, and many more were wounded. And in that air, in that foetid closeness, cuts and wounds healed poorly if at all. We held an extraordinary small meeting (as if we were hierarchs), and the particular technicians (myself, and the thruster-woman who was called Tatja, and the three geophysicists and land-maintenance people) convened a commune panel to weather the storm of so much self-harm. Some tried to encourage group panels, assemblies of people to talk and play; some tried setting up football matches. And, to be safe, we denied shuttle duty to all but ourselves, which was not popular. There was talk. They said that I did so because my name had not come up on the rota before – as it had not. But I had no respect for that rota, on account of the way it had been abused, with favours and promises traded to those notified of duty to pass it over silently to others.

It was this way that I took my first shuttle duty, and flew upcable to dock with the *Senaar*, with messages and what they call 'tradeables'; mostly it was cages of birds and bird-meat, because the *Senaar* had not brought birds. And it was on this occasion that I first met the Captain Barlei. I think, indeed, that he and I had spoken once or twice whilst the ships were assembled but when I had liaised with the *Senaar*'s tether-person at the beginning of the voyage, there had been a different captain then. Understand the *Senaar*, where they live by the hierarchy and they passed their acceleration time with politics and intrigues. The captain that had been before was called, I think, Tyrian, or Turian but he was dead when I flew upcable that time.

They washed me in their airlock soda-shower and then gave me paper clothes and invited me through to talk. And they gave me a glass of lukewarm vodjaa, except that it was barely a glass, hardly a thimble. And they sat and crowded about me, with all their uniforms and rank-insignia, that meant little to me, except that it made it difficult for me to know to whom to talk. And Barlei was there, and introduced himself. Oh yes, I met him. He was a flabby man, but his clothes refused to recognise the fact and pinched at his flappy throat, and squeezed his fluid belly. Accordingly, his face was grape-coloured, and his eyes bulged forward out of his face. But he had played their game, whatever their game was, and risen to the top of the hierarchy, and Tyrian, Turian, was no more.

Of course, all they wanted to know about was the death of Katarinya. Every ship had cast eyes upon it, naturally. It was the event of the voyage. But where another ship might have poured us cold vodjaa, or whatever their drink, with the liberality of the wake, and wept with us, and laughed with us, and swapped stories of the dangers of cabin craziness – where another ship would have done this, the *Senaar* did not. The staff officers all sipped their drinks, and scowled and put the thimbles down on the table as if they were unpleasant things, and then Barlei began talking with a rasping voice about the dangers to the voyage that our ship had brought with it.

'Cabin craziness is indeed a dangerous thing, Captain,' I agreed.

And he replied but did not, as I had done, address me by any title or name. This, according to his own schema, was a bad error although it could hardly bother me. He said, 'We must take precautions to safeguard the voyage as a whole. What if this person had flown upcable? What terrible damage could have been done then?'

I had thought this myself, of course, but I said (because this is how the game must be played on *Senaar*), 'You misunderstand the case. This Katarinya was sick, homesick. She had left a baby girl with a partner who refused to join the voyage. She lost her mind over this baby and thought to rejoin it. But she was a poor pilot and burnt out the engines, and so she crashed.' There was an awkward silence, and

9

the staff officers looked at me. So I said, 'You may replay the visuals to see for yourself.'

'Our problem, Technician Petja, is . . .' began one of the officers but he was clearly a junior one, because another broke in upon him.

'It is clearly a matter of discipline, is it not? It is inconceivable that one of ours would do such damage with a shuttle.'

'Is there no cabin craziness with you?' I asked, in mockery. But they have no such irony in *Senaar*, and shook their heads with serious expressions. 'I am indeed impressed.'

'You can follow our way,' said the officer. 'You can begin to train your people as we are trained.'

This was an insult, and nothing less. So I drained my vodjaa in one gulp and stood to leave. But the Captain, Barlei, held up his hands to usher me down again. 'Must we quarrel, Technician?' he growled. 'Can we not remain allies and friends? You understand our concern. It is not for ourselves, but for the voyage as a whole.'

'We have convened commune meetings, and . . . adjusted the shuttle rota,' I said. 'There will be no further jeopardy to the voyage from us.'

'Sit down, please, Technician,' he said. I sat then, but it was not the right thing to do. He nodded, and said, 'We think it would help the voyage if your commune of command were made permanent.'

'Permanent?'

'A full-time body, charged with the duties of governance.' He began, at this, to lecture me on the *Senaar*ian way, of politics and hierarchies, and I grew offended and spat on the floor.

He pretended hurt at this, and said, 'Can we not even offer you advice?'

'To recast us in your image? I think not.'

'Surely we are already part of the same federation? Surely we will all be living on the same world? Surely,' (he said this last with a wheedling voice) 'surely we all serve the same God?'

I stood up again, and left. As I made my way back to the airlock in my ridiculous paper clothes, Barlei came after me, with all his junior officers scurrying after. He said, 'Before the voyage began, we saw a free and fair interchange between our ships. Many of your people came and visited *Senaar*, and many of ours spent time upon the *Als*.'

I stopped here, because I was uncertain what he meant.

But then he said, 'I believe several of my men' (note possessive!) 'fathered children aboard the *Als*.' His voice was sterner now.

'That,' I said, 'is a matter for the mothers. The child begins life with the mother, of course.'

'The child *belongs*,' he said, stressing the possessive word, 'to the family of the child. And the father is a part of the family.' It was in this way that the whole question of the children of Senaarians was inaugurated between us.

As I piloted the shuttle downcable with a parcel of software and some 'traded' foodstuffs, I thought little of this. I decided that we faced only five months of acceleration and then we would be cruising; these worries would fade away as we entered our trances. But this thing about the children, this was a seed planted.

The craze for suicides burnt itself out, of course. As we neared the end of acceleration people became distracted by the possibilities of trance. We disbanded the commune, and society returned to normal. And finally we were travelling at the cruising speed. Our gravity dribbled away as the accelerators petered out; we walked with larger and larger strides. We jumped higher and higher. And now spirits were high, because we felt as if the back of the journey had been broken.

When you go from full gravity to no gravity your blood pressure rises. You feel heavy-headed. But after a day or two the pressure comes back down, and then you are ready for trance. This is what you must do: you climb into a suit that pumps a cream in at the neck and out at the left foot, because you will be suspended for decades and you must keep the skin and upper derma softened and supplied with nutrient or you will age. Then you inject another pipe into the carotid, that allows the passage of a soup of hyper-oxygenated molecules contained in a nutrient fluid into and out of your blood stream. Now, these molecules are micro-crafted, and release oxygen slowly during their time in your body; passing through a slow filter they will spend a few months in your bloodstream, and will keep all muscles and tissues supplied with oxygen, just as the medium in which they move will allow cells the energy to function. The final thing, before the mask goes over the face, is the pneumelectrics in the suit; these will slowly build muscle resistance in a long stretch, like a cat stretches but extended over days, and then a slackening, and then the stretch again – every muscle in your body, in sequence – over and over, for the length of your time. Because your muscles must not sleep, or they will waste. Now it is time, and the trance technician pulls the mask over your face, and you feel the slow seep of the cream, like a sludge, up your chin and over your nose, your cheeks, your forehead. And now you take the tablet, which you have kept under your tongue (or swallowed immediately, depending on your preference), and you let it go down your throat.

Some people say they do not like the onset of trance, and indeed, some people do panic when they can no longer breathe, or earlier even, when the mask covers the eyes and they can no longer see. But I have always found it the most delicious of sensations. The tablet takes effect slowly, and you drift away, but it is the most relaxing feeling, the abandonment of everything. You do not need to move, the suit is stretching your muscles slowly, with an infinite care and the most sensuous precision. You do not even have to bother with the slow drawing of breath – have you ever stopped to consider how wearying it is to have to draw breath, every second, awake or sleep, for the whole of your life? With the muddling in the head of the tablet, like the finest vodjaa, it is a relief to abandon the breathing. Everything slips. Consciousness dissolves.

A wave lifts, c-curves and falls against the infinite beach with a perfect sound of white-noise. Another.

Another.

The tablet encourages you to fall asleep, of course, but you do not sleep through the thirty-six years of trance. Other ships practise that form of medically-induced coma, as perhaps you know, but not us. Lock a body in a box and put it into coma. Startle it awake at the end

12

of the process. The problem with such techniques is the mortality percentage. Depending on which technique you use, this can reach as high as twelve per cent. This represents too great a toll on the whole crew. Worse than this, it turns hibernation into a death lottery. Would you go to sleep knowing that there was a one in ten chance you would not awake?

Mortality rates for trance are much, much lower. On our voyage, our ship lost only two people in trance. Because it is not a coma, consciousness is never really lost but it does enter the weird world of sensory deprivation. There is not even a heartbeat by which to orient yourself, not even the heaving of the chest with breath. The mind does not exactly go out, but neither does it exactly stay switched on.

Shall I tell you what it feels like? To begin with, it is simply like falling asleep in the comfortable darkness. It is being a child again. And, at some stage (although it is difficult to say when) you wake up and it is still dark, and dreams are bothering you at the margins of your thoughts. And you sleep again, or wake again, but your mind is not settled. It processes the thoughts and the memories, and puts them together in odd ways, and stores them away. You sleep again, or you wake again, or one of the two. But you are dreaming less and less and memories bother you less and less. You are nowhere, you are nothing. Nirvana. There is no distant roar of engines to capture your senses; no tug of gravity to force your mind to constantly orient itself. No breath, no heartbeat. There is no sense of time. Moments of darkness and quiet exist, they blend seamlessly together in the mind, and who knows how many years exist between each one? Only the slow, slow rhythm of the stretch, the cat-like stretch of your body, and then relax. But although this happens so slowly it takes days, it becomes what your breathing used to be. A peaceful, background thing; and soon you cease to notice it.

But then, the body begins slowly to convulse, a jagged awkward sensation, and you become aware of waking up, and it is an unpleasant itch, a crotchet. Then you are handled, and the mask comes away, and the dim lights hurt your eyes. So you cough, and blink; you retch up the fluid in your lungs; you take a shower to wash the slime from your skin, and you dress yourself, and float out.

You have been in a trance for twelve years; you feel as though you have slept but a single night. And now it is time for your six months of ship duty. Maintenance, shuttle duties, in weightlessness; sitting around with your half-dozen other awake colleagues. You play, you copulate, you work, you exercise your stiff body in elastic harnesses to simulate gravity, and you know a boredom that trance had made you believe was impossible. But your detail is over eventually, you can climb back into the suit, and return to the trance.

Another wave slowly ascends, bends, breaks on the red sands. Another.

Another.

Then time has dissolved altogether.

In zero-gravity, and supplied with moisture, the body ages barely one year for ten. In the dark, the mind rests.

I put my name to the documentation for the voyage at the age of thirty-one; I was seventy-two by the time of our arrival at Salt, but at the same time I was not even forty.

We covered the distance between worlds at .7 c, which meant a long period of deceleration at the journey's end. But for this arrival year we were all awake, and full of excitement. So we connected computers, and burnt our thrusters to turn the whole fleet one-eighty degrees, and, with the comet behind us now, we reignited the burners and began to slow. Deceleration pressed us against our ship floors with .2 g at first, which was hard enough on our soggy bones, but we began to recover, and week by week we increased the deceleration thrust, and the gravity climbed, and the hard torchlight of our new sun, silver-bright, was visible clearly.

Barlei

The planet we know today as Salt was originally designated Nebel 2. Naturally, this was only ever going to be a temporary identification, an astronomer's tag, and it would not serve as the name of a homeworld, but I still regret the name that has superseded it. It strikes me that it concentrates unduly on the negative, the bleaker features of our planet, and therefore it contributes – subtly, but surely undeniably – to a lowering of morale. My own suggestion to the fleet panel was *Keseph*: the word is the Hebrew for 'silver', and reflects the appearance of the world from space. The white-silver shine of the planet, in the gleam of Nebel's whiter-than-sol light. Silver is also precious, which might encourage inhabitants to value the splendour of the world God made, and made (let us not forget) for all of us. Exodus 26:19 tells us that the sockets of the pillars in God's tabernacle were made of silver; and in Zechariah 6:11 the holy crown is made of silver. All this, and other examples, suggest to me the Divine blessing that silver carries with it. But *Keseph* has not gained popular currency, and so I must talk of *Salt*.

Salt is a planet with a gravity of a little over .8 g. It has no moons, or rings, or other associated phenomena. Indeed, the Nebel system possesses rather fewer of the standard requirements as specified by Paulo's Law. It has only three planets, one in a close orbit, one at almost exactly one astronomical unit, and one gas giant on a very wide and slightly elliptical orbit. The gas giant, an argon world clearly visible in the night sky, is known as *Hadros*, the Greek for unicorn, although the name strikes me as unnecessarily fanciful.

Clearly, according to Paulo's Law, the absence of sufficient and deep enough gravity wells to attract away stray asteroids and cometoids should have resulted in the relentless bombardment of Salt, and the pulverisation of all life upon that world. There is, our scientists tell me, a certain amount of evidence that Salt has been extensively bombarded, but the tenacity and complexity of vegetative life suggests that it has been several millennia since the last major impact. The system is strewn with a large number of small orbiting bodies, comets and meteors, it is true but most of them follow a wide orbit at several degrees from the elliptic. We were concerned, at original settlement, that asteroid bombardment might pose a serious threat to life, and even went so far as to plan Senaarian orbital defences to try and screen the larger bodies (which we have never built, what with their expense). But since settlement, meteor falls have been relatively rare.

We have transmitted this information back to Earth, as is proper; but it is twenty-five years before they receive any transmission, and another twenty-five before any reply might be picked out of the infinite night. At such distance we do as other colonies have done, as is the right and proper and holy thing: we dissociate ourselves from Earth. You are young and have never known that world, and it means little to you, although I understand there are organisations of youths in other cities who define themselves as Earth-patriots. But even for those of us born on Earth it is difficult to feel the connection in the heart. We are a new world, a new beginning. The dawn cannot be always concerned with the moon at midnight.

The trouble at settlement began much earlier, of course, before any plans for asteroid defences were mooted, and it is my duty, I suppose, to trace the pedigree of this war right back to the long voyage, and even before. I take no pleasure in this. Nor do I have even the littlest desire to occupy this time, these files, only to justify myself and my own actions. Everything I have done has been done for the good of my people. For my community, my tribe. For this nation and its dedication to God. History, they say, is more than a chronicle. A history empty of justification, of politics and belief, is a blind history.

Perhaps the best way to start is to try and explain the sense of harmony, of the necessary balance between order and freedom, that prevailed upon the *Senaar* during the voyage, and which has prevailed within Senaar since we arrived at Salt – to explain it with an analogy from music. I love music. Music is the great passion of my people. It requires discipline, application, hard work and self-denial to master the skills of the keyboard, my own instrument of choice.

But once you begin to achieve that mastery, the playing grants you freedom beyond the possible dreams of Alsists. In the same way, the music itself contains the tension, between the rigidity of the notes themselves, each one precise in its evocation of a certain tone, and the tumbling freedom of their combination; between the path you must follow that was set out by the Master Composer, and from which you must not deviate (who would dare 'improve' the writing of a Beethoven, a Bach?), and the channel you must find to express yourself, your own individuality, and without which music might as well exist only on computer disk. A nation is a composition, a sonata in people. It must possess harmony or it is nothing. So, to me, this history of my people, this narrative I bequeath to you all, is a sort of symphonic poem, a major-key hymn to the energy and achievements of our people.

Before I begin the narrative, I must add one further thing, in answer to the slanders that have come from the Alsists. It is true, I concede, that we packed needleguns from the very beginning. But to assert that this in some manner contradicted the terms of the accord all ships signed before committing themselves to the project is absurd, and propagandist. The accord allowed each prospective settlement to make provision for its own self-sufficiency (although it was expressly stated that settlements can expect any and all reasonable support from other settlements – something ignored, or perhaps flouted, by the Alsists); and self-sufficiency, clearly, includes self-defence. Neither did we 'hide' the fact that our cargo included needleguns, as they claim. To say 'hide' suggests a deliberate attempt to mislead, but are we truly bound to itemise every single piece of cargo? Surely that is contrary to the spirit, and the reality, of organising so large a project. Besides, any objections voiced by the Alsists to needleguns are voided by the fact that they stole (mark the breakage of divine commandment!) a whole bartel of our guns at the earliest opportunity upon landing, and have since duplicated many more. Clearly they have no principled objections to the use of such guns. Too many of my people, some of whom I considered members of my family, have died at their hands, let us not forget.

I cannot forget.

Representatives from all eleven communities met, and all satisfied the Convention and Allied legal establishment that we could live in peace together. It is no small undertaking, to travel to another star, to make home upon another world. At this early stage in the pre-voyage, spectrographic [*intertext has no index-connection for a%x '1895spec-trographic' suggest consult alternate database, e.g. orig. science*] data suggested there was more water on Salt than in fact there is (and, the logic went, where there is water there is abundance and plenty). Accordingly, it seemed likely that we would be able harmoniously to share the planet between us, to build another outpost of Zion in the skies. Pre-voyage negotiations were accordingly smooth.

I met Petja Szerelem twice before the voyage actually began. At this time I had not risen to the rank of Captain, and was an over-lieutenant in the ship's crew. As such it was my duty to liaise with the command officers in the other thirteen ships, to set up channels of communication should we need them during the voyage. In most cases this was straightforward: *New Florence* and *Eleupolis* were similar enough to our own. And my stays aboard *Yared* and *Smith IV* were particularly stimulating and pleasant. But no ship was as awkward as the *Als*. To begin with, I had dealings with a woman called Marta Cserepes, but she had no official standing, because (of course) the Alsists have no concept of officialdom, or government, or anything else. This Cserepes had been assigned the job of liaising with other ships in a work rota allotted by a computer program that could not (amazing!) be rewritten without destroying all its files. There was so little flexibility in this arrangement that, midway through my initial connection, the Cserepes was assigned on some other task, some menial cleaning chore in all likelihood. I was presented with another liaison officer, whose name I forget. But I took action. I approached Szerelem, who was at that time chief technician. He had been voted by all the ships as best qualified to supervise the tethering operation, making certain that we were all securely attached to our comet. It seemed to me that, as the most eminent, or at least, the most famous among the Alsists (of course, we didn't think of them as a nation at that time, but it is convenient to use the present terminology), he should assume the mantle of command, at least for the duration of the voyage. It seemed to me then, as now, that the rigours of deep space require a firm hand, a structure of command; and that if anarchy were so precious to these people, then they could reinstate it in their own kingdom when we arrived at our destination. I explained this to him, cordially. But he frowned, like a child.

'I cannot comprehend,' he said, with his clogging accent.

He was then much younger, a small man, rather too dapper for my own notions of manhood. He wore the peculiar accumulation of thin clothes, many ripped and dirty, layer piled on layer that is so characteristic of Alsists (of course we offered him some disposable clothes after he showered). But at least his face was washed and his hair clean and cut (unusual amongst them, I believe). His face was narrow, and his nose came down like a ship's anchor, straight and clearly defined. The lines running down to the corners of his mouth, those lines that divide the upper lip from the rest of the face (what are they called?) were very deep and pronounced. But his eyes were a woman's eyes, soft and blue; they had none of the steel of true leadership, the blue I am confident I shall see when I look into God's own eyes at the day of my death. Still, I found his attitude bewildering, and possibly he was insulting me, in that serpentine, awkward manner of Alsists, who take such perverted delight in bending language, in laughing secretly at you, behind their teeth.

'I cannot comprehend,' he said, with his sneering voice, but I was, then, a diplomat and I said nothing. Only smiled.

'But surely,' I pointed out, 'as a scientist, you understand the importance of order in any organism. There cannot be such a thing as a chaotic organism; it is a contradiction in terms. Surely you can see that together we will form a huge organism, tied together on the umbilicus?'

But I was wasting my speech. He lectured me a little on the 'freedom' those people profess, on the incapability of human governance, of the need to abdicate all such political structures, to trust the primacy of the individual (he said the word 'political' as if it

19

were some mild blasphemy). There was more in the same vein, but of course we know that their professed theology of abdication is only a licence to allow themselves any and every immorality.

Whilst the ships were being constructed, there was a certain amount of fraternisation between peoples. Some ships (*William de Morgan, Grey Lantern* and *Crow* I remember) imposed curfews and denied access to all but essential crew. Usually such quarantine was for religious reasons, and as such we respected it. But the *Als* had no restrictions at all. Many people came and went, many of our people included. Now, the immorality we all associate with Alsists has a particular sexual component. Many of our men were tempted, and many fell.

This is evidently an awkward matter and whilst it must be faced, as the egg out of which all that destruction hatched, I have no wish to dwell upon the specifics of so sordid an affair.

Unlike most civilised society, the people aboard the *Als* deny contraception to the men. The men have access to none of the divinely sanctioned forms of birth-control. Instead, contraception is completely the business of the woman; she need not even tell the man whether she has decided to conceive a child or not, nor would an Alsist dream of asking such a question. Fathers have no rights. We might remember that human beings have no 'rights' as such in Alsist anarchy, and these two facts cannot be unrelated. But, however repelled we may be by the behaviour of some of our people, the point is that there was a misunderstanding between a number of my crew members and women on the *Als*. As a result, there were a number of pregnancies.

This occasioned my second visit to the ship, a few weeks before final launch. I spoke with several technical members of the crew in an attempt to reclaim these children as ours: according to all rules of law, the fathers have rights equal to the rights of the mothers. Several possibilities existed; we were prepared to offer homes on *Senaar* to the mothers, or even to set up reciprocal arrangements such that fathers could visit. But nobody would meet my diplomatic mission on any official level. Wherever I went on *Als* I was met with blank faces, non-comprehension. Not only did they seem certain that children belong only to the mother until puberty (after which time, it seems, they belong to nobody), but they seemed incapable of understanding that their perspective was anomalous, or even unusual. I argued over and again the rights of fathers, of families (for what is a tribe if not a family written large?), but nobody would listen. Or, to be exact, they would listen, but they would not *hear*. And here is another habit of the Alsists that demonstrates their lack of civilisation. When you engage them in conversation they will listen, with their head tilted slightly, and answer, but only if they are immediately interested. If they are bored, even bored a little bit, then they will simply walk away, without so much as a polite goodbye. I encountered this rudeness many times.

The business with the children was a great scandal at home, and it was only the fact that we were underway, chasing our comet (with all the hurry and business associated with that) that crowded it out of our minds. The timing was unfortunate. Once we were underway, all personnel were recalled to *Senaar* and contact with the children was lost. I sometimes think to myself that had we struck then, early, and recovered the children before the voyage, the current state of affairs need never have happened. But there was nothing to do. We caught our comet, and soon we were away, leaving the system of our birth for our new world.

The year-long acceleration is a difficult time. There is little work that is necessary, and too easily idle minds will brood on injustice. So it was with the business of the children. The officers (there were some) who had fathered these boys and girls were disgraced, of course; but they were still part of the crew. The most senior was the under-Captain, who was reduced to Major; and I was promoted to under-Captain myself. Most of the fathers were military men, some were civilians and technicians. They banded together, would meet after chapel and at other odd moments and grieve together. Many sympathised with them. It was in large part the environment of the ship during acceleration, the close confinement and the ensuing nearclaustrophobia, that encouraged this dissolute thinking. Perhaps it was also the closeness of the scandal to high command. I had known under-Captain Beltane personally, and had once respected him. But his wife had recently died, and some Alsist woman had worked her sensual spell upon him. It was as if his career meant nothing.

This was a time when people were combustible, and with such a spark, something approaching a scandal, matters could easily have got out of hand. It was a time that required strong leadership, an immediate example. But Captain Tyrian was a brooding man, a difficult individual. And this was a troubling time. He could only see the betrayal of his men; he could not see the larger issues.

As under-Captain I attempted to settle the people. I organised sporting and musical competitions. Chapel choirs competed for a silver cup. There were individual piano recitals. A football league, consisting of seven teams, was assembled and two separate competitions were set in motion. The football gaming was especially popular, so much so that I agreed to turn over part of the central parkland to construct a second football pitch. Military physical regimes were set up, and ancillary training regimes opened to those civilians interested in perfecting their bodies.

Let me describe to you how the *Senaar* was before we landed it and converted it into our beautiful city. It was a small space, then: a dome hung within a larger semi-vacuum canopy in which cargo was stowed. The dome was laid out around a central park of great beauty: green lawns dazzled, crisp white paths of marble paving cut sharply through. There was a central canal, winding from fountain to lakelet (and, through underground piping, back to the fountain) stocked with large carp and trout, who swam lazily and sometimes turned their pink bellies uppermost at the water's surface. Open lawn stretched up over hillocks; shrubs and trees promised shade, quiet, mystery. There were three bandstands; an athletics track. People swam in the river, and tickled the bellies of the docile fish. People walked with their lovers through the park, and kissed in the shade of trees, or listened to recitals, sitting on the lawn. From the very centre of this Eden rose a single silver needle, four hundred metres tall (kept in place by a wire that went on upwards to the roof of the dome), and at the summit of this needle was a golden ball of light, the finest artificial sun money could buy. It gleamed out upon its little world, and people basked in its brilliance. It even possessed artificial clouds, the size of toys, that came out from a device in the top of the sun to dangle in front of its face, and cast immense shade upon the world, according to a carefully programmed routine. And at sunset, the light slowly glowed redder and redder, and then faded slowly to dusk and darkness. And at sunrise, the light would begin in a pink-pearl glow, and build slowly to the bright sunshine of day. I mean it quite literally when I say that no expense had been spared.

Around this park, carefully planned and structured, were the residential areas: dormitories for single men and women, apartments for the partnered or married. Apartments were available to anybody willing to accept the associated work regime, but most unattached people were content to stay in the dormitories. There were seven chapels, each spaced equally, and all were full of a Sunday, with hymn music shining in the air. The two chief barracks were north and south (notional compass points, of course, but helpful for orienting oneself), and backed onto training grounds: a mock-town, all stone and concrete in the south, a wilderness of scrub and trees in the north. And, some might say, the most important of all was the complex of government buildings. They were westward: court-house, Parliament and civic centre. The court-house sat every week, not every day as is now necessary: but with a proper sense of discipline and purpose, crime was small-scale and infrequent on our voyage. The parliament was open to all. Every citizen had his or her votes, bought with their own monies or earned in lieu of wages for work, to spend as they wished on whatever motion was called. And, perhaps because of the lack of real work, many citizens took a healthy interest in their government, and attended all debates, whether legislative or merely planning and anticipatory. To the east were the shuttle bays, the airlocks, and the hibernation tanks.

All was carefully and orderly in its layout. A perfect town, an Eden.

Of course, there were losses. It is one of the perennials of space travel, of any travel that involves locking people into a small space for decades. Sadly, one or two accidents, and from time to time a citizen who lost their sanity, resulted in death. But keep this in proportion: understand the overall mood of determined strength, of the depth of our joy at this Divine Mission, this journey to another star! You will never undertake such a journey, and it is unlikely your children will, either. Maybe your grandchildren, or great-grandchildren, but this is a privilege that comes only every four or five generations. We worked as a community; we maintained the infrastructure and interstructures of our ship; we kept the gardens, operated the necessary machinery; we prayed and worshipped; we talked with friends and spent time with the people we loved; we played sport and competed with love in our hearts; we played music, and listened to our friends and spouses play music. Children were born, bonds strengthened, but because of the cross-section of people we had chosen to undertake the passage there were no people to die of old age, no senescence. Ours was a youthful, vigorous Eden.

It was also true that I was in touch with the will of our people, where the Captain was not. He became increasingly reclusive, locked away in his apartment with only his partner for company. I was forced into the position of seeming to canvass the people; of walking amongst them, chatting with them in the park to learn their unofficial opinions and views; of attending many open-floor debates in the Parliament; or visiting the technicians. I felt this my duty. I also issued a number of community-service broadcasts, explaining various aspects of the ship's functioning. Naturally this gave me a higher profile than the Captain, which some of the other senior officers thought objectionable. It is true that I was the member of senior staff that civilians and ordinary military ranks felt they could approach without inhibition, to tell me their grievances or express their opinions, or even simply talk. It is true that my popularity was high. But I considered it important that at least one member of the council of six have this degree of susceptibility – for the good of the ship. Of course, I spoke to the Captain on this matter, several times in fact, but little I could say made any difference. He became odd, even quirky. He took to cutting out the pages of his Bible and rearranging them at random, working on the mistaken belief that God made His will known through such random things. He tried to read significance into the gibberish this made of holy writ.

I suppose it is true to say that, as Captain, and given the generally good morale of crew and citizens, there was little for Tyrian to do. This does not excuse him, of course: rather the reverse. It is more important, much more, that a captain demonstrate fibre and character during the quiet times than at the pitch of incident or excitement. Anybody can lead in a crisis; it can be easily trained into a person. But to maintain the courage and leadership at all times, to keep people on the road, the purposeful road that leads them through life with joy: that is the real task, the point of leadership. Was Moses the greater leader as the salt water parted and the Egyptians hurried at their back? Or was the greater task to keep his people together, focused and straight, during their decades of Sinai exile? Was Napoleon [*intertext has no index-connection for a%x'50Napoleon' suggest consult alternate database, e.g. orig.historiograph*] the greater before or after Moscow? [*intertext has no index-connection for a%x'60Moscow' suggest consult alternate database, e.g. orig.historiograph*]. The question answers itself.

Well, it seems that Tyrian was not capable of facing the demands of the quiet, happy time that I had engineered. As is common with leaders at such moments, he grew restless with his people's happiness and tried to force change. He called council meetings to talk about establishing military schools for all children, both during the voyage and after arrival; about altering the hierarchies and routes for promotion of army officers; about setting up a panel to vet all possible marriages. Naturally, at these meetings, I was forced to speak against such absurd suggestions. I could do no more than point out how little the people would welcome such oppressive statutes. It was not that I wished to prevent the Captain from proposing legislation – which was, after all, his right of command – but (and this was the length and breadth of my disloyalty to that once-great man), I insisted that such legislation be placed before Parliament, for the people to spend their votes upon if they so wished. Tyrian wished to pass the legislation under the Necessity rubrics, which would have meant no vote.

It was, I remember, a difficult session of council. Two of the over-lieutenants sympathised with me, although they had to preserve decorum and side with the Captain. One of the over-lieutenants, a man named Gauster, was vocal and unpleasantly loud in his support of the Captain to do whatever he wanted. Two were undecided between us. The Captain – let me say this, to give some sense of how far he had lost the necessary grip – was unshaven. He was a tall, thin man, and he grew a great deal of facial hair; unchecked his beard would have been extremely thick, and would have covered his neck, chin, lips and grown up his cheeks almost to his eyes. Obviously he shaved, twice a day, but for this meeting – a meeting of all senior staff, I need not remind you – his face was blurred with stubble.

Under normal circumstances council meetings are held in camera, and proceedings are secret. When (for instance) military secrets are at stake such a policy is only common sense but in this matter, directly relating to the welfare of the people, I could not keep silence. I refused to betray the community and I left the meeting determined that the people should know the truth. This was the occasion of my football stadium speech; you may have read it, may even have studied it at school. How little I relish the thought of children being schooled to learn my little speech! There are so many other great figures from history, so much more deserving than myself. Of course, the actual speech was rather different from the version that has come through history; there were many more hesitations, words stumbled over, than the records tell. But the basic thread of the speech was as true then as now: that the people's freedom is paramount. Such hard-won, such expensively-protected freedoms, cannot ever be subject to the vagary of one man, no matter how eminent that man might be. The occasion was a volatile one, I grant: the two most popular teams on *Senaar* were coming together to contest the most important football cup. Almost everybody not otherwise engaged was there, and hearts were alive, spirits were thrilled with the excitement of the occasion. I took the micphone because I had organised the original

26

tournament. And what I said received a great roar, the whole crowd shouting their approval of what I said. Tyrian, also present with me on the stadium balcony reserved for command, was furious. He stood up, and would certainly have tried to grab the micphone from me, made some counter-speech, perhaps announced my arrest. And that might have provoked a civic disturbance, maybe even a riot, so fiery was the people's spirit in defence of what I was saying. So I made sure to round off my speech by calling the players to position, and starting the match off. With the players rushing around, and the crowd roaring for one team or another, there was nothing Tyrian could do but sit and watch. I was absorbed in the game but even so I could tell that Tyrian's eye was on me the whole time. It was obvious now that Tyrian regarded me as nothing short of a traitor as if personal loyalty to him outweighed my duty to the people!

Still, it would have been foolish of me to neglect my personal safety after the speech. It was only the next day that Tyrian's men came to place me under ship arrest, and my men were waiting. Some histories talk of the battle of the parkland, but it was no battle, if that term be strictly applied (and I have seen some real battles since that time). Men were killed, regrettably, but much was at stake here. Such fighting as there was mostly took place in my quarters and the surrounding alleyways. Anticipating an attack, I had positioned six of my best men on an elevated walkway; two stood by the door, and more waited inside. Tyrian's people were taken by surprise. Five were killed, five wounded, and the remainder fled over the parkland, where my men pursued them. It is true that a civilian was killed in this secondary encounter but the needle that killed him came from one of Tyrian's men.

Once the first blow had been struck, events assumed their own momentum. Tyrian, less and less in touch with reality, publicly denounced me as a traitor; ordered all the people of *Senaar* to rise up against me. I do believe he would have welcomed the sight of me bound and gagged like an animal at slaughter, carried shoulder-high by a swarming mob. But his actions had undone him; he was clearly no longer mentally fit for the high trust of ship's Captain. My loyal over-lieutenants rallied to my cause, the people's cause, and brought their troops with them. More soldiers confined themselves voluntarily to barracks, under orders from the more cautious of commanders. Tyrian's personal troop, and Gauster's, assembled and took control of, in the west, the government buildings and surrounding houses, and in the east the technical installations. I made my base in the southern barracks, and posted my troops in the central park. It was my most earnest wish not to involve civilian habitations in battle but Tyrian was attempting to force my hand. If I tried to take on both forces, my own army would be fighting a war on two fronts, yet if I concentrated on only one, the other could pass easily across the parkland and catch me in a vice. Heavier ordnance was available to us, in bartels in storage, but there was a clear and unavoidable danger in deploying them that the very fabric of the ship would be damaged. Fortunately, I had control of the storage, and sewage/recycling tanks, so I could prevent this eventuality. It also gave me military leverage: with food stores in my control there was always the option to starve Tyrian.

In the end, Tyrian's own strategic positioning was his undoing because he had sealed himself away from the people. True, he held the Parliament building, but no citizen would approach, knowing it was held by hostile troops. I was able to move amongst our people, to reassure them, and to gain the confidence and trust that has carried me through the high duties of leadership ever since. I was also able to post men in civilian housing throughout the north and north-east, for the people's protection and reassurance. Of course, this also gave a base from which to strike down into the technical centres in the east. So, I planned my attack carefully, to minimise damage to the territories of *Senaar*, and extinguished the sun one day at noon. In the darkness my men broke through the walls and into the airlock hangers in the east; the fighting was fierce here, but expert command on the ground won the day. The bulk of my troops then stormed the east and claimed a swift victory. But my real genius lay in the west, where I organised a mass civilian rally outside government buildings. Tyrian could not counter-attack without first breaking through this unarmed crowd, killing many. He was too weak-willed to take such an action, and by the time the sun was re-ignited I controlled everything but the western buildings. From that moment on there was no doubt as to who would emerge victorious. The remaining over-lieutenants emerged from their barracks and swore their loyalty to me. Two days later, Tyrian resigned. I was ready to put him on trial before the people, and possibly incarcerate him for the remainder of the voyage, but he took his own life with a needlegun.

Naturally, I needed to punish some officers, but for the men: well, men are men, they follow orders. I stripped all rankers of insignia, but allowed them to re-enlist, swear loyalty to me and go about their business. Business which was, in the first instance, clearing up the damage for which they had been largely responsible.

And so it was that Tyrian lasted only a little under three months; the tasks of command during so elongated a voyage were too great.

It may seem strange to you that I arranged to have all the bodies of those soldiers who had fought against me buried with full military honours. They were my enemies, I suppose, but my concern was always for the good of the people of *Senaar*. These soldiers had only been following the orders of their superior officers, and as such they had done their duty. What more can be asked of any person in our community, even of me? So the bodies were cocooned in military tape, their families awarded the proper military pension of monies and votes, and there was a day of official mourning declared. The bodies were released into space.

I am not ashamed to say I cried at this ceremony. I consider it a sign of strength in a man that he is able to cry.

The month that followed was not easy; I had to struggle to rebuild the harmony *Senaar* had once enjoyed. I reordered military rankings, and set up specific project targets for people to work towards, with various rewards. But the greatest danger to our voyage was not the struggle to assert the popular vote by right: the greatest danger came from outside, as it always does. The anarchy of the *Als* put the entire mission in jeopardy.

One of their women, demoralised by the dissolution of life aboard the *Als*, experienced a psychotic interlude. She became violently insane, murdered several of her crewmates, and stole a shuttle with the intention of doing further damage to the fleet as a whole. Whether she hoped to collide her shuttle at full speed into the next ship downcable (the *Babulonis*) and so breach the hull and kill everybody inside, or whether her intention all along was to try to wreck the ore-anchor and so jeopardise our chances of successful colonisation, it is difficult to say. What cannot be denied is the malign determination with which she set out: witness the way she fired her shuttle's engines to full thrust and aimed herself at that section of the fleet downcable from her. Had her engines not overloaded and her drive buckled, I sincerely believe she would have done much more damage. As it as, we must thank God that she managed only an oblique collision against the body of the ore-anchor.

Still, this was a near-disaster, and clearly demonstrated that the system by which the *Als* governed itself was inadequate to the job in hand, the task facing all of us. Of course, I believe in the rights of self-determination of the various peoples of our world; and on a planet, such liberties can be indulged to a much greater extent. But in the fragile, communal world of a starship (which is, after all, what we were) indulgence is only weakness, and the good of the all must supersede the good of any one people. I talked with most of the Captains of the various ships, and we all agreed that either myself or Dauid, the Captain of the *Babulonis*, must summon a senior member of the *Als* to a meeting, at which the united voice of the other thirteen ships could be expressed. Only a madman would wish to stand against the majority decision.

I decided to summon Petja Szerelem. Because he had once been the tether-technician he was amongst the most recognised of individuals from the *Als*, and since I had already had dealings with him I assumed – wrongly, as it turned out – that I would be able to treat with him. He came, carrying some bird-carcasses as a kind of peace-offering (to be fair to him, I think even he, with his ingrained social ineptness and anarchistic disregard for the feelings of others, even he had the

30

good grace to feel sheepish and ashamed at the action of his crew member). I returned the compliment, gifted him some of the produce from our Fabricants (we have always possessed some of the most sophisticated software for Fabricants amongst any of the ten nations) – magnifiers, a Solidus, some traction-alerters and an Aglet. We also brought out some of our supply of alcohol, and served that up, without so much as hinting at payment: it was an action of the purest open-heartedness, a gesture of friendship.

Try to imagine the scene. Despite the hardships we had endured, including (let us not forget) a war which badly damaged a great deal of vital equipment; despite this, we prized our personal cleanliness and hygiene above everything. Senaarians are renowned for appearing neat and clean at all times. Try to imagine the stench which greeted our noses when this Szerelem came out of the airlock. The tramp-like accumulation of layers of swathed clothing, many of which were frayed and dirty, and none of which were in any sense style- or colour-coordinated. He had shaven his head bald, perhaps to appear more menacing, although the effect on his thin face was to make him appear undernourished. And the smell! The foetid rush of sweat-gone-bad and uncleanness affronted us. My officers are well trained, and did not betray their revulsion, but to think of embarking on a diplomatic mission without first washing! To go forward as a representative of your people when you smell like rotten meat! We provided him with washing facilities, though they had little chance against the accumulated grime. We also provided him – again, free of charge – with some clean clothes. To all this, as to the food and drink we provided, he said nothing. No word of thanks from his blistered lips.

He guzzled our offered hospitality as if there were shortages of food and drink aboard his own ship (perhaps there were: I have heard no good things of the ability of Alsists to organise themselves and their supplies). He grunted and sniffed when we made polite small talk. It was, genuinely, as if a particularly well-trained animal, an ape, say, had come to visit us. My junior officers were beginning to bridle; they are, after all, military men, and their blood is hot, howsoever well disciplined they are about it. They were beginning to sense a deliberate insult to our ship, our people.

'Mr Szerelem,' I opened, 'I trust you are enjoying our hospitality.' I said this, not to bait him, only to remind him of the generosity we had shown him. Fresh food and real alcohol are not so easily stored and transported that a travelling starship can afford to give them away every day.

But he said nothing to this. The principle of gratitude has been almost bred out of the Alsist mentality.

I explained to him that, having consulted with the other ships' Captains (a process of consultation which omitted the *Als* only because that ship had no proper command structures, and so was unable to tender a representative to the videophone Captains' panel), we had decided to offer certain suggestions to his people, in the purest spirit of friendship, to help safeguard the whole fleet. He snarled at this, his chapped lips sliding up his teeth like an animal. There were stains on his teeth. I believe the Alsists used a great deal of their storage space for alcohol (important to Alsist culture, they claim) and a special kind of weed, a sort of herb that they chew to narcotic effect. Perhaps this Szerelem was affected by this drug at that time.

I assured him that our interest was offered in the most tender spirit of commiseration for their loss; that we wished no inappropriate curiosity into the internal arrangement of their ship; but that the safety of the whole fleet had been challenged.

At this he coughed, or laughed, or barked, perhaps. 'This is not concern,' he said. I remember the ungrammatical nature of the sentence particularly. When pressed, it transpired that he meant: this is no concern of mine. This was a reflection of the philosophy of these people, that the community bears no responsibility for the evil of the individual. Perhaps you begin to see why it is so difficult to relate to this nation, and why the hard path of war has been unavoidable.

I explained the decision of the Captains' panel, that the *Als* institute government of some sort, to instil some degree of social order and prevent catastrophes of this nature happening again. He bridled at this, but I pressed on: after all, I reasoned, it was only a few months before acceleration would be complete, and then with the crew almost all in stasis, government would become an irrelevance anyway. Besides, strong government would help address some of the unpleasantnesses inside the ship. Rumours had reached us of the high rate of crew suicide down there, and the generally low morale.

He seemed impressed by this last argument. 'I concede that your system has meant that there has been very little suicide, very little cabin craziness amongst your people, Captain,' he said. 'But it is not our way, to be governed.'

'You will adhere to this "way", then, even at the cost of your life?'

'Yes.'

'And the lives of the other ship-members? Of the fleet?'

'That means nothing to me.'

One of my officers pointed out how important discipline was going to be in setting up a city, a civilisation upon the new world, as much as in a ship. Szerelem scowled at this. I swear he prodded at his nose with his little finger, like an ill-trained child. He scratched at his shaven head, with an astonishing vigour, as if he wished to draw blood. Then he spat into the palm of his own hand and (horrible to watch) wiped it against his sleeve.

'You people have no spirit,' he said. 'You could not understand.'

'At least my people would never endanger the well-being of the entire fleet, as one of your people has done.'

At this he drained my drink in one gulp and lurched, rather unsteadily, to feet. I tried to pacify him. I could see several of the junior officers were on the verge of striking him; understandable, perhaps, in the face of his calculated insults to the *Senaar* and those who flew her. But I tried to calm him, assured him that we wished only to reach a settlement that was agreeable to both sides.

He stood, looking down at me. There was an awkward pause, and I decided to use a little of my authority. 'Sit down, Technician,' I said, firmly but not rudely. The effect was striking: he obeyed, like a dog, [*intertext has no index-connection for a%x'1000dog' suggest consult alternate database, e.g. orig.historiograph*] almost without thinking.

'Our interest in your ship is motivated by more than disinterested concern for the fleet as a whole,' I told him. 'We do not forget, even if you do, that there are twenty-one of our people aboard the *Als*, the children born to fathers from *Senaar* and held hostage away from their families.'

'No concern of mine,' he said.

'Perhaps you are unconcerned,' I told him, 'but the welfare of our people will always concern us. We are not a people to abandon our own; least of all little children, who are unable to look after themselves. We must insist that proper safeguards are put in place, to prevent the less stable of your fellows aboard the *Als* from committing any further crimes against the fleet, and to ensure that the twenty-one grow to the adulthood where they will be able to choose to return home. To *Senaar*.'

He seemed stuck on the word *crime*, which is not a concept they possess in Als. His eyebrows were twisting with the difficulty of understanding it. You can see how little attention they pay to their Bible in that place!

'I must also insist,' I said, 'that the fathers of these children be granted the rights to visit the children up to the time when hibernation begins; and again, during the deceleration at arrival.'

He seemed equally puzzled by this, but also a little belligerent. 'You can see the children if the mothers agree, but I cannot speak for the mothers.'

'We must put in place a body that can overrule the selfish desires of the mothers, if such get in the way of internationally accepted law . . .' I said. But at this, for some reason I have never really been able to fathom, Szerelem leapt to his feet. He seemed raging, furious, almost possessed. My junior officers surged forward to hold him away from me but he cowered back from them.

I stood. 'What do you mean by this?'

His only answer was to spit on the floor.

Some have said that, at this affront, I should have imprisoned

Szerelem aboard the *Senaar*, perhaps used him as a pawn to force the Alsists towards reason. But this misunderstands the nature of Alsist society. Each individual cares for nobody but himself, and they would in no way be distressed by the loss of another. Perhaps I should have detained him anyway, or perhaps had him executed. Had I been able to see into the seeds of time, as the phrase goes, I would have known then that such action could have saved our people a skyful of trouble. A skyful of trouble.

2

The Fox and the Lion

Petja

Ours is a world with very little landscape. It is largely salt desert, with some localised rock formations, and the Sebestyen mountains that back us are the only real mountains. There are three small seas. Before our departure from Earth, analysis of the spectrographic data from this world suggested there was a great deal of free water on our destination world; but there is too little water. It was water that threatened, in the end, to become a currency with us – to be, that is, monies, although such a thing is alien to our way. But scarcity will disrupt the proper order of things.

Whether there had been more water on Salt fifty years ago and that water had in some manner become lost, or whether the original data were corrupted in some way, it is difficult to say. I have heard conspiracy stories from time to time, stories that suggest that Earth authorities falsified the data to encourage us to go. Perhaps such things happen. And life here has been hard enough for me to be resentful, if I were given to resentful feelings. But the finest beauty is to be found in desolation, and our world is a piece of the finest beauty. It is the silver-salt jewel of God's creation. Smoke stretching itself in lazy curls against the mirror at three in the morning – even though you know the smoke to be toxic and bad-for-health, even though it is very late and you are exhausted, even though you are stunned with weariness over the talking that has gone on so long – despite all this, the smoke against the mirror will shake you suddenly with its exquisite beauty. Just as a man may look down at his life's blood draining away, and see the sun glinting in the wetness as a glossy red perfection. So it is that the green claustrophobia of the Earthly oasis, the free-standing water and the heavy wet air, the buzzing insects and the sweat; all these things are ugly, for all that they represent fertility. So it is that the wide stretch of the desert, blank and glittering in a sun that will steal your moisture and kill you, the emptiness and the waste; all this is beautiful, for all that it represents desolation.

In saying this I am out of touch with the younger generations, who want nothing more than to change the face of our world altogether, to introduce life and growth to every part of its dead face. This is a noble aim but I will be dead before it can ever happen, if it can ever happen, and I am glad of that. Do not think me perverse! A man may walk out on the surface of an alien world, and his eye may dwell on the emptiness, the desert of white aching towards the horizon, and he may feel at home for the first time in his life.

We arrived in orbit, a great procession of ships, strange and new, from another star. And we celebrated for three days and three nights; but even in the middle of celebration there were people too impatient to make merry. Those who had been allocated shuttle duties took themselves and their friends down to the surface; flew down to the shoreline of the Aradys sea, and danced in its powdery salts with masks on. They came back with chlorine irritation to their eyes, but they were envied. I went down myself, and walked for an hour and a half, wearing goggles and breathing mask; walked away from the sluggish water and past the mountain peak at the furthest end of the range. Walked into the bright east of a new day, with the sun iridescing in the early air.

It was this impatience that caused us to break with the fleet before the others, and bring our ship down to the seashore. The world was here to fulfil us; this was our chosen land. And, at the same time, we were here to fulfil it: we are its chosen people. This world had never had a moon, and we (the fleet) brought it three. The comet, star-shaped now with its loss of bulk from its twelve thruster-sites, like twelve bites into its edge. It circled the world, and on some mornings you could glimpse it, a shining star that swooped low over the sky. Then there was the ore-anchor, placed in a polar orbit; and the frozen oxygen. Three moons. There was little life on Salt, no biology and only some botany, and what little there was lurked in the mountains, or floated insentient in the lakes, insignificant. Over time we set about our great tasks, to begin soaking up the free chlorine, filling the sky with air, bringing down water and trace elements into the world. We brought our own life, adapted and tweaked it, and let it begin its slow colonisation. And we brought the world ourselves. We added soul, God's most precious quantity, to a soulless place. We were the spirit of Adam, passed through the finger of God into his limp body. We were creation; the morning star and the evening star. We would burn down from the heavens, balanced on a spear of oxidising rocket-fuel, slowing to meet with the ground, a shuttle filled with materials and with soul.

Barlei

The calendar dates from the very date of landfall but many of us had put foot upon Salt before the *Senaar* landed on our new homeworld. In the months after arrival, and after we were settled in orbit around the planet, I was again very busy. The tasks that faced us were large, but it is the large task that draws the human spirit upwards. Humankind will always meet the challenges that face it, and will overcome, with the strength of righteous purpose and by God's will.

The world was not as hospitable as we had hoped. Our gathered data, purchased before the voyage, had suggested plenty of free-standing water on the world. The great problem with stellar colonisation – and should you, or your children, ever think of harnessing a comet and moving to another star, then you must bear this in mind – the great problem is that data is always received out of date. Our information left the sun twenty-five years before we began the planning for our voyage; by the time we had mobilised ourselves and arrived, another forty years had passed. The moral is: be prepared to be adaptable. You must play the music God has composed for you, and sight-read if necessary. When you stand before the great Creator at the day of your death, and he demands you explain your conduct on this world, do you think you will be allowed to stutter and mumble? No, you must sing out your life; you must read off the notes of your moral behaviour. You must make your life into music, and that music must be a hymn of praise to authority and to God. Salt was our symphony.

The more immediate problems were not those of insufficient water. There are three bodies of water on Salt, and although the water in them is supersaturated saline it is easy enough to desalinate. Of course, the lakes are not very deep, nor very wide, but they are there; and they were deeper when we arrived than they are now. But even more importantly than the native supplies, we had brought our own ball of dusty frozen water with us in the shape of the comet that had pulled us the immense distance between our worlds. The majority of the comet's bulk had been dissipated in the process, naturally, but there were still several hundred thousand tonnes. Comet activity in the inner system is low but there are a great many comets on wide and distant orbital trajectories, and it will always be possible, if the water situation becomes too grave, to mount an expedition and retrieve one.

So I was not too worried about the water supply for our new world (these were precisely the terms in which I talked in the early days, as if our world were a house, and water merely a pipe that needed to be properly fixed; such talk raises morale). No, the water supply was not the greatest worry. More pressing, it seemed to me, was the atmosphere. The concentrations of free chlorine were relatively high, as were one or two other poisonous gases; the rest of the air was a cocktail of inert gas and fifty per cent nitrogen, but there were only trace levels of oxygen. We had hoped for more oxygen; or, at least, we had hoped for enough water to be able to derive our own oxygen. It seemed for a time that the oxygen we had towed with us from Earth (actually from Jupiter) was not going to be enough to raise global levels but we discovered a certain amount of frozen oxides under the South Pole, protected from sun by the sheet salt-ice, and we were able to liberate the oxygen from them. And then we pushed our orbiting ball of pure oxygen downwards out of its orbit, into the atmosphere.

What a spectacle it was! I have seen visuals from above, which show it streaking like a great firework [*intertext has no index-connection for a%x'9705firework' suggest consult alternate database, e.g. orig.historiograph*] round and round the world, spewing more and more of a tail and shrinking. But I do not have to rely on visuals, as you young people today do; I was there, I was on the ground. The *Senaar* was still in orbit at this stage, but we had established a home base on the eastern shores of Galilee with two shuttles, and I chose to watch the spectacle from there. It was a splendid sight, a chariot of fire and steam passing faster than sound to the north, along the equator. After it had gone over the western horizon its sound-wave boomed, with a great sound of tearing, like a mighty cloth was being rent in two before the temple of God. We waited expectantly, and it emerged again, much lower in the sky. And then it crashed, away over the horizon, to the north. It came down as we planned, almost exactly half-way between Galilee and Perse. Some of our people took trucks and drove out to examine the site. They said it was possible for them to stand in the mists it gave off and remove their masks, to breathe the air directly.

Never forget your heritage, my children! Never forget that the first women and men to breathe the air of Salt unaided were Senaarians!

The diffusion of this mass of oxygen fully into the atmosphere took several months; and the liberation of oxygen from such oxides as we could find took most of the year. But long before the end of the year concentrations in the atmosphere were up to fifteen and sixteen per cent, breathable though thin; we had raised atmospheric pressure by several points. The atmospheric scrubbing of chlorine and other toxins was a more complicated task, though.

The difficulty here was that our eleven nations were settling, mostly, around the three great lakes, Galilee, Perse and the Pale Sea (those who were not settling directly along the shores were choosing sites close enough to the water to lay a pipeline without much expense). Much of our early energy, after we brought the *Senaar* to ground, was spent in building the desalination plants. Water settles in the depressions and chlorine, more than twice as heavy as air, settles in these depressions too. You will have seen, as I have, the banks of yellowy-green gas rolling as chlorine fog from the waters. But my people, and the people from the other ships, had spent decades cooped up in their hulls. We could not hide away, as if still voyaging through space: we had arrived. We had to get out. It is our nature to want to break any bonds placed upon us. Samson in the temple.

We did two things. The first was to dedicate our Fabricants to manufacturing converters for an entire month. These were catalytic-ally-charged buoys, powered by the sun, that locked up the chlorine as solid bricks of chloride plastics. We launched hundreds of these floating detoxifiers on the broad, calm waters of Galilee. The other Galilean nations (they were young then, hardly the great nations they have since become! Still, it is right to talk about them as nations, for such they were, in their essence, in their potential), the other nations along the coast, Eleupolis, Yared, New Florence and Babulonis, contributed funds towards this project. They lacked the specific Fabricant software to be able to produce these buoys but New Florence created some solar-powered catalyst rovers, to travel the depressions and dry sinks in the desert and do the same job there. There were, I believe, other projects launched in the north. But this business of clearing away the poison was very large-scale; it was going to be many years before we saw a significant reduction.

So there was a second strand to our approach. We fitted our people; we altered ourselves! If Moses will not come to the desert, the desert must come to Moses, a proverb of which my old grandmother was particularly fond. The devices we used are antiques now, of course; at the time they were the highest of high-tech. We would take a person, and sedate them, and under surgical conditions we would remove much of their sinuses and fill the space with a carefully grown filter. An organic substance this, derived I think from coral (you will not know what coral is, of course, but you can check it if you are interested), that scrubbed out the chlorine. And because it functioned as a sinus, the removed chlorine was washed out of the nose again in mucus suspension. A self-cleaning lifelong filter-mask. Perhaps you say: what was wrong with the ordinary masks? Was it so much bother to have to put them on? Well, today (and because of us) you can walk about your homeworld as God made you, you don't understand the irritation of the masks. The way the edges rub the skin, bringing out welts and infections in the flesh. The uncomfortableness, the sense of constriction. And, of course, the danger: they could fail, fall off; you could be at home when your window is breached and your mask not to hand. Worst of all, I suppose, they were symbolic of our incapacity; they squashed against our faces, artificial pig-snouts, a reminder of our imprisonment. How could we bear to be imprisoned on our own world?

Of course, the Alsists mocked our new technology. It is in the nature of anarchy to fear new technology. Their propaganda satirised us: whenever the visuals were set in Senaar the people always had runny noses; always dirty noses when they represented us! But they did not understand that mucus was only produced when one had been in contact with chlorine; and then it was simply a matter of carrying a handkerchief in order to wipe it away, in the thoroughly civilised manner. With some people, it is true, the implant would cause minor infections, and this would involve them in continual production of mucus; but whatever the Alsists have said, for most this was not a problem. I myself was fitted with an implant (it has since been removed) and I experienced no discomfort or side-effects at all.

My first walk in the open air was televised throughout Senaar, of course. And what an experience! I fitted my contact lenses, and put in place a gum-guard, to inhibit me breathing through my mouth (it is surprisingly easy to forget to breathe only through the nose and a lungful of chlorine is an unpleasant thing). Then I stepped through the airlock on the crystal-salt beach. To be able to walk down to the water, to feel the wind gently on my face, to breathe deeply (through the nose) of the air of our world! To watch the sun, still white, settling towards the horizon, throwing long black shadows behind us all. I would have stayed longer, but the Devil's Whisper starts up at dusk.

You may have seen the representation of me contemplating Galilee, with the sun just clipping the horizon, and a crowd gathered to watch me. They were going to put it on our banknotes, but I stopped them because I considered it would have been vainglorious of me to allow such a graven image on something so important as money. But it is commonly reproduced, and there is a mosaic of the scene, assembled from different shades of salt, glued to the wall of the primary debating chamber.

Petja

Our solution to the chlorine problem was a mini-mask. It was a clever thing. You would wear it about your neck at all times, like a pendant, but when its sense-cell detected chlorine, at even the most minute levels, it would leap up. Like a live thing, like a salmon, which is a fish that used to hop out of the waters for joy on Earth. A receptor was embedded in your tooth, a tiny device: the homer was in the mask. And it would leap up towards its mate and there the mask would be, clamped over your mouth. You needed to remember to breathe through the mouth only, of course, but it became a sort of reflex. To feel the gentle smack of mask over the lips, and then to take a deep breath through the mouth. Then you had the leisure to take some nose-clips out of your pouch and fit them over your nostrils. Chlorine up the nose is not a pleasant thing. It is a gas that irritates the lining of the nose.

Barlei

It was characteristic of the Alsists that, without compunction, they stole the land east of the Perse Sea. It is true that protocols signed before the voyage were, shall we say, vague on the subject of exactly how the land was to be allocated although they did stipulate that all nations were to have equal access to water, arable land, mineral resources and the like. But on arrival, it was generally accepted that all ships would remain in orbit until negotiations had reached a consensus concerning land apportioning. Of course, I agreed to host such negotiations aboard the *Senaar*. But the Alsists, and Szerelem in particular, flouted the process of democracy. They took their ship down and landed on their present site without so much as informing the other captains of their actions. I remember the day; being woken by my PA in the early hours of ship-time, and hustling up to the command bridge in my uniform dressing-gown to watch the *Als* bruising the atmosphere purple and red with the heat of their entry. And by then it was too late to stop them.

Today, when it is generally accepted that Senaar is the most advantageously positioned nation (rooted as we are on the fertile east coast of the eel-rich Galilee), it may be difficult to understand why this Alsist manoeuvre caused such outrage. But think yourselves back. With so little by way of geographical features, Salt's weather is dominated by the coriolis force. The winds in the northern hemisphere are prevailingly western; and Als is positioned at the back of the Samson mountains (the Sebestyen, as they call them), which represent a sort of natural windbreak. But the winds in the southern hemisphere come mostly from the east. East of Senaar there was nothing but a thousand miles of salt desert, stretching on and on until eventually you reach the broken hills north of the De Morgan Sea. Often the weather was calm, but when the winds got themselves roused up they could be fierce indeed.

There were two times of great wind, of what used on Earth to be called *typhun* [*intertext has no index-connection for a%x'160typhun' suggest consult alternate database, e.g. orig.vocabhyp*]. One would happen shortly around sunset, when the cooling air of the night-time out east would sink and push great howling winds towards us. These would last for an hour or so. Then there would be a dawn wind, less savage but just as unpleasant. And wind off the desert is much worse than wind off the water. As you know, the waters of Galilee are supersaturated and will barely take on more salt; salt blown on to them sinks to the bottom as a sort of sludge, which is one of the reasons why the Galilee is so shallow at our end, and why the water is constantly, yearly, creeping westwards. But in open desert, the driest place in the world, winds break the tiny particles of salt into even smaller microparticles of salt that can be as little as a few atoms across. On exposed bluffs, which act like rock anvils for the hammering wind, these tiny specks are blown up by the billion, a stinging, coruscating blizzard that looks like smoke and feels like a million insects eating the skin from your flesh. At its most intense, the east wind will blind the unwary watcher; will make any exposed skin bleed from a thousand scratches. It makes a high-pitched hissing as it moves over the ground. It will entirely devour corpses left in its path within months; and, of course, there were to be corpses (but I will not hurry my narrative forward). It is known, still, to those who have to venture eastward beyond the Great Dyke as the Devil's Whisper.

We very quickly learnt to stay indoors during the dawn; to retreat to our homes for an hour as soon as the sun had vanished behind the horizon, but the wear on our equipment was very great. Machines clogged up with the fine salt; our plastic windows became so scored with fine lines as to become opaque grey filters that scattered light in sunburst-rainbow patterns.

And so we built the Great Dyke. It is officially called the Barlei Dyke, in my honour, but I am uncomfortable with such tributes. And 'Great Dyke' accurately enough describes what it is: a Pharaonic feat of engineering, massive and beautiful. We excavated a kilometre east of our furthest settlement (fortunately the very severity of the wind meant that the topsalt was thinner here than in most places, and we

45

did not have to dig too deeply to reach bedrock) then we carved out great slabs of quartz and saltstone and lifted them by shuttle to lay a great wall. This we built upon with small stones, and then bulldozed the salt from east and west to create the dyke. Finally, we secured the whole with (to the east) saltstone capstones, a solid bluff, and (to the west) a layer of engineered topsoil which was planted all over with salt-grass.

The whole was the single most expensive undertaking of the pre-War period. It was paid for with a special tax, willingly paid by all Senaarians, as well as by contributions from the other Galilean nations, which were (even at that early time) allying themselves with the strength of Senaar. I contributed a million from my personal fortune. And the dyke meant that the severity of the eastern winds was abated.

Well, to be truthful, for about a year after the dyke was built matters did not greatly improve. The aerodynamics of the thing were not perfectly figured, and for two of the years's three seasons the winds were high enough to breach it. They would be sucked closer to the ground by the shape and come whipping into our land. More than this, the natural strains of salt-grass were poor things. Plant engineering came a long way, very quickly, but the indigenous strains were brittle and thin. As soon as the stems were a finger's-length long, the wind would rip them from the sand and throw them downwind. At us. You know how sharp-edged salt-grass is? Imagine a flurrying tornado-wind filled with them. They gave the Devil's Whisper a growl. We had to plant great pillars of quartz, quarried and lifted at huge expense, to break up the profile of the dyke. And the plant-engineers tried many strains of vegetation, adapted from Salt's natural growths or adapted from Earth strains: salt-bamboos, which grew tall but spindly, easily broken by the wind. Scrub and web-algae that clogged the spaces between spars. Finally, a stronger salt-grass that held the leeward side.

But what did teething-troubles matter? The dyke was a symbol! It was a hymn in stone and salt to the Lord, a statement of our power to build, to change the world.

And how we built! Sometimes I think no nation, not even ours, will ever recapture the burning energy of those first few years. We dismantled areas of the ship as it sat on the salt shore of Galilee, leaving only the great central dome: this we kept, partly as a monument to our tremendous journey across space, but also because the gap between its double-shell was filled with fluorocarbonated water as a shield against deep space radiation. Our new sun was brighter than the old and put out more life-harming radiation, and the upper layers of Salt's atmosphere were poor in greenhouse gases. The buildings were converted to hospital and creche facilities, and young children and the infirm – those most at risk from the higher doses of rads – were kept under the dome. There were three hospitals, actually, even in those early days! One was a standard medical installation, and took most of the insured and wealthy patients; but there were two smaller endowments made by wealthy Earthers who had been too old to accompany us, and these two centres of healing were set up on a nominal percentage fee basis. It was my proud boast in the early days that Senaar possessed the greatest provision of healthcare and pre-school facilities on the whole of Salt. This is still the case, although other nations have made certain advances. And although the War set us back.

The typical dwelling-buildings, that grew all around the central dome, were of the sort familiar to us all from history visuals; those flat-topped, heavy stone structures. They look primitive (indeed, they were primitive) but they did the job. The job was providing shelter, from the wind on the ground and from the radiation above.

Sites were initially all owned by the state, to be leased to the inhabitants for twenty years. After that they would revert to the inhabitants and the inhabitants' descendants. This encouraged people to think medium-term, but did not tie them unreasonably. And so, in the spare time they could manage from their various jobs, people began to come out of the tents in the shadow of the dome, and pick their plots of land. They began to build their own houses.

People could quarry their own saltstone, or have it quarried for them fairly cheaply: saltstone lies close to the surface, under the topsalt. So, they would build their walls of saltstone, lay out the rough plan of the dwelling. But the quartz lies deep, outpushings from the granite core of our world. The individual could rarely muster the means to quarry it himself. It is at such moments that the individual can draw on the strength of the whole community, the whole congregation.

I dedicated one of the ship's shuttles to quarrying and ferrying monumental blocks of quartz from east of the Dyke and I established a scheme whereby citizens could purchase these blocks from the state with a money deposit, the balance to be redeemed either in money or else in community work. The shuttle would carve a six-metre thick chunk of quartz from the quarry and airlift it to the dwelling, lower it gently onto its laser-points and let it settle. I know all about this procedure, because I built my own house. It was a good scheme: people got good houses, and the community got a great deal of public works at no cost to the treasury. We owe the North Coast Spinal Railway to this scheme, or at least the first fifty kilometres of it.

Can anybody claim to feel at home until they have experienced the joy of building their own house? As head of the government, of course, I had quarters inside the dome, in the government buildings, but I decided this was not appropriate. It might have looked as if I was hiding under the protection of the dome, as if I was too frightened to brave the dangers of radiation like my people. Worse (in political terms) it associated me with the weak, the sick and the children. So I chose a site on a raised plateau, five metres above sea-level, overlooking the Galilee (enemy propaganda suggests I had the police evict two families to vacate this space, but this is not true: both families were very happy to give the ground over to me). I brought in half a dozen workmen and workwomen – in fact, I had to insist they took their wages, so keen were they to do the work for nothing. But I reminded them what it is the Bible says about the worker being worthy of his hire. Together, we quarried the saltstone and built the walls; we laid out the interior with bedroom, kitchen, dining, reception room, guest rooms, study, bunker, lumber room and bathroom. Then the shuttle hovered in, the copestone dangling

48

massy beneath it. I can barely express how satisfying was the sound of the *thuk* with which the quartz greeted the saltstone.

This, my first house on our glorious new world, was a place of great happiness to me. It was, perhaps, a little dark inside, but that was necessary in the face of the radiation hazard. Windows were few, the ceiling felt lower than it actually was. In the winter it could become rather cold. Still, I have only happy memories of that house. From inside that house I co-ordinated the building of a city. At evening I would sit on my porch, watching the sun set over the Galilee, with my advisors around me. Or, sometimes, just old friends; or perhaps ordinary citizens, sitting at my side and sipping herbal tea. Talking. Admiring God's beauty. Somebody might play some music, an air on the pipes for instance, or a sonata on the keyboards I kept by the window overlooking this porch. These were the times of tranquillity for me.

But tranquillity can only ever be enjoyed if it is sandwiched between times of great work. And how we worked!

There were epic meetings in the Parliament, during which the various plans for the city were debated. Tempers ran hot. There had been many plans for the overall layout of the city submitted, by qualified architects and planners as well as by ordinary citizens. Most favoured a cross-shaped design, with urbanisation branching in four directions; not very practical, I am afraid, to dissipate buildings so widely. Others expressed self-consciously musical motifs, or at-tempted to pick out a pattern on the ground, of a face or the Eagle of St John, or some such. Some were more mathematical, grid-patterns or circular grilles of streets. I consulted with my advisers and shortlisted six, which were then defended in Parliament by their designers and ultimately voted upon in a special pre-season debate. The vote treasury had never before, and has never since, taken in so many votes! It was remarkable how fervently people cared for this issue. The debate went on for three days, and each day I had to suspend discussion because no pause in the proceedings presented itself.

When the particular grid was decided upon, there was an intense period of building. People would work all day, and then spend all night building, taking only a few hours sleep at dawn before going back to work. Nobody was idle. Adolescents, who would normally be at school except that the schools had yet to be built, lent a hand constructing their classrooms. Pregnant women worked during their rest-time. The sick would do what little they could, programming netscreens from their hospital beds. Only on Sunday mornings would the work stop, and people would gather, in the open air at first, and later in the first churches, to give praise.

We built houses, and we fused down the topsalt between them to make roads. People scoured the topsalt of their garden, laid plastic in the pits they made, and hawked and traded their organic rubbish and the algae cleared from the bays of Galilee to spread over it: a foul-smelling stuff, but the first slow stages in building the mulch we think of as soil, the first step on the road to growing Earth plants. We programmed out Fabricants to produce bicycles, to be sold at basic government price, and the streets were crowded with people making their way to and from work. Houses came into being along the road. Every day seemed to bring in another shuttle flight, with another huge piece of hewn quartz from out east. Everybody was busy, everybody contented. And although you could see the strain in people's faces, the physical exhaustion, nonetheless we all tapped into the energy and resilience of youth (for we were a *young* nation). Concerts happened without planning; a woman with a guitar and two men with pipes would start playing on one of the scrubby open places that still pocked the city. A crowd would gather. People would be talking, laughing, cheering the music. Or else, the word would go round the net, or even by word-of-mouth, that a quartet was going to be playing in such-and-such house, or that the children's choir was practising in the dome, and people would slip away from their work for half an hour, and gather by the wall to listen. Music is the soul of mathematics, somebody once said, and work is mathematics; energy expenditure, efficiency curves, technology and science, the geometry of building, the topography of city-plans. And people would sing as they worked, God's plan manifesting itself in this new city. Music would soar from the half-finished houses, the squat office buildings without roofs, the public areas.

Praise.

For the first month I was busied with establishing the superstructure of government: another building, if you like, but a metaphorical one, set up on the base of my people. But I also travelled. I visited the building of the dyke many times, and put myself about amongst my people, often physically lending a hand. Everywhere I went were happy faces, joyous women wiping sweat from their faces to shake me by the hand, reedy men laughing at my jokes. I visited the hospital many times, greeting the sick and confined. Mostly it was the radiation-foolish, people who were too sloppy with the necessary protocols. Many burns, depilations and cataracts; but even in the venue of sickness there was joy. People would grasp me by the hand with tears in their eyes, even though the skin of their palms was coming away beneath their bandages. I remember particularly leading a ward in prayer; one woman sang loudest of all the worshippers, and the nurses told me afterwards that they were astonished by her vigour, that until my visit she had hardly been able even to raise herself from her bed. She died later that day, I believe; I like to think of her exertions as proof that the spirit can be stronger than the body.

Within a month of the landing of the *Senaar* I was beginning my first Galilean journey. The number of times I have travelled around and over our sea but I shall never forget the first time! I flew by shuttle to Yared, on the north coast: from the first, our closest ally and dearest nation-friend. I was there officially to initiate negotiations for the North Coast Spinal Railway, but in fact there was more joy, celebration and praise – and more trade negotiated – than can be suggested by that rather bland official label. I was banqueted every night, shown the plans for their city. The land north of Yared is bitter, without even the limited algae fertility that we enjoy east of Galilee. Accordingly, Yared hemmed the coast, kept close to the water that gives life: few buildings were more than a hundred metres from the waters, and the Yaredish had their gardens in the front: not faux-grass and flowers growing weakly in hastily-assembled soil, but portions of the shallow sea boxed off and desalinated, places for waterlilies and big-fronded leaf plants, for eels and tiny genengineered sticklebacks. I visited many of these homes, met many of the Yaredish people. There was a great televised summit meeting between myself and the Yared President, Al-Sebadoh, at which the treaty of accord was signed. In all the vicissitudes that followed, the years of war and hardship, this treaty between our two great nations has never been breached.

Of course, Yared is a much poorer nation than are we and most of the trade we undertook on that first visit was symbolic; from the Yaredish artefacts and statues that do indeed possess a certain beauty but are of little practical use, from us Fabricant programmes of tremendous and immediate use. But although enemies of mine have sometimes stigmatised my dealing with the Yared as unprofitable, you must understand that profit is not always measured in terms of money. With Yared we have always had the staunchest of allies, and our alliance is partly founded on their sense of indebtedness. And if some of the more hot-headed Yaredish factions have resented the Senaarian dominance of the Galilee basin, most have recognised the force of necessity, have understood the good order and harmony that comes out of a single recognised authority. And after all we do worship the same God, which can hardly be said of the puerile individualism of faith practised amongst the anarchist Alsists; a faith which in practice amounts to atheism.

From Yared I flew over the waters (I can still remember pressing my face against the shuttle porthole as the pilot banked to catch the thousand glittering fragments of sunlight thrown up by the waves, as if our sea were molten, brightest platinum waves) to visit Eleupolis. They were having their teething difficulties, problems that marred their foundation, and I have no wish to slander one of our allies by dwelling too harshly on that time. Suffice it to say that I did not stay long, with the volatility of the political situation so severe. Eleupolis was a poor place then, with too much squabbling and fighting to allow time for building. Things have improved there now, and I understand that it is now quite fashionable for our young people to take trucks round the south-east curve of Galilee and visit. But at the beginning the people of Eleupolis bickered and fought and argued amongst themselves, and there was little by way of building. And the people paid the price for this lack of strong leadership. Living in tents is all very well as a temporary measure, but without solid roofs to fend off the radiation you will not prosper. Sickness and death began its slow growth curve. And instead of recognising this evil and banding together to combat it, the Eleupolisians only bickered and fought and argued the more. I understand from historians that this nation suffered the greatest proportion of deaths in the early decades. The workforce was decimated, the land was stunted. I established alliance protocols with the provisional government, but I believe that same government was overthrown within days of our departure.

From there I flew along the coast, and then south-west over the shrugging broken hills of Gant to Babulonis. This was a more stable community. They had decided not to build by the shore, and instead carved their homes from the Gantian hills. Their first great public work was the great pipeline, running from Galilee to their city, powered by solar pumps. They preferred the hills partly because it made building their homes easier, but also because there was an indigenous sort of salt-grass there, less harsh and useless than our East Coast variants. We tried transplanting this strain, of course (we traded Fabricant software and some other technical knowhow for various Babulonis goods), but it did not thrive in the windier east. Babulonis was centred on a long, winding valley, fairly sheltered from the whipping winds. The pipeline deposited some water in a pool at the head of this valley, and it ran (by means of certain cleverly-concealed pumps) up the course of an ancient riverbed to a reservoir at the far end. Strange to sit by a stream and watch it run uphill! But I sat there, in the white light of midday, patting at my face with a silk handkerchief in the heat. The chief of Babulonis described the process by which they created this stream: resurrecting the dead planet, he called it. And it was a beautiful sight to sit in the mouth of an elegant Babulonian cave-home, looking down past meadows of cropped salt-grass and over municipal buildings to a river, sparkling in the sun. Some call this Babulonis Canal, since it is an artificial waterway; but, as they themselves point out, the riverbed was a natural Salt feature, not of their construction, so it is not appropriate to call it a canal.

After settling treaty details with Babulonis, I shuttled up the coast and visited Lantern, on the western coast. A strange community Lantern, built around only three families such that every citizen is a member of one or other of these families: The gene pool, clearly, is not as diverse as it ought to be, and Lanternians do suffer amazingly high incidences of congenital and inherited disorders. Neither, I think, is the younger generation of Lanternians happy with the claustrophobic feel of their community. Many leave their families and homes, and move to other nations. Of course, few lands are as welcoming as Senaar. Most resist all forms of immigration, and those few that do not have strict regulations governing who can come. With Senaar, though, we have always welcomed the immigrant, provided he or she brings money (or money's portable equivalent in skill and labour), and provided he or she is prepared to do their share of the work that is to be done. And over the years several thousand Lanternians have, I believe, tramped up to New Florence, boated to Yared and finally caught the spinal railway to Senaar. Some have even navigated their way there along the full length of the Galilee in home-made boats, a perilous undertaking but one that demonstrates the pull of a perfectly harmonious nation such as ours. We are the envy of Salt, my children, my people! It is no sin to take pride in this. It is, after all, God's doing.

With my visit to New Florence, and the signing of the final element of the treaty (with a great deal of public celebration all about the shores of the Galilee), the Southern Alliance was formally consti-tuted. How little did I then know that this alliance, headed as it was by Senaar, was so very shortly to exist in a state of war with the nations of the north. Indeed, upon returning home, I was advised to travel north, to see whether some of the nations building themselves about the shores of the Perse might not also be encouraged to sign up to the Alliance. And I planned this; my people began talking to northerners by radio, setting the terms for the first visit. But about the Perse the Alsists were already establishing their malign hold.

At home, in our beloved Senaar, the group of interested parties passed a Parliamentary motion expressing their anxiety regarding the kidnapped children. Ageing one year for ten in stasis, and living for a year's acceleration and two year's deceleration, these children were now biologically nine or ten years old. We were concerned that they had already been warped by the culture of Als, and the feeling was now commonly articulated that unless we could recover these infants before puberty they would be lost to us altogether. Senaarians are a people that value the family above almost everything, save God, and the prospect of never again seeing their children greatly distressed the fathers, many of whom were in the military. Of all the issues that were debated amongst friends, and by the nascent web all around Galilee, this was the most hotly contested.

Some said we should negotiate; some said we should mount a raiding party and take the children back, whether Als liked it or not. The army was busy, but trained soldiers consider themselves warriors, and grow restless when they are being employed as engineers and sappers, building bridges and putting quintiglass windows in the facades of shop-stores. At monthly meetings of squaddie representatives there was, my subordinates told me, a great deal of grumbling. Whilst we struggled to make the gale-picked barrenness of the eastern Galilean plain fertile, stories were coming down of the easy life of the northerners. It was said that the Alsist settlement of the Perse basin was an illegal action, amounting almost to theft. It was said that the Alsists were using underhand methods to bring Convento and Smith into their sphere of influence. It was difficult to know what to believe: empire building ought to be flatly contrary to the anarchist philosophy of Als, but I had had many examples of their evil intent. And it seemed clear to many, even during those early days, that there was going to come a time when our two nations would come into bitter conflict; when the white deserts of Salt would redden with spilt blood.

Petja

When we realised the magnitude of the task before us, some of us wept. Salt tears fell upon the salt ground. We had dreamed many dreams as we travelled through space, foreseen many versions of our world, but we had foreseen none so bleak.

Consider the desert God had seen fit to test us with. There was little water. The air contained poisonous levels of chlorine and some other noxious gases. The upper atmosphere was insufficiently stocked with greenhouse gases, and the average Salter was exposed to twenty or thirty rem of radiation a year. The topsalt was completely hostile to all the forms of vegetation we had brought with us from earth: cultivation of the plants we were familiar with could only take place in tiny plots laboriously reclaimed, boxed at the sides and underneath, filled with the mulch of our own organic waste. There were many species of native plant and algae but none of them were edible or in any major way useful to us.

The salt-grasses, of which (I believe) thirty-three varieties have been catalogued, are barely plants at all, more a brutally primitive arrangement of salt crystals with a few organic traces, virtually no cellular structure. The sea algae, of which there are many dozen strains, are no good by themselves as food, although it is possible to use algae as a fertiliser for growing modified versions of various vegetables. The land algae is more interesting, but is only to be found in the mountains and (I understand) in the broken hills of the far south.

Close to the water, and in the uplands, where a relatively high proportion of magnesium chlorides, magnesium sulphates, calcium sulphates and potassium chlorides are to be found, there is a certain amount of aboriginal vegetation. But in the desert nothing grows; not even salt-grass can survive the parching barrenness, the regular scouring of savage winds. And deserts cover more than eighty per cent of our world's surface. Our younger generations talk of transforming the whole world and many changes have taken place, even in my lifetime. I can stroll through the seashore arcologies on the north coast without a mask, I can run my fingers along the broad and waxy leaves of new plants, I can crush the tiny peppercorn bulb-heads of frogflowers between my fingers and smell the bitter perfume. The vista along the seafront of Smith is one of greenery, a lush and cultivated stretch of land beside a sea so dark it is purple-black. But we have barely touched our world. It is only a ten minute stroll south or eastwards from the seashore to pure, aboriginal desert: the unending acres of salt dunes, the world-girdling emptiness of the Great Desert.

People wept because our first months of life on Salt might as well have been a continuation of the confinement of the voyage. We still spent most of our time inside, cowering under the dome of our ship or digging windowless homes into the ground to escape the solar bombardment. We still ate recycled foods; meagre meals bulked up with processed shit. My vision had been of spreading my shit on fertile alien soil, of growing large spinach and cabbage plants, but for the first months even our shit was too precious to waste on the soil. We held various scientific colloquia to discuss the best way to scrub the chlorine from the atmosphere, to build up an ozone layer, to create enough topsoil to provide sustainable arable production. But often as not I would leave these meetings early and find my only solace in a bottle of vodjaa and the bed of a friend. It seemed as if the task was beyond us.

But – we must never lose our faith in that conjunction. But there were positive things about our world, too. It was mostly temperate; too hot in summer (and in the midday equatorial desert much too hot, without shade, humidity or breeze), and a little too cold in winter (except at the poles, where it was below freezing for much of the year), *but* for the lengthy spring and autumn the ambient temperature was perfect. Then there was, at least, some water. It is conceivable, I suppose, that there might have been no water at all. And, as a lover of mine once told me, if we had been sent to a world with oceans of water but without any salt at all, we would have surely died. I think she meant it as a sort of joke.

Let me tell you how we first organised ourselves upon this new world. Work rotas were reinterpreted in terms of the tasks before us: those allocated agricultural duties spent our days marking out fields and clearing the topsalt quite away until the quartz-granite was visible underneath. This would create deep, empty swimming-pool shaped holes in the landscape, and these we would line with ship's plastic, cover with double-layered plasglass, and begin to fill with laser-pestled ground-up rubble from the mountains, a fine shingle, topped over with such waste and mulch as we were allocated, which wasn't much, because the recycling bins still claimed most. We were trying to create an agricultural soil; which is no easy thing. Soil is a balance of minerals and decaying organic matter that took millennia to come to being on Earth. Unless it be perfectly right there are almost no plants that will grow in it. For months all we could grow were boltweeds (useful as food only in a heavily processed soup-form) and, oddly, tomatoes, which seemed to do well. This food was rather radioactive, of course; but we ate it anyway.

Achieving a sufficiency of grown foods, rather than having to rely on dwindling ship's supplies and the tasteless horror of the recycle bins, was a priority. Work rotas, then as now, could only ever allocate a quarter of a person's day to work, and that only if a state of emergency were declared. But in those early days most of us did not stick slavishly to our rota. If the second half of morning were allotted to agricultural work, then we would turn up early and stay all day. I spent a month on soil work, and then was shifted to livestock, and then roads. Normally, livestock would have meant birds, but our birds were confined to the dome of our ship. Those few who flew away died in flight of the bad air and the high radiation, and fell to the earth like tied-up bundles. In this enclosed space there was little call for bird-farmers, and so I devoted my time instead to the eels. We hollowed out pools, and pumped partially desalinated water from the sea into them. Then we took out the frozen eel embryos, genengineered them for a while with a modicum of easy-splice materials, and then released them to swim and grow in the tented water.

'If we can desalinate the Aradys, even only so much as partially'

58

Eredics said to me as we bobbed in this warm bath, with the eels wriggling against our waving feet, 'then we could populate the whole sea with these eels.' Eredics was a friend of mine, and we were rotaed together creating eel ponds.

'There's still the radioactivity,' I said, my head back, my eye on the tent roof. Its envelope was filled with blockading gel, but it still did a poor job of protecting the eels from the solar buffeting. The ambient radiation was still too high, and mutations were common.

'Not really,' said Eredics. 'They are bred to swim down. At a sufficient depth the water itself will shield them.'

But this was to ignore the bigger problem, which was the desalination. The only thing that could survive in the seas of Salt at the beginning was the aboriginal algae, and even it found it hard. It was only to be found in the bays, where the water was still enough to allow a partial crystallisation of salt at the surface in the heat of the day. The algae would grow underneath this crust, where the water had been partially cleared. This made it easy to harvest by simply cracking the bumpy sheets of white and upending them, to grasp the beards of blue and green and pull them away. The algae made a reasonable fertiliser, although the amount of processing it required was too great for it to be eaten directly. Besides it tasted foul, even triple-processed.

More than this, practice had never taken the salt out of water; it had always taken the water out of the brine, and collected it at some other point. But we could not do this with the whole Aradys; we could not boil away an ocean of clean water and accumulate it somewhere else. And so, other plans, more or less absurd, were hatched by people sitting about the night-time fires, sipping their vodjaa or dancing or telling one another tales.

But this was not to come next. Next, we built the home dormitories. We were mining some metals from the hills around and we stored these in trenches on Istenem Hill. And we dug the three main dormitory caves underneath Istenem Hill, so that this metal store, and the saltrock of the hill, could help shield us from ambient radiation. Most of us were happy to move from the ship, which could now be devoted wholly to livestock and birds. Of course, some wanted other than to live in the public dorm, and to these people then as now the same remedies were available. They could live where they liked. Then as now, this gave little freedom to the individual, for a single woman or a single man can work only very slowly at building their own home, particularly in the inhospitable conditions of Salt in those days. But many people did leave the dorms, and set out to make their own homes, by themselves or in groups. Small spontaneous collectives grew up to establish rock-roofed halls, or churches, or larger dwellings. Some people wanted still to live in the dome, which meant they had to endure the stink and company of livestock; but it was true that the dome provided the most efficient radiation shield still, and for some that was the most important thing.

One dorm was allocated to women and to women-and-children. The other two were general, although the hospital was located in one of these. For the first few months I lived in a general dorm with my then lover; but towards the end of the first year she was pregnant and moved to the women-and-children. We would still meet, of course; still eat together sometimes, but we were more Purist in those days. Today's fashion for cohabitation was unthought of.

Her name was Turja. Our relationship started the week after the *Als* was brought down to land on the new world. She moved very gracefully, like a dancer, although she was actually rather squat physically. She was less defined by curves than most women: her figure was more square, and her breasts had the solid squareness of car headlights. Her legs went straight down, and her waist did not dip inwards. But she was still extremely graceful; she moved on the front of her feet, tripping forward and back as if in a perpetual dance. And her face was very beautiful.

One week her rota took her into the dome to tend the birds. After feed had been laid out for the flying stock (something that took only moments) this chore revolved chiefly around feeding the geese. I wandered in one morning. I had spent most of the night roofing a new eel pond. Of course roofing was tiring work, physical work, and I had tried to get a little sleep after dawn. But I was still high from the job, the mania of prolonged effort, the talking with the other members of the team. Do you know how that is? Laughing together, singing, telling bad jokes.

There had been four of us, two men and two women. Sometimes workgroups click, sometimes not. How else would it be with the random allotment of the rota? This group had clicked, and we had finished the job in a single night, instead of the two days scheduled. That is how it is, when workmates jolly one another on, set one another impossible targets, laugh at failure and accident. I cut my arm against one of the supports, and the others jeered as I hurried off to the dorm to get it sealed. But when I came back they were in even higher spirits. We finished so rapidly that we were left with a sensation of discontinuity, almost of dismemberment. There was a sense in which we wanted the delirium of the job to continue, to carry on the high. But there was nothing more to be done, save check the finished dome more times than it required; and we ended up sitting in the paling of the dawn laughing and talking, sipping celebratory vodjaa.

They were Hamar, Sipos and Csooris. I had spent some time with Csooris on the voyage, but we had spoken little to one another. She had the most beautiful hair of any woman I have known; it was so black it seemed to shine. Cutting it off during the voyage had seemed a great loss; but it had grown back during trance and deceleration, and was now down to her shoulders. Apart from that, there was the joy in discovering a bond, a connection, with people I had previously been happy to nod to in passing, to smile at in the dorm. We talked about the radiation, the thing our little dome was supposed to block.

'Of course,' said Hamar. 'There is no substitute for several metres of heavy metal. Our little envelope with its gel will do something, but little enough.'

'Our work is useless then!' said Sipos, but laughing as she spoke. The thought that we had quite wasted our night seemed hilarious to us, and laughing spread round like a ripple of flame.

'You can't use heavy metals to generate electricity,' I pointed out. That was the trick with our design: two layers of tough plastics and the space between filled with a polymerised composite gel that soaked up solar radiation, grabbed the passing particles like a playing child snatching a thrown ball out of the air and set up a resonance-excitation pattern that sensors at the base of the structure converted to electricity, which in turn was used to power the pond; keep it heated at night, keep it aerated, supply the food and so on. It was an elegant machine, although the gel lost its protective properties after time and had to be replaced every five months or so.

Hamar was a large man, with a great deal of red hair on his body, chest and back. This hair sprouted up his neck and throat, but he kept his chin and mouth shaved, and he was completely bald, so that when he stripped to the waist – as he had done that night, with the heat of the work – his head looked oddly smooth and clean on top of his ruggish torso. He was sipping his vodjaa through a straw. He used to drink it through a straw because (he said) it increased the rate of absorption of the alcohol, although I never understood the logic of this proposition. His mood had shifted down a little now, and he was more reflective.

'It is strange to think about, though,' he said, 'isn't it? Perhaps it is the invisibility. Now!' – and he pointed, with his left hand – 'all around us, the radiation is falling, raining onto our heads.'

In fact, we were sitting under the dome beside the gloopy pool, into which we had just unloaded the baby eels (though they were too small to see), and so we were sheltered to a degree from the environmental level of radiation exposure. Sipos started to say something to this effect, but Hamar started again.

'Particles, it is,' he said, as if we didn't know. 'Tiny torn-up pieces of the sun, torn up and spat out at the speed of light. Down they come, all around us, like a never-ending blizzard of dust.'

This was not exactly true either; the indications were that we had happened to arrive to Salt in the middle of an unusually intense period of solar storm activity, and that in a decade or so the rem count would drop to less punishing levels. But none of us pointed this out. Perhaps Hamar's odd and poetic conceits had spooked us. We all sipped, sipped. The vodjaa warmed through us.

'You can't see it,' he said in a lower tone, 'or smell or taste it; you can't feel it with your fingers. Only your DNA can feel it, feel the little dots as they hurtle through, dislodging atoms in the amines. Setting up patterns of disease, neoplasm. Pushing the dominoes over, and letting the cancer tumble along. What a strange thing it is when you think about it! That infinite dust, settling all around us, now, tomorrow, onwards.'

'I read in Lucretius,' said Csooris, suddenly, 'that this is the nature of the universe.' Csooris had a passion for Old and New Latin. 'So the ancients believed: an endless rain of dust through the universe, falling from nowhere and falling towards nowhere. Lucretius says that this is all reality is, except that something has introduced the slightest of swerves into the falling, so that the atoms begin to move about, come together, move apart.'

'He didn't mean radiation though,' said the more literal-minded Sipos. 'He was one of the ancients; they surely had no such conceptions.'

'It was a poet's conceit, I think,' I said.

Csooris seemed angered by this. 'What do you know of it?' she snapped.

'I have read the thing,' I countered, bridling a little myself. '*The Nature of Things*. I read it in my mother's dormitory.'

'But in translation,' she insisted. 'Not in the Old Latin.'

'Latin!' I scoffed.

'I can read a bit of New Latin,' said Sipos, trying to defuse the situation. She had travelled amongst the Vaticano Republics when she was a young woman, I think.

But Csooris was not impressed. She spat. 'Kindergarten tongue!' she scoffed. 'You can learn it in a day.'

Hamar was harumming, clearing his throat. He was being made uncomfortable by the sparring. Sipos didn't like it either; she was a straightforward woman, more comfortable with facts than fancies.

'The big question,' she said, her voice a little too loud, to try and bully the other conversation out of the way, 'remains. What are we going to do long-term about the levels of radiation? We need more than domes and holes in the ground.'

Hamar was nodding. 'We need two things. We need an ozone layer, and we need a magnetosphere.'

'In that order?'

'Other way round,' said Csooris.

I confess I was a little heated by the occasion, and perhaps angry with Csooris. 'Of all the stupid things to say! And how do you intend to create a magnetosphere?' I said, sneery.

The situation (but I am sure you know it): Salt possesses a very weak magnetosphere. Our world has a nickel-iron core, molten, and a granite mantle, mostly quartz. The core revolves at a different rate from the rest of the world, and this differential generates a magnetic field, as it does on Earth. But the differential on Salt is not great, and the field generated is not strong. There were many theories, but the most likely explanation was that our world is a very old world. That its core has been slowing down for billennia. This would also explain certain other features. Maybe the surface of our world was once covered with a salty sea, but the water has been lost over many years. Maybe life once crowned our world, maybe even intelligence. There were people who boasted that they intended to dig out fossils of our Saltian foremothers; others who insisted that there had never been backbones on our world before, let alone intelligence. Other still refused to believe that our world was a dying one: and indeed, there were other possible explanations for the state of things.

A magnetosphere is a very effective protection against the rigours of solar radiation. But ours was not strong enough, and there were no ways to increase it, short of reaching into the heart of the world with a god's hand and giving the core a great spin.

'We must work at pumping ozone, or similar screening gases, into the stratosphere,' said Sipos. The conventional response.

'I'm in a dorm group,' said Hamar, 'and we have a plan. After all, we don't need to shield the whole world, just ourselves. Why not build a filter, a huge filter kilometres across, and position it in geosync orbit over Als?'

The rest of us laughed and scoffed at this, of course; but Hamar seemed quite genuine, and tried for a while to flesh out his conception. It could be constructed out of crystals, grown in orbit; it would make the midday sun more bearable; it would introduce temperature variants into the atmosphere that would break up the punishing morn and evening winds. After a while, getting a little heated, he said, 'What else do you suggest?'

'Build a gel-filled blanket and wrap the whole world in it!' I said.

'Dig underground and live like moles,' said Csooris, happy again.

'God will provide,' said Sipos in a gloomy tone. Atheism had increased among us since our arrival, you see. Mostly, I think it was to do with the disappointment in discovering that our Promised Land was so flawed, that God had not provided for us. Of course, atheism is no business of anybody else's. Many of us had only agreed to the religious protocols in the first place so that we would be allowed to join the fleet. (It is ancient history now, but the original initiative for the fleet had come from the World Ecumensis of Christian churches. We had joined because no more political grouping would have accepted us.) On the other hand, there were many deeply religious, or at least spiritual, people with us. I was one.

We sat for a while in silence, with that sudden soberness of the spirit that can come with too much drink. I pressed my face close to the inside wall of the dome we had just built. Outside, invisible to everything but the eyes of our DNA, as Hamar had said, was the incessant rain of solar particles. I tried to visualise it. I tried to think of it as a rattling rain, like minute hailstones, or deadly bullets falling thousands to every millimetre. But I could not. For some reason my eyes could only see in terms of a softly tumbling snow, flakes of radioactivity blown about like a blizzard; like the swarming of an invisible hive. The sun was only just up, so perhaps that informed my fantasy. I thought of the dust landing on the ground, like snow, instead of hurtling on through the rock and into the planet, as was the truth. I thought of it building up over the millennia, great drifts of hot particles, dunes of white-hot sands.

Later Hamar and Sipos wandered round to the other side of the pool to have sex in the water. I sat for a long time in silence with Csooris. I found myself recalling the times we had been together during the voyage, the places we had found to have love. We had almost fetishised secrecy, privacy, and had sought out places where other people were not. I was looking again at her hair. The dawn light, filtered through the dome, was almost pure white; it made strands of white reflection in her black hair. I reached out to touch it, but she batted my hand away.

She seemed oddly maudlin, and was sipping away at her vodjaa with a great purpose. For a while I was content with the silence, the clarity of the moment. I thought of us in her universe, in her Old Latin poem, all of us falling together, forever falling through nothingness towards nothingness. The most we do is only a reaching out, a trying to grab our fellow fallers, trying to swim through the air the way novice spacepeople do in weightless, thrashing pointlessly about our centres of gravity.

'Do you want to have love?' Csooris said to me suddenly. Without waiting for me to reply she added: 'I thought you were going to ask.'

I shrugged. 'I was thinking of other things,' I said. But, now that she mentioned it, I found the thought exciting. I was getting hard. Perhaps it was the remains of the buzz from the night's work, a continuation of that out-going energy. I reached out to touch her hair again, but again she slapped my hand away.

'Leave my hair!' she said.

'I was only going to caress it a little,' I said, offended.

She said nothing, only shifted herself over towards me on her bottom (we were sitting cross-legged beside the lip of the pool) and began to kiss me on the mouth. This was very pleasant. So we had love quickly, with most of our clothes still on, and with Csooris on top. But as I lay there, acting the solid earth to her pounding, I began to feel weirdly insubstantial, as if Csooris above me, coming down upon me again and again, was actually falling through me. But maybe it was a good thing, being distracted, because she came twice before I did, and then came again when she saw me climaxing.

Afterwards she fell asleep straight away, and I lay next to her. Maybe I dozed for a moment or two, but my consciousness refused to disengage. I stared at Csooris' face for a while, at the little lines underneath her eyes, and the pores in her cheeks and nose. That moment is very clear in my memory now. The light was like water, somehow; clear and fresh, reviving like a cold wash of the face. Soon enough I got up and climbed through the little doorway of the dome to the outside.

My mask clicked up over my mouth, and I fidgeted for a while with my nose clip. The air was still cool from the night and I was struck by how quickly the air under the dome (a dome we had only finished a few hours earlier, after all) had already become greenhouse-heated. It was pleasant to feel my skin chill. I wandered over to a nearby pile of stones, and climbed up to sit on them for a while. This was a little foolish since, clearly, it was dangerous to spend unnecessary time out of doors, and to rack up rems on the dosimeters we all carried hung about our hips. The dosimeter was checked every week, and the exposure was then factored into the work rota. If I had thought about it, I would not have risked being allocated a month's indoor work, since I enjoyed being outdoors: but I was fascinated by the sun. It was still only just climbing over the mountains. A great wedge-shaped shadow lay over the surface of the Aradys, on which the chlorine fog roiled and played. The white and pink skin of the mountain, of Istenem, looked darker in the morning. The other mountains, on the far side of the water to the west, gleamed where the direct sunlight fell upon them and seemed to bleach the rock.

Soon enough I got up and wandered over to the dome, more to get out of the radiation for a while than anything else. There were people playing football in the area behind the entrance, so I wandered further back and into the goose farm, still wanting to be alone. This was where Turja was just beginning her morning shift.

She had scattered seed for the airborne birds, and was cleaning out the water from the troughs. I watched her do this for a while, propped under one of the trees newly planted in this part of the dome. I still felt no fatigue from my night's exertions; if anything, I felt rather hyper, rather keyed-up by the excitement of finishing the project ahead of time and by the morning sex. There was something soothing in watching Turja go about her duties. She moved calmly, gracefully. From the trough to the goose-gate, and then into the compounds to shoo the geese out. They came, hissing and croaking as is the goose way, and she followed, waving her arms in great sweeps and whooping to make them go. These geese were genengineered; they were the height of a man, and most weighed more than a man, but their brains were still tiny goose brains and they were easily scared. The flock started feeding, and Turja moved among them, poking and checking. She noticed one with a septic leg, and had grabbed the huge bird and up-ended it in a moment. I was transfixed. Such grace, combined with strength. She didn't even need to sit down: the beast's wings unfurled and struggled against the floor, its cross-looking face twisting away, its legs up in the air. Turja cleaned its wound and applied a steripatch.

'You've worked with geese before,' I shouted across the yard to her.

She wasn't startled, which suggested she had seen me come in and had been ignoring me. But once she had right-ended the goose and watched it scurry away to join its lanky fellow, she wandered over and sat down beside me.

'It's on my list of preferential jobs,' she said. 'I've always liked birds.'

'Birds, yes, I have always liked birds also,' I said. 'But not geese.'

'Really?' She turned to look at me with eyes narrowed, ready for mockery. 'Why not?'

'I'm not sure,' I said. 'I think maybe it is the teeth. I find it hard to like birds with teeth. Teeth are surely for animals. They look sinister lining a beak.'

She laughed at this. 'What a rigidist you are!' she said. The reference was to an old sect from before the voyage had begun, a group who had preached a sort of religiously-endorsed essentialism; it was only used now in jest.

I laughed with her. 'You're very beautiful,' I said, feeling warm.

'You're not handsome,' she replied. 'Not to my eyes. Although there are some who think you are.'

'There are?'

'Of course.'

'So you know who I am?'

'Of course,' she said again.

'But you don't find me attractive?'

She shrugged. 'I like my men with more muscle, larger bodies,' she said.

'What a shame,' I said, laughing. 'Because I was going to ask if you wanted to have sex, as soon as your rota shift is finished. But now I find that you only like over-developed men!'

She smiled. 'Well, perhaps I will have sex with you,' she said. 'But not until after my morning's work.'

It was as simple as that. I fell asleep under the tree, and Turja went back to her job. It felt remarkably secure, just sleeping there; popping into consciousness for a moment and noticing her about some other chore, and then slipping away into sleep.

Barlei

Part of the purpose of this document is to tell what I knew of the hero, jean-Pierre Dreyfus. You will know his face, so there's little need for me to describe it any detail, but I can say that the visuals do not capture the versatility of expression, the lively vigour of his eyes and his mouth. He was a handsome man, the perfect army officer, and there is a reason why his memory is cherished, even to the present day. That reason is that he represents something, the embodied essence of Senaar. Strong, brave, light on his feet, always courteous and glad to be of use. With his white skin and pale hair he always looked as if he belonged on this world, as if he were a true native. And in his dress uniform he was so handsome! There is no shame in a man admitting the handsomeness of a man, if there is

69

nothing impure in that admiration; and there was nothing but a pure delight in my breast at the figure of the warrior that jean-Pierre cut.

I promoted him from his lieutenantship to a captaincy soon after our landing, when it became clear that his skills were of an above average calibre. Sometimes people think that the soldiers of an army exist only to kill, but of course the truth is very different. The true soldier loves life, his own and others, almost as much as he loves freedom. The true soldier works and plans to avoid war, to safeguard life. The attributes he possesses are the power to command, the strength to carry out his will, and the bravery to face any consequences. jean-Pierre had all these. Superior officers would find themselves following his suggestions as if they were orders, so forcefully and expertly did he speak. His men loved him with a passionate dearness; they would have died for him at the merest hint. And the women adored him from afar.

By the second week I had put him in charge of the job of building the barracks. This took priority over even the building of domiciles, since the army must be settled and strong before it can usefully hold the umbrella under which the rest of the community may shelter. So jean-Pierre had the power, which he used judiciously, to take civilian workers on secondment (of course they were paid at the army rate, according to their skill) to help construct a secure area with all the necessary facilities. His was a model command. He was up before dusk every day, immaculately turned out in uniform, to greet the evening reveille (most construction took place during the night, of course, when the radiation levels were lower). Then, throughout the evening, he co-ordinated teams, personally gave them their orders, and ensured that the raw materials were delivered, that the Fabricants were positioned and programmed, that the site supervisors knew what was what. Throughout the night he worked tirelessly, bullying-up his men, rebuking the civilians for falling behind the military, encouraging and bringing together. The barracks and all the necessary inner installations were completed a full week ahead of schedule.

He helped me with the building of my own house after this: the man had tremendous energy. After the first month I organised a festival to celebrate our progress, and the whole of Senaar turned out in the cool of the late evening (once the wind had died down) to cheer the torchlight parade of our army. And the loudest cheer went up for jean-Pierre.

In those early days we were all too much preoccupied to watch many Visuals, but some enterprising individuals were setting up Visual companies nonetheless, using their voyage capital to invest in transmission equipment and going door to door in the new town to sell subscriptions. The pre-recorded shows were all old news, of course: we had all had many years during the voyage to watch the soaps, the sermons, the practical shows. In order to whip up an audience the Visual companies – there were two I think: Senaar Visual and one other, that sank into bankruptcy shortly after beginning trading – anyway, to entice an audience SV hit upon the idea of Visualising our growing community. A sort of real-life soap, you see. They approached me, through my agent, the ensign Preminger, but I declined: I valued my privacy too much to consent to being filmed the whole time, and I did not need the money. I suggested they contact jean-Pierre: he was an up-and-coming man, a popular figure, but I knew he did not have a personal fortune. And so it was that jean-Pierre's life became a Visual programme.

He came to me about a fortnight after this had begun, to ask my advice. On this occasion, I had to ask the man with the camera-spectacles to wait outside my house. I like my private conversations to be private.

'I have come to ask your advice, Mr President,' he said. He always called me 'Mr President' at the beginning of our conversations, and I always had to correct him with a 'Call me Barlei, my dear Lieutenant.'

'What advice can I offer you, my friend?' I asked him.

'It is a question of romance, Barlei,' he said.

I laughed. 'Of all the topics on Salt, that is the one I am least qualified to offer advice about! I have had so little experience of love affairs that I am a mere child where such matters are concerned.'

'Nonetheless,' he persevered. He was so pure, so manly, that the

71

mere contemplation of the subject was making him blush. 'I am wondering about taking a wife.'

'Splendid idea,' I said, heartily. 'You have been single long enough.'

'Fifty years!' he joked. This was a common joke amongst those who had come through the hibernation of the voyage. In fact jean-Pierre was biologically a little over twenty-five.

'Why do you need my advice, my friend? Should you not rather come for my blessing?' His parents had both died in the hibernation tanks, and on landing I had taken a kindly, parental interest in his welfare. I regarded him almost as my son.

'Well, Barlei,' he said, shifting in his seat. 'I have had several offers, from several ladies. Some of them less than decent.'

'Beware this sort of temptation, my friend,' I suggested. 'Particularly now that you have signed your soul away to the Visual companies! But joking aside, it would harm the morale of our nascent community if word got about that you were a man of loose morals.'

'All the more reason for me to marry!' he said.

'I agree.'

'Then this is my problem: two first daughters from prominent families in Senaar have taken a fancy to me, and I cannot decide which I should marry!'

I laughed at this. 'Which do you love?' I suggested.

'I love them both,' he said, sighing. 'They are both wonderful.'

'Which is the more beautiful?'

'One is dark and one is fair,' he said. 'But could you say that day is more beautiful than night? Or that red wine tastes sweeter than white?'

'This is a predicament indeed, my friend,' I said, still laughing. 'I think I will hold an exclusive banquet, here in my house, and perhaps I will happen to invite both of these families, and then I can really give you my opinion.'

Preminger was against this idea: he thought it would appear too elitist, too extravagant a gesture this early in the life of our land. But I overruled him, although I did concede him one point and invite the Visuals to cover the occasion. What Preminger did not understand (he was a man of brilliant intellect, but only a narrowly conceived understanding of humanity) was how a little high living can raise a people's spirits, even if they can only experience it at second hand. The banquet took place one night the following week, in the still air after the Devil's Whisper had died away. The nine richest Senaarian families attended. The food was provided by my own chef, although the numbers were such that he had to borrow the skills of another three cooks from neighbouring families. A military quartet provided the music: Bach and Schubert, which I consider the most easeful for digestion. And, naturally, jean-Pierre came, with two of his fellow officers, his friends.

There was a great deal of conversation and laughter, with glasses of wine (red and white, in jean-Pierre's honour, a little joke between the two of us; although I'm afraid it was only Fabricant wine, water-mixed powder, which never quite tastes the same) and a little dancing. Both Visual companies were there, and a large crowd gathered outside my front door, to cheer each new arrival. It was so liberating, so civilised.

'We might be back on Earth,' said Herr Warnke, to me.

'Not at all,' I countered. 'This is distinctively Saltian.' And, indeed, there were great dishes of differently-coloured salt, all gathered from the topsalt of the surrounding territory. There were many kilos of the stuff in each bowl, clearly much too much for condiment, but in those early days, when the food we ate was still being taken and reconstituted from the ship or the recycle farms, people used to add a little salt to taste. Nowadays, of course, everything we eat (more or less) is salty enough already, coming from the environment it does. But the platters of salt were more than a mere gesture in those days.

And so we filed in to the dinner-hall, and ate delicious food beneath plastic candles that burnt to give off the perfume of lavender and cinnamon. The light glowed on the polished quartz of the table, the Visual camera people hovered discreetly out of the way, the conversation murmured around the table. At one point I proposed a toast to our new life, our new world, created by God's Grace in the face of such difficulty, and everybody cheered.

But neither did I forget why I was there. I made sure to be sat within talking distance of both the women jean-Pierre was interested in. One was the eldest daughter of Herr Warnke, a very wealthy man who was already making good business from the manufacture of sorel cements, particularly promising for construction purposes and much cheaper than always mining quartz slabs, with a side-business in trace elements taken from the salts. I knew Warnke fairly well: he was a large-bodied man, with a taste in black suits and orange shirts, a fashion I was not afraid to tell him was too young for his maturity. But at this he would simply shake his balding head and laugh. We had had several meetings, because Warnke Inc. had agreed to take on board two dozen refugees from the chaos along the coast in Eleupolis. Many people wanted to get out, and as the most prosperous nation, even at that early stage, many people applied to come to us. Of course, there would be little point in them coming unless they had money (why would they want to come just to starve in the streets?) or else a guaranteed job of work. Accordingly, Warnke had sent representatives down, and the first two dozen Eleupolisians were due to fly back. This was good for them, because they got to escape the horrors of their homeland; and it was good for Warnke, and for Senaar, because he obtained the very cheapest workforce. He had explained the situation to me, and I (after all, only a military man) had not been too proud to learn.

'Almost all native Senaarians had come on the voyage with fairly sizeable fortunes,' he reminded me, rubbing his bald head with the flat of his hand.

'Few as sizeable as yours, my friend!' I told him.

He laughed. 'But the economy cannot really subsist on pure wealth, you see. We need an underclass, people to do the menial jobs. There are few enough of those, but we suffer employment difficulties at the bottom level. I know I do.'

'You think these migrant workers will be the solution?'

'Oh I wouldn't think of them as migrant,' he said. 'I think we should grant them full Senaar citizenship, with a clause to revoke citizenship and expel them if they become bankrupt.'

'Bankruptcy to be defined by . . . ?'

'If they cannot pay their taxes, I suppose. If they have no money.'

'But they'll come to us with no money! Should we expel them straight away?'

'If,' Warnke corrected, laughing, 'if they have no money and they lack the patronage of an employer. As long as they're working for Warnke's, they'll have enough money to pay their taxes, and to eat.'

And so we arranged it. Warnke built workers' dormitories, and shipped in his cement workers from Eleupolis. But I am straying from the point, which has to do, of course, with his daughter. She was the fair-haired beauty, like a golden child. Slim, elegant, with the prettiest laugh, and perfectly bred. More, she was accomplished as a flautist. Her name was Kim.

'My dear,' I called to her over the table. 'Tell me, which uniform do you prefer? The regular army, or the technical corps?' The army uniform was the deep blue it has always been, and the pilots and sappers from the technical corps wore green.

She laughed. 'Such is the question a woman has to answer!' she called back. 'Nothing to do with affairs of state, or the priorities for building railways lines, or anything like this, but blue or green!'

'You haven't answered my question.'

'The blue of the regular army, of course.'

And jean-Pierre sat there, in his immaculate dark-blue uniform, with his gleaming gold pips of command on his shoulder, and blushed like a schoolgirl.

The other woman in the contest, as it were, was the only child of a man called Hardison, who was establishing a school and a college. There were virtually no students in the latter, although there were some children for the former, but Hardison's plans were long-term, and his personal fortune large enough to enable him to wait for profits. I applauded the public spirit of his enterprise, because the effect was to provide education for the few children of our community by running the school at a loss. When the birth rate rose (we

75

confidently expected a great burst after the initial business of settling Senaar into the new world was finished and people could turn their thoughts to such things) more schools would clearly be established: by then Hardison's school would have the longest pedigree, and would be attracting the best students. And would be able to charge the highest fees. So perhaps Hardison's altruism was not so short-sighted!

His daughter Coventry was tall and lovely, hair as black as deep space, skin a delicate brown, the colour of the desert at dusk. She too was tall, lithe, lovely-looking, with a beautiful long face and eyes of such depth they drew the watcher in. I leant in her direction, and called to her.

'My dear! Which is your favourite instrument?'

'I beg your pardon, sir?'

'Your favourite musical instrument?'

She smiled at this. 'And must I pick a favourite? Isn't the point of musical instruments that they do not compete, do not strive with one another, but play together, in harmony?'

'Still, you must have a preference?'

'The piano, then!' she said, laughing. 'My own instrument!'

After the meal, Coventry and Kim played. It was a Mozart concerto and was exquisite. There was a perfect hush in the room, and we were, for that time, transported away from our worries, our anxieties, even (if I could speak for jean-Pierre) from our loves and human passions, into the realms of pure music.

The next day I saw jean-Pierre again, just before he was due to inspect a parade. 'Well?' he asked me, as he straightened his collar.

'You are right,' I conceded, laughing. 'How can I tell them apart? They are both as lovely as one another!'

'Perhaps I should marry them both,' he said, laughing. But this joke was a little too low for my tastes.

'I cannot advise you, my friend,' I said. 'You must follow your heart.'

Three weeks later the engagement was announced, between jean-Pierre and Kim. Their wedding was the social event of the community; hundreds attended, and most of the rest of Senaar watched the Visuals. He asked me to be best man, but I decided that this would not be compatible with my position as President, and so a brother officer stood next to him in church. But I was present too, in the front pew, and I am not ashamed to say that I shed some tears of joy for my brave boy as he spoke his vows in the presence of God and that congregation.

Petja

For a while Turja and I were happy enough in the large dorm. Actually, since most of her rota came up during the day for the first two months (caring for the livestock and so on), and since most of mine (basically construction) came up during the night, we only saw one another for morning and evening meals. But after two months I was rotaed onto road duty, something of which I had absolutely no experience. Accordingly, I spent five days or so on the simulators, familiarising myself with the design and construction aspects of the job. Strictly speaking, I did not need to spend so long, but I chose to learn the job as thoroughly as possible because it suited my purposes. Clearly, I could choose whichever time of day I liked to work the simulations, and so I started sleeping with Turja through the night.

The dorms were mostly empty at night, because it was night that saw most of the outside work being done, to reduce the radiation hazard, and most of the early work of the settlement (construction, open-mining and so on) was night-work. We would cuddle together under the duvet, giggling like children.

'You are most deliberately being slow in learning your new rotation,' she would say to me.

'I am, I am deliberately boring myself stupid so that I can be with you.'

That was the point, of course: I could have stayed on the simulators for the whole rotation if I liked. If I liked, I could have stayed on them for the rest of my life (except the next rotation would have thrown me off; and except that people would have been unhappy that the roads weren't built, and might have shunned me, or beaten me up maybe). There was no compulsion or, rather, the only compulsion was internal. The simulations are boring. They occupy the hand and eye, true, but they achieve nothing; they are merely computer pixels moving around. Who, in their right minds, would want to spend their quarter-days climbing into a simulator cab to go through the same routines over and over, when they could get out into the real world; when they could plan real roads, and then build them, and climb out of the cab at the day's end with a weary but profound sense of satisfaction?

In other lands, I know, work is a chore. People hurry through it, or drag their feet so as not to get too wound up in it, and yearn for it to end so that they can go off and do whatever else they want to do. But in other lands work is distributed poorly, with jaded workers who have spent their lives doing the same job until it has worn a groove smooth in their brains and they can no longer summon up the energy to do the job properly. With us, we work a quarter-day, and the rest of the time is ours.

And we discover this: that there is not enough to do outside work to keep ourselves busy. That we find ourselves wandering off to other people on work duty, offering to lend a hand, wanting to be useful again. With us, nobody gets into the rut of the eternal working return, every day the same as every other. With us, we are given a new job every few months. If we do not know how to do the job, then we learn; it rarely takes more than a few days. And after a few years we discover we can bring skills from all our areas of expertise to bear on any problem that confronts us. It keeps our minds alive. Only with extraordinarily specialised jobs, that require not a few days but many years of training – as with my expertise in tether technology, that had proven so vital during the voyage – is the labour limited to one person.

But in the bliss of those first few weeks with Turja, everything else was blotted from my head, except the joy of holding her and having her arms about me. Under the duvet, in that warm dark space like twins in a womb, so close our breath blurred into the air together; and one day we woke to find that our hair had become entangled and we had to pick it apart with a comb, laughing the whole time. We would have love before going to sleep; and then we would wake together, and have love again, a sleepy delicious kind of sex. I loved the way her skin smelled, the taste of her hair in my mouth, and the back of her neck. I loved the gentle roughness of her legs, where her hairs grew, and the dark narrow hairs that lay along her pale legs like cracks in enamel. I would run my hand slowly up the left leg, and she would squeal with ticklish delight. I loved her feet too. Often I do not like a woman's feet, perhaps because there is something awkwardly unaesthetic about them – the strange combinations that a foot represents: hardened toughened skin on the heel and ball of the foot, but with that soft, vulnerable baby-pink skin in the arch in between; the pure line of the top of the foot and the messy fringes that are our toes; the sheer gnarled size of toenails. I don't know what it is; a person is allowed their quirks and tastes, I suppose. But Turja's feet were perfect, quite large but for some reason every element of her feet was perfectly balanced with every other element. I could tickle them for ages, kiss them, rub my tongue over them. She liked my body too, for all that she had said she preferred more muscular men.

Our lovemaking fell into a pattern, a pattern as natural and satisfying as breathing. In the evening she would be the dominant partner, moving me around purposefully, egging me on, squatting on top of me or grabbing me and adjusting my rhythm when I was on top of her. In the morning it was different, because I woke slightly earlier and with a deal more energy than she did. Then I would take the initiative, and she would lie in a delicious helplessness. I would get out of the bed and go naked to one of the dorm Fabricants to fetch some breakfast, then I would bring it back and the two of us would eat in bed, spilling crumbs and splashes of ersatz-coffee on the duvet, laughing like little children again. Then she would dress and go off to the farm, and I would go off to the simulator, and work through the technique of operating a road-roller. In the afternoon we would wander through the dome, simply talking, or else lie under the tree in the goose-yard.

She must have pulled out her contraceptive patch within the first week, to judge by how soon she had the baby. She did not tell me she was going to come off her contraception, and clearly there is no reason why she should have told me. It was her business, obviously. But perhaps there is some significance in the speed with which she made her decision. After she had gone to the woman's dorm, I was thinking about this. I knew that she had never before removed her contraceptive patch with any man. There was an unspoken compliment there, I think.

But she did not tell me, and for several months I had no idea about the foetus inside her, and we carried on like teenagers. She was moved off the farm rota and given a diplomatic and programming job instead, something she had done before several times. I finally grew too bored with the sims, and went off with my road-roller. Most of the roads from Istenem to the rest of the settlement were already finished, and there were no urgent road-requests for me to address, so I could decide to build a road where I liked. Or I could decide not to build a road, but the boredom would not be pleasant. So I set off in the smaller car, driving a path northwards along the bank of the Aradys, clearing rubble out of the way (there wasn't much) with my small fitted crane, and putting down road-markers. This was quick work, and within days I was driving back along the coast. Back at Als I called the mine, told them I was building a road, and the operator at the other end shrugged: they were flying most of their processed minerals down to the settlement, and had no urgent need of a road, but (I told them) the shuttle flights were absurdly wasteful of energy, and in the long term a road would be a great boon. At least they did not actively object to the road, and neither did anybody else when I posted my plans in the dorm on my return home. So the following week took me away from Als, and away from Turja.

I fired up the great bulk of the road-roller (rebuilt and upgraded from an old shuttle chassis, it was), and set off north: the under-carriage lasered, rodded and grazed the salt beneath me, and the after-roller applied a layer of superdur plastic that bonded with the sink-rods. The whole process happened as I drove on at about seven k.p.h. I needed most of my attention on the first day, moving through the north of our settlement, to avoid the farming robots left lying since I prospected the route, or to detour around the site of somebody's home (a dingy, tiny-looking hut-in-the-ground, usually with a pile of rubble on the low roof for radiation protection). But by day two I had gone past habitation and I could spend more time looking around me. I spent the morning watching the scenery; the dark waters of the sea with their shifting banks of green fog were illuminated brilliantly by the rising sun. To my right was the bulge of Istenem, with our buried dorms, and the stockpile of metals like a bizarre snowcap. North of it the mountains rose, step by step, until by day three I could only see the peaks by pressing my face against the side window of my cab.

At lunch I would eat pasta, or chew a reconstituted bread (shitbread, it was called, with a superfluous literalism), and with half my eye on the way ahead I would compose elaborate, flowery voice-mails for Turja. I would tell her how she had set my heart aflame, how I could not wait to see her again, all the things I wanted to do when we were together again, all the usual romantic clichés. I sent these after lunch, and I know that Turja must have received them directly because she worked her morning shift at the message/visual computers. She never replied, but replies were not her style, and I know she enjoyed receiving the messages.

In the afternoon I would read. Sometimes I would step out of the truck, and walk alongside in my mask and nose-peg, but there was little to do or see, and it seemed foolish exposing myself to unnecessary radiation. By early evening I would watch the scenery again. The setting sun was now behind the mountains, and the palette of colours had changed completely. The eastern sides of the Sebestyen mountains were richer and darker in colour, features more clearly visible; the quartz-granite was rusty-red, with patches of tomato-coloured regolith. The Aradys was inky in the shadow of the mountains, and a glorious purply-blue out of them. To my right, the direct sunlight showed the salt patches over the skin-coloured granite.

But then I would stop and batten down. I was quite sheltered from the Devil's Whisper but it still came rattling the sides of the roller and throwing salt against the windows like gravel. And when it had passed; I would set the roller going again, putting the control on its most sensitive setting, and go to sleep. The machine would stop and wake me perhaps three times in the night, sometimes because a stone the size of a fist (say) had been blown into its path, sometimes for no obvious reason. I was never angry with these interruptions to my sleep, and I was never tempted to adjust the control to a coarser emergency setting. Rather the machine wake me at the slightest thing than I go ploughing into a great boulder and breaking down.

On the fifth day I arrived at the outbuildings of the mine, and met up with the workers. There was quite a community there, a hundred people or so, and they seemed happy. Many had paired off and there were even some obvious pregnancies, which rather suggested that people had been trading their work rotas to stay together on the site. Either that or quite a few people had been very lucky in their allotments. I have a particular dislike of trading work rotas, as do many of the first-generation Alsists, although I know it is a common enough thing amongst the young, but I was in too good a mood, with the relationship with Turja in its early stages, to want to make a fuss. Besides, it seemed clear that the other mine workers were not offended by this behaviour, so in all likelihood I was going to find myself making a noise all alone, and I might well have risked a beating.

I stayed in the mine for two days before I became bored. There was little work I could do without training up in the simulator, and I was not moved to do this. I went on, and laid more road to the next mine along, which was following a seam of silver into the heart of the mountains. This team had hollowed out a great hallway under the mountain and played football there often. I joined in, and was glad to give my body some physical exertion after its week sitting cooped up in the cab of the road-roller. Afterwards, I got into a fight with a drill-bit co-ordinator, who took exception to what he called my self-aggrandisement; a reference, I suppose, to the prominence I had once enjoyed during the voyage as tether expert. This was strange, because since the landing I genuinely believed I had faded out of general consciousness; but this man – he was called Lichnovski – was shouting and yelling and spitting at me. To begin with, I shrugged and tried to leave his company, but he followed me, and then he made a swing for me with an aluminium spar. I have an instinct, something in the sub-brain, that serves me well in fights. I was able to rush him, feint, pull the spar from him, and then start to pummel him with my fists upon the back of his head and the small of his back. He lay down upon the ground crying (probably because of the excess of vodjaa he had drunk rather than the damage my fists had done), and I let him be. But later that night he came at me again, when I was sitting cross-legged, discussing politics with a group of miners. This was not so good: he surprised me with his fist and broke the skin on the side of my head, just before the ear, so that the blood came out very liberally. This time we wrestled and broke apart to aim great swinging punches at one another, most of which missed. The rest of the miners shuffled away, embarrassed by our display, but one of Lichnovski's friends came to try and pull him away, and a few more miners stood about, watching. Our scrap took us staggering along and out through the main entrance, where nobody followed (it was night, and cold). Outside, we fought a little more, but there was blood all over my face and in my eyes, and I was not watching very closely when I punched his face. I connected with his mask which broke away and fell useless to the ground. Lichnovski fell too, coughing and howling. The chlorine levels were low, since we were halfway up a mountain, but they were enough to poison him. Worse, I did not realise what had happened for a little while, because of the dark and the blood in my eyes. When I did I hauled his convulsing body back through the swing-lock and into the mine; but his lungs were badly hurt. He was flown down to Als on the next shuttle. I did rather regret the whole business.

After the fight I felt antipathy towards that mine, so I left and visited another two, carrying on the road. Then, after only a few days I started back, laying a parallel carriageway south, back towards Als.

Seeing Turja again was a joy that almost made the intervening absence worthwhile. She had been involved in negotiations with the other settlements around Aradys over plans to pool resources and build some gigantic chimneys in the mountains, to pump greenhouse gases into the atmosphere. The southern hemisphere settlements were also talking with us. She had also fielded requests that Als appoint a diplomat, a somebody to greet the various visitors, official and otherwise, who wandered into our land as well as a somebody to go off on diplomatic visits. Visitors were sometimes puzzled, and even angered, by the lack of hierarchy or formalised relations in Als. They expected to be met; they were bothered by the fact that nobody demanded to see passports or threatened to throw them into gaol as illegal immigrants; they disliked the lack of police, the absence of restrictions, all those chains that reinforce in slaves their sense of themselves. Because Turja asked me, I did agree to respond to some of the official advances, particularly the ones from the south. There were no diplomatic spaces allotted to the work rota, because the business of relating to other nations cannot be reduced to a timetable in advance. It is supposed that foreigners approach the relevant person, such that if they wished to 'trade' hogs, they should approach whoever has been given the job of raising hogs at that particular time. But the circumstances were unusual, it is true.

For a time, Turja and I moved out of the general dorm and slept in the dome with her animals. This was a whim of ours; to make love under a tree instead of under a rock roof. After a week or so we began to miss the comforts of dorm life and moved back.

If I think back and am honest I must confess that I hurled myself into this relationship with Turja. I clowned to amuse her, and bullied her into pastimes and jollity with a manic desperation. And this was because, even so early, I knew that she was withdrawing from me. I was busy with the road-roller for another week, laying down a road that had been requested around the settlement. I would come off duty and hurry down to the dome, but Turja would not be at the place we had agreed to meet; or else she would shoo me away, saying that there were chores she had to attend to; or we would be together, but her manner would be distracted, awkward. Sometimes she would blush.

I took another work rota, this time as a medic (a rota I had done previously and which needed little training anyway; the netscreen provided all diagnosis and treatment). This was good, except that it brought me back again to Lichnovski with his chlorine-blasted lungs. New lungs were growing in a special Medical Fabricant, but it was taking weeks; in the meantime, Lichnovski could do nothing but lie about, breathing pure oxygen through a mask, glaring at me with his fierce eyes over the top of this plastic snout.

Barlei

Tragedy struck a mere two months into the perfect marriage. Our whole nation wept. My beloved jean-Pierre was on manoeuvres, practising grouping and regrouping his men in the salt desert, without air-cover (I was already thinking ahead to the possible necessity for raids upon Alsist territory); life in Senaar was gradually assuming a normality. A party of women, jean-Pierre's wife among them, set out in a rover to explore the lands to the south of Senaar. Such parties were common in the early days; the wives and daughters of the wealthy had few enough pastimes, after all, and a rover, driven by a military man, was a useful and exciting way of acquainting them with their world. They left the salt-flats in the late afternoon and climbed the rover onto a rocky hillock; and there the Devil's Whisper caught them. Their driver had gone outside to secure the clamps but the design was faulty (he said) – or he was incompetent – and the rover was blown over. The side windows shattered on the rock and three people inside died. Those fitted with internalised sinus-masks survived, of course; a shuttle picked them up twenty minutes after the disaster, weeping and dribbling mucus but alive. The driver survived for the same reason. But Kim died. She had never had a sinus-filter fitted, for reasons, I am sorry to say, of vanity – she didn't like the idea of her pretty face disfigured with some of the less pleasant side-effects. We may deplore this prideful self-regard but, well, she paid her price. As for the driver, there were differing views on his culpability. The rover was standard Fabricant ware, and as such was obviously of tested and reliable design. But the truck-clamps, that pinioned the vehicle to the rock, were not. We had not known, until coming to Salt and experiencing the severity of the Devil's Whisper, that we might need such things. And so the army, and other truck owners, had put out tenders to several possible companies (all still nascent in these early days), and the cheapest and best design was commissioned. As is usual, the driver (I am afraid I cannot remember his name) could not claim faulty parts against a company-owned product without risking a lawsuit; and rightly so. That sort of claim, that the company's product was criminally liable for three deaths, would be a serious blow to that company's trading potential, and as such the company would be allowed to challenge the possible loss of revenue in court. But a man in the driver's position would, of course, not be in a position to fight a lawsuit; the cost would ruin him. Admitting personal liability would only result in a fine, in most cases, and was the preferable option. Certainly, I remember that the fellow talked wildly of shearing plasdesigns to begin with but was more sober after he had bought a little legal advice, and admitted re-sponsibility.

It goes without saying that jean-Pierre was heartbroken. I felt for the poor man. I granted him a fortnight's compassionate leave, and he spent three days, Achilles in his tent. He came to see me personally to request reassignment; his face was salt-coloured, his features frozen. There was something manly in his determination, in the strength of will to conquer his grief. I sent him back to his corps.

Perhaps it would be true to say that I have lived aspects of my life through others. Now, old as I am and given to musing on the past, I cannot be sure whether jean-Pierre was a son to me, or whether he was an empty shape into which I could suture my own sense of self, my own identity as a man. Was it myself that marched, at salute, from the house to take a shuttle out to a tented camp in the Great Salt Desert? Was it jean-Pierre who stayed behind, weeping small, painful tears in a darkened room? Were we that interchangeable?

The same small tears are there, now, as I speak these words. And they cannot be for jean-Pierre, since he is long dead. And how can they be for me, when I am still alive? Perhaps there is a nothingness that summons tears. Perhaps that is what they are.

I grow fanciful in my old age.

Sometimes I dream of my bright boy; dead, dead. God's will.

It was shortly after this that I officially opened the new Parliament building, an impressive twin set of quartz towers a hundred metres tall. The towers were mostly for show since the Parliament chambers were buried under the topsalt and under a ceiling of bedrock to protect the proceedings from radiation. It was a great day. There had only been one opportunity for the people to vote on any proposal since settlement, and that had been on the shape of the settlement, an out-of-the-ordinary referendum; the normal procedures of our democracy, the patterns of political living we had been used to on the voyage out, had been denied us with the pressures of our new life. I made a speech, for those there in person and the Visuals, a powerful one I think (although if I am honest I think Preminger wrote it for me), about the potency of this establishment of democracy on the new world. There was a sizeable crowd present but most people stayed indoors, away from the dangers of the sun. The speech was Visualed throughout the Galilean basin.

The Vote Treasury came on-line at mid-day, of the third day of June, P.A.5. A great day. There was some small disturbance in the fortnight that followed, which I think is mentioned in the history books. Or perhaps not, since it was only a small-scale business. It had to do with the conversion rates of ship-vote stockpiles to new vote currency. Earning, and hence taxation, had been limited in scale during the voyage out, for obvious reasons; and therefore people had not been able to accumulate votes at what might be considered a normal rate. There was a pressure-group formed to agitate for conversion from ship-votes to new-votes at a double rate, or even a triple one. Naturally I held firm on this point: vote inflation is one of the things any reasonable ruler needs to guard against. And, this being a constitutional matter, I was able to veto any attempt to have this proposal itself voted through, but there were one or two small demonstrations.

jean-Pierre headed a small platoon to police these demonstrations. There was steel in his eyes on that day. I remember taking him to one side to talk with him and being struck by how fierce and manly his repression was, how firmly and precisely he kept hold over his boiling emotions of rage and hate. The Visual company was still paying to broadcast details of his life to the Galilee basin, and so there was a man with camera-spectacles following him always, even at so trying a time. I shooed this fellow away for five minutes of privacy with my friend. 'My friend,' I told him, 'soon there will be a time when you can give true voice to yourself, in actions not words. Soon you will have a chance to redeem the honour of all Senaar, to go heroically against the enemies of our people and rescue the hostages.'

3

The Raid

Petja

I became obsessive, that worst of things. I tell you this, not because I am proud of it, but because perhaps it helps you understand what happened. I fixated on Turja. I became a rigidist, by instinct, by accident. Nowadays, perhaps it is less unusual but in those days there was something almost scandalous about it. I spent all the time I could with her: I spent every moment during which she did not actually push me away. My work rota had been specialist-overridden: representatives of the other nations settling around Aradys were approaching us. Turja received requests from other governments to meet and discuss international co-operation; she fed the request into the computer, and my previous experience at tether work signalled me for diplomatist, and so I was assigned. To be truthful, though, this rota was thin indeed. There was little enough to do as diplomatist, and so I spent much time with Turja, and when she sent me away (as she did often) I went back and assisted in the hospital. The level of sickness was rising, with cancers and cataracts beginning to come in greater numbers, and chlorine poisoning also, so extra help was welcomed. The man I had fought with, Lichnovski, was still there and he scoffed at me when I returned to the ward. His voice was still wheezy and full of coughing, but he strained to shout to me.

'So you have become a rigidist in work, as you are already in sexual matters,' he said. 'I have heard stories about you from the other nurses.'

'At least,' I retorted, 'my lungs are fully functional.' We had almost finished growing back his lungs, but in those days (and today as well? It is a long time since I have had a medical rotation) regrown lung produced only tiny alveoli, and the lungs were less than half as efficient as natural ones.

Lichnovski turned red at this, his sputum coming from his gasping mouth in little specks. 'You rigidist fucker!' he grated. 'When I'm off my back I'll kill you! I'll kill you with my own hands!'

'Or I you,' I replied. 'My lungs are stronger, after all.'

'You did this to me!'

'And I would do it again.'

'You rigidist fucker! Do you think I don't know you? What you are doing?' And he started shouting to the other people in the ward, hoarsely haranguing them. 'He has a diplomatist's rota, does he? He'll set himself up according to the hierarchy! He'll turn us into a Senaar, into a slave network! Can't you see what he is doing?'

This was too insulting, so I went over to his bed and pushed a pillow over his face. His hands leapt up and gripped at my wrists, but I was much the stronger. I held him this way for twenty seconds perhaps, a long time for a man with half a lung; then I let him breathe again. His face was purple, and he had no energy to even curse me. He stared at me with red-veined eyes popping out of his head, hate in the look.

But at the time I had no thought for him. I went back to Turja. For once she was in a good mood, with a glow in her eyes. We wandered out into the bright sunlight and the fierce, salty air, deciding to walk from the dome to Istenem; and as we walked I hooked my arm through hers, like an old-fashioned couple. Even the snout of her filter-mask could not reduce her beauty in my eyes; even the contacts we all wore, which protected the eyes from the sting of the chlorine, even they could not dull her glance. As we walked, we talked about Lucretius. I had told Turja what Csooris had said about this author from the ancient world, from a world now impossibly distant from us, and Turja had become interested and had got a Fabricant to print out a copy for her to read. It required translation, since Turja could not speak Old Latin. And so I had read the work, or read it again, and so we talked of it together. I considered the whole thrust of the work insufficiently religious but she insisted that when he spoke of the vital power of a human being's spirit winning through adversity, finding its way through the flaming walls of the world and spreading throughout the measureless whole, that Lucretius was talking about God.

'God as you understand It,' I said. 'Of course,' she said.

Then she quoted, rustling the Fabricant printout flimsies from her satchel; her voice was blunted by her mask, given a strangely tinny timbre. She said '*medio de fonte leporum surgit amari aliquid quod in ipsis floribus angat*,' reading with ponderous precision from the page.

I said, 'What does this mean?'

She laughed, the sound stifled by her mask. 'You must learn Old Latin and find out.'

So I lurched at her, laughing, to snatch the printout from her and see for myself, and she laughed and ran off. I caught up with her, and we pressed our foreheads together, the convention that had grown up to express kissing when outside, where the masks prevented access to the lips. We were still laughing. The disappearing sunlight was on her face, given a blue-green tint by the chlorine clouds gathering on the water, through which it shone. It made her eyes seem deeper, her hair darker. The sound of the evening wind, the Devil's Whisper, beginning to gather in the east. A sound like a huge giantess, tall as the stars and a long way off, gathering up a titanic rustling dress from around her knees. I slipped my hand inside Turja's shirt and under-shirt and ran my nails softly over her breasts. She loosened her belt, and we had love very rapidly, hurriedly, leaning against the rock at the foot of Istenem. As I climaxed, I felt a sense of falling, an inward falling away, almost a tumbling. Afterwards she said, '*sunt lacrimae rerum.*'

This was our last happy time together.

We went to the dorm, and slept for an hour. Then we joined a large party, and played games in the dorm hallway. After this was drinking and eating, people talking and laughing together. It grew dark. Some people set up a bonfire, and we all sat round it, laughing and drinking, playing a telling game where we had to give names to the shapes made by the fire. I lost track of Turja, and went to find her later on, in a side room away from the party; but she was quiet, her eyes red in the sudden brutal light of a ceiling striplight.

Three days later she told me she was moving to the women's dorm; that she wanted to close off the relationship with me; and that she was pregnant.

'Which amounts to the same thing,' she said briskly, as if speaking common sense. 'Because, when it comes to term, I shall be living in the women's dorm anyway, and the child will begin life there.'

'But that's many months in the future!' I pointed out. The pregnancy was barely visible yet in the curve of her belly.

'But it is over between us,' she insisted. Her face was calm, her eyes looked hollow, as if I could see directly through her without touching her at all. I pressed the point.

'Why?'

'It is.'

'But why?'

'Because of what I want.'

It was on the edge of my mouth to say *and what about what I want?* But this was too ridiculous a thing to say, of course, even in my emotional state. I sat down heavily. We were in the dorm, I think. It may have been the dome. I cannot remember precisely.

'You must acknowledge,' she said, her voice a little gentler, 'that you have been acting almost in the ways a rigidist might.'

I had heard as much from several people, usually as a jibe, as a dart thrown at me to try and puncture what people saw as my self-importance and ego (another archaic term, but one too complicated for me to elaborate here). This happened at the same time as I assumed diplomatist duties, and became in the eyes of other nations the 'hierarch' of Als. With other people, such as Lichnovski, I was able to throw the accusation back, but from Turja it struck deep. Hurt.

'I have been obsessing,' I acknowledged in a small voice. 'You are right to end the relationship. But you have no need to go to the women's dorm if you would rather stay here.'

'I want to be with women now. I have started a relationship with Csooris.'

I am ashamed to say I felt a corrosion in my soul, a feeling of resentment at the transfer of affections; but I 'suppressed' it. It was an awkward internal manoeuvre, like holding down vomit. 'This explains your interest in Lucretius,' I said, and my voice was strained.

She said, only, 'yes.' Then she fetched out the flimsies from her satchel, the same ones as before, and gave me them. The page that happened to be on top contained the following:

How lovely does it strike us, when the wind churns up the waves on the great sea, to watch from the land and see the great labour of somebody else, struggling with the controls of a boat or trying to keep the sails under control; not because it is enjoyable or a pleasure to see another human being in difficulties, but because it is good to realise what difficulties you yourself are being spared. How lovely is it also to witness great battle plans at War, carried out over the plains, without you yourself being in any danger from them.

I have kept that page, bookmarked, on my own notepad.

For three days, or more, I was in a raging and angry mood. I picked fights with people, and when passers-by or other people noted the injustice of my rage they sided with the other person, and would beat me. But, looking back, perhaps it was exactly this punishment I was searching for. After one tumble I broke a collar bone, and admitted myself to the ward to have it sutured; but luckily Lichnovski was asleep, or else he would certainly have baited me and laughed at me from his bed, and I might have killed him in my retaliation.

But this is not the narrative. It was at this time, towards the end of the relationship between Turja and myself, that I first received the embassy of Rhoda Titus, and her guard of six men; and it was during this time that Senaar made official advances towards Als. At the beginning of this embassy I was happy with Turja, and at the end of it I was raging with her absence. And history records the truth of the Senaarian plans, that this embassy was the cover for the Raid.

Barlei

I anticipated, as it is the duty of a leader to do, that the Alsists would not respond to diplomacy, and so I brought training and planning for the Raid to fruition during the time of the diplomatic mission. But, for the purposes of show and in the nature of politics, I gave the embassy all my backing. I met in military council, broadcast throughout the Galilee basin on all Visuals, and debated the best actions. It was decided that, Als being in effect a matriarchy (for all its pretensions at anarchy) the best thing would be to send a woman, but as Preminger pointed out, it would be madness to send a woman alone into such a place (the stories of sexual immorality that filtered out were truly heartbreaking). It was agreed that an honour guard would accompany her.

Rhoda Blossom Titus was the president of the Women's League of Senaar, an organisation she had herself put in motion during the voyage. I had consulted with her myself after I had assumed the burdens of command, and she convinced me – most straightforwardly, with none of the evasions and flatteries that women are prone to – that her dearest concern was for the unity and order of the nation. She held back from actually joining the Women's Corps of the army (although, she said, she was happy swearing public allegiance to me), and I suppose there was no official reason for me to expect her to recruit. I was, after all, convinced then of her devotion to our nation.

I made her a public offer of this embassy, and she accepted; and in conference afterwards I made plain to her that I had little hope of success, and that it was paramount she discover the disposition of the hostages. Our best men were ready to fly in, release them, and be back in Senaar within the hour. They had been training under jean-Pierre for many weeks.

Petja

Rhoda Titus came in great pomp, in a shuttle plane. It contained her and a small retinue of personal servants and secretaries, all army people; it also contained a body of blue-uniformed men, with visors to cover their eyes and make them look more inhuman, more alarming to their foe. Each of them carried a short ceremonial sword strapped tightly to their back, between their shoulder blades, so tightly indeed, that I remembered wondering whether it was possible for them to unbind them in the heat of battle. Each of them wore a sidearm dangling from a holster. And each of them hefted a needlegun, bearing it at all times in their hands. They marched down the ramp of their shuttle in order, and stood like trees along a country road as Rhoda Titus walked down. There was that smile on the face of Rhoda Titus that I recognised then as the distinctive expression of high caste Senaarians: the smile of pride.

I had been contacted and told of her arrival (the Senaarians had specifically requested me, and it was chance, fortunate for them, that I was on rota) and I was waiting for her. I think she expected a crowd to have gathered, or for there to have been other members of the diplomatic party, but there was just me. This was my rota, and I was fulfilling it. In fact – and this will seem ironical to you to hear – I was grateful for the visit, since this work rota had hitherto presented me with little to do, and I was bored.

There was a crowd, that day. A few people stopped what they were doing and came over to look when they heard the approaching shuttles; and then when the soldiers marched out, they were struck by the sight. Some went to fetch their friends, and people began speaking to one another. One or two even picked up rocks and started throwing them at the shuttle, which caused the soldiers to take up offence positions, aiming their needleguns at Alsists. But the rock-throwing stopped, and name-calling began, and the Senaarians lowered the sights of their needleguns. But before this I met the diplomat.

The first thing Rhoda Titus said to me was, 'Where is the rest of your delegation?'

I only shrugged and smiled at her. Remember, at this point I was still happy in my relationship with Turja, happy in my rigidist paradise. I looked and I saw a neatly-presented, short but pleasant-looking older woman. Womankind delighted me in all its forms, because Turja was a woman so I was minded to be polite to Rhoda Titus. 'There is only me,' I said.

'I am Rhoda Blossom Titus,' she said.

'I know who you are,' I said. 'Who else would you be, arriving in a military shuttle with armed invaders?'

She bristled up at this. 'This is my honour guard. They are here purely for my protection.'

I shrugged again.

'You are Petja?' she asked.

'I am.'

'Well,' and her official mask fell away a little, 'why don't you tell me so? This is most awkward, standing about like this.'

'I clearly didn't need to tell you,' I said, 'since you knew anyway. But if you feel awkward we can go inside. It is doubtless not good to be standing in the sunlight, soaking up so many rems.'

'You have facilities prepared?' she asked, straightening up again. 'Why?'

'What do you mean?' she said. 'What do you mean, "why"?'

She wore no mask, even though we were outside, because the Senaarians had this sinus technology; she simply mopped at her nostrils constantly with a handkerchief, and squinted at me in the high-chlorine sunlight by the lake. It meant I could watch the precise motion of her face. Her mouth wrinkled up prettily when she was puzzled.

'Why do you want facilities?'

'Isn't it obvious?' she snapped, her official mask dropping a little again. 'So that we can begin negotiations! Unless you have prepared a reception for me? Food? Drinks?'

'If you want a drink,' I said, 'then I'll stand friend. But we have nothing prepared.'

'Well, are we to negotiate out here? In the radiation, and the heat?'

'Negotiate?' I said.

At this point somebody threw a stone, and it clanged noisily off the side of the second shuttle, sitting by the waters. The guards twitched. Another stone came flying. Another. Rhoda Titus whirled around, and around again.

'What are you doing?' she demanded.

'I am doing nothing,' I said.

'You are attacking our shuttle! This is an outrage!'

I shrugged. 'I'm not doing anything of the sort.'

The captain of the guard of six muttered something, an order clearly, and the soldiers adopted their positions: three dropped to the ground, the remainder standing behind them. They had lowered their rifles at the stone-throwers.

'Tell them to stop!' insisted Rhoda Titus.

My mask was itching me a little, so I shifted it slightly on my face. 'It really has nothing to do with me.'

The rock-throwing had stopped now; maybe people were bored with it. It was a hot day, and throwing stones is heavy enough work, but the commotion had brought a few more people out, and some were calling names and shouting abuse. The soldiers, I suppose, did not speak our tongue. But they looked nervous.

Rhoda Titus made little noises in her throat, as if nervous. She hurried back over to the soldiers, and the captain of the troop started, as if electrically jolted. He moved between the stone-throwers and Rhoda Titus. It occurred to me he was protecting her but the crowd was in flux, people coming and going now, and there were no more stones. Rhoda Titus was looking at me. I was laughing, indeed, with the comicality of the bustling Senaarians.

She came back over to me, cross now.

'Perhaps,' Rhoda Titus said to me, 'perhaps you think this suave, but believe me, no leader in the sight of God would tolerate such lawlessness.'

'What can you mean?' I asked. I was not asking her, I was merely speaking my thoughts aloud. But her bleary eyes lit up.

'I'll tell you what I mean. I mean the divinely ordained duty of leaders to provide a good example to their people. I mean the necessity of order and harmony. Why did you not restrain those hooligans? The stone-throwers? What if they provoke my guard? What if they were to get themselves killed? What then? This would have stained your honour and mine, both, and possibly started an international incident. Why are you not calling your police, to have these people arrested?'

But I was bored by this time, so I turned to go inside. In those days it was never a good idea to stay too long in the sunlight.

I heard Rhoda Titus give a little yelp of outrage behind me, and then she hurried to catch up. I could hear the *klink klink* of the uniform buckles as the honour guard jogged into position behind us.

'Are you trying to insult me?' Rhoda Titus demanded, pulling alongside me. 'Are you trying to insult Senaar?'

'You said you were thirsty. Shall I stand friend and get you a drink? Your people too? But they are soldiers, so perhaps they have their own rations.'

We came under the Istenem overhang and so out of the sun and into the dorm entrance. There were people gathered, sitting in the shade and watching the comings and goings by the seashore below; people standing and talking; a game of five-a-side played over by the other wall, with a goal chalked against the rock. But people stopped what they were doing when I came in followed by half a dozen armed soldiers. There was some muttering, a sense of communal displeasure. The Drinks Fabricants were on the other side of the seal-door, so I went through, and Rhoda Titus and her entourage followed.

I keyed in the code, and stood friend for Rhoda Titus; the Fabricant poured us two fruit-tint drinks, and I drank mine straight down. It was hot, and I had been standing in the directness of sunlight. Rhoda Titus looked at hers with suspicion, as if perhaps I had poisoned it. She handed it to one of her honour guard, who sniffed it, sipped it, waited, handed it back. This struck me, again, as comical, so I began to laugh, after which I could see this commanding officer and several of the men frown with distaste, even scorn. Understand this about the Senaarians: they lack humour.

A friend passed, and I chatted for a while. She was called Haefner, and was on a Fabricant technical rota. 'Who is this?' she asked. 'Somebody from Senaar,' I replied. 'Rhoda Titus.' 'And soldiers!' said my friend. 'I know,' I said. 'They are jumpy. But this is the manner of things in the hierarchy.'

'What are you saying?' interrupted Rhoda Titus. 'I heard my name – you are talking about me. I demand you tell me what you are saying.'

'She is angry,' said Haefner, still in the home tongue. 'Perhaps she is angry like this all the time.'

'I understand so,' I replied, in home tongue also. 'I think it is a function of the hierarchy they practise down there. Everybody is frustrated at some level, everybody is prevented from doing this and that by law, or by the person above them in the hierarchy.'

'It is interesting,' said Haefner. She scratched at the space between her eyes, as she did when puzzled. 'What of the person at the top of the hierarchy?'

'He too is thwarted, I believe,' I said. 'Even though there is nobody above him in the hierarchy, he is constrained by his duties and responsibilities. Their last Hierarch was killed, you know, for failing to treat his duties with enough respect.'

'You *must* speak to me in common tongue,' Rhoda Titus squalled. Her hands were flailing in front of her, giving pathetic emphasis to her words. 'As diplomatic representative of the People's Republic of Senaar I *insist* you accord me the respect due to my status.' She turned to her Captain of Guards, but I suppose even he would have found it hard justifying killing a person only for speaking their own home tongue.

'She is angry,' said Haefner, in home tongue, 'and yet she does nothing about it. There is something inside her that prevents her from taking any action.'

'It is curious to see,' I agreed. 'The hierarchy is internalised.'

'How bizarre,' said Haefner. She mulled over the idea for some short time. 'Why would a human being internalise such a thing? It cannot be healthy.' She started sniggering at the absurdity of it.

Rhoda Titus puffed out her breath several times, regaining control. 'Will you force me to return home to report this insult? By ignoring me, you are ignoring the entire people of Senaar! By insulting me, you are insulting the entire people of Senaar!'

At this Haefner tumbled into laughter. 'Why?' she demanded in common tongue (which, actually, she spoke better than I). 'Are they all in your belly?' She laughed again, at her own joke.

'Rhoda Titus,' I said to her. 'How can I insult the entire people of Senaar? It would take me many months to go amongst them all, insulting each one to their face.'

Rhoda Titus was silent. After a short space she said: 'You are mocking me, I think.' Her expression was dark. Her guards shifted their weapons uneasily from hand to hand.

Haefner had grown bored. She shouldered past the guards and plugged her applique into the Drinks Fabricant. I ushered Rhoda Titus to follow me, to allow her the space and quiet to do her job. Rhoda Titus came after me, her face dark with the heat of her anger; her guard trotted after her, a great unlikely crocodile of people. We came to the cot I was sharing with Turja, and I pushed off my outside shoes, each foot prised off with the toe of the other. Then I sat, cross-legged, on the wide bed.

Rhoda Titus stood for a while, glaring at me, and her guard huddled behind her. For a while neither of us spoke, but eventually she broke out with, 'What is the meaning of this?'

'Rhoda Titus,' I said. 'I shall explain the way of things here. There is work to be done, and it is allotted by rota; programmed rota, not a human one. It so happens that I have been prioritised for diplomatic duties. But I take no pleasure in them. I am doing this because my rota requires it. Shortly the work period will be over, and then I shall go off to spend some time with the woman I am seeing.'

Rhoda Titus did not know what to say to this. 'You are going to abandon me?' she said. 'What are we to do? Where should we go?'

'Do you need me to tell you what to do? You don't know yourself what you want to do?' I said, chuckling at the oddity of the conception.

'Have you at least assigned me proper diplomatic quarters?'

I shrugged. 'I'll stand friend again, and you can have a cot in the general dorms. Not all your men though, but they can surely bivouac themselves elsewhere.'

If it were possible, I would say that she seemed even more outraged. She looked about herself, and stared at the dorm. The cots spaced out, the glowlamps bobbing against the ceiling, marking out splashes of light that disappeared with perspective into the distance. It was day, so many of the cots were occupied; in the silence it was possible to hear some moans from couples having love. Rhoda Titus cocked her head, not recognising the noises, but understanding at some deep level that they were offensive to the Senaarian prudery. 'You are suggesting,' she said, as if with tremendous effort, 'that I stay . . . here?'

I shrugged. I was greatly bored now, and on the point of giving up my work rota for the day and simply going off.

'In the same building as . . . men?'

'You could go to the women's dorm and see if somebody would stand friend for you there,' I suggested. 'But you'd have to leave your soldiers behind.'

'I expected specifically designated diplomatic quarters,' she shouted. It was really a shout. 'I expected quarters that we could have to *ourselves*!' Note the possessive! Rhoda Titus's speech was truly littered with possessives. *My* mission. *My* men. *My* country, even. To think of *possessing* a country in entirety! But she was blind to the comicality of her expression.

'If you want such a thing,' I said, very bored indeed at this point, 'then you can go out into the wasteland east of here and build it for yourself.'

I left her then, and went over to the dome to see Turja. I am not sure what they did in the end. I suppose they went back to their shuttles and slept there. The following morning I put Rhoda Titus and the whole Senaar mission to the back of my mind and spent an hour or so contacting the other Aradys settlements by voice-mail. But Rhoda Titus came to see me anyway. She must have overcome her shyness and asked directions.

'My dear Szerelem,' she said, and smiled at me. 'I have come alone.'

I shrugged. I could see there was a tiny twitch in her brow every time I did so, so I assumed that my shrugging was irritating to her. But she did nothing with her anger, only squashed it down inside her, so that it pulled at her face with its invisible string. Of course, this was fascinating to me: that somebody would have an anger inside them and make every effort to prevent its emergence. Naturally I took every opportunity to shrug, to see this internalisation in action.

'I have come alone,' she said, her voice a tiny bit harder, 'as a sign of trust. I have sent my bodyguard out to train in the wastelands east of the settlement, which leaves me unguarded in your presence.'

We were in a chamber off the dorm, where the voice-mail equipment was. I stood up and went out, wandered over to the Fabricant and fetched myself a drink. Rhoda Titus came hurrying after me. 'Perhaps you don't understand the significance of what I have done,' she said, high-pitched.

'Tell me,' I said, settling cross-legged on the floor. She looked down, thought about joining me, thought better of it. Senaarian women are trained to think that their dignity is the most precious thing, so she could not settle herself on the floor next to me. But at the same time they have codes that force them to be uncomfortable, ill at ease, standing awkwardly and talking down to me, that dissolve that dignity entirely away. A paradoxical people.

'My men,' she began (possessive!) 'are more than a practical guard against things happening to me, although heaven knows there's a real enough danger of that in this anarchist place.' She looked about her, anxiously. 'But they are more than that. They are a symbolic representation of the might of Senaar. They are the . . .'

I stopped her. 'I cannot say I am interested in your metaphysics.'

At this she stalled, blushed a little. But she seemed to have come to a resolution not to become hysterical as she had done the previous day. She still stood, but was looking around now for a seat, for something to sit on. And then, giving up even that hope, she settled herself gingerly upon the floor. There was a pause, whilst her face was lowered towards the ground. Then she raised it, and she was smiling bravely.

'Mister Szerelem,' she said. 'I have decided that our mission began badly yesterday. It seems to me that our two cultures are so very different that misunderstandings have occurred. You have mis-understood how totally the honour and dignity of Senaar informs everything we do. You did not appreciate the honour guard for what it was, simply as a reflection of the importance with which this mission is regarded in Senaar.'

I was shaking my head, and Rhoda Titus stopped talking, inclined her head, asking. So I drained my drink, and said, 'You seem to think I care enough about your mission to misunderstand it. But I do not care, one way or the other.'

She coloured, and then pressed her palms together. 'Please! Can you not see how difficult this is for me? I am trying to make concessions to your way of life. Surely you can help me a little in this difficult task?'

I shrugged.

'Today I am resolved,' she said, in her carefully paced speech, as if reciting something learned in advance, 'to try and reach out to the culture of Als. Today I hope to learn something of your way of being, your mode of society. Once I have done this, I hope it will draw our two peoples a little closer together. I hope it will draw you and I, Mister Szerelem, a little closer together.'

'Well, I have stood friend to you already,' I said. 'I am willing to do so again today. But I cannot comprehend why you should wish to dance this dance.'

At this she leaned forward, her eyes intense. 'For the sake of the children!'

I was a little startled. 'You have children?' I said.

'Me?' She sat back again. 'Me? No. No.' I noticed that her eyes were now glistening, as if she were about to cry.

'What is the matter?' I asked.

'How could you ask me such a thing! Why do you continue to play these games with me?'

'I am truly baffled,' I said. 'What games?'

'You know who the children are!'

'I do not.'

'Then why do you think I am here?'

'I have no idea. Really I have not. I have received you only because this is my current work rota.'

Then it all came out in a rush. 'Why else would I be here? Why else would somebody from Senaar come all this way, with all the pomp of a diplomatic mission? Only to try and bridge the gap between us, only to try and heal the wound, and have the children put back in touch with their grieving fathers. Only to help make whole again the terrible breach in God's family.'

'Does this have to do,' I said, 'with the children fathered by Senaarians before the beginning of the voyage?'

There was a pause.

'You are playing a game,' she said, coldly.

'Certainly not.'

But the puzzle was assembling itself in her head. 'All I can say, Mister Szelerem,' she said, 'is that the issue of the children has been a continual thorn in the side of the Senaar nation ever since the voyage began. These fathers have mourned their lack of access to their babies. The entire nation has grieved. Whole factions have grown up within our body politic concerned only with the question of retrieving these children – the hostages, as they are called – and bringing them home to the land of their fathers. Some would see the army invade your land to bring this about. Your people are represented on all Visuals as wicked, almost satanic, without law or respect for humanity, with evil designs upon the flesh of the infant, as pigheaded and sunk into group-insanity, as living like beasts with no thought to the welfare of others.'

'I can't recognise the land you are describing,' I said.

'Oh I know there are exaggerations in the reports we hear. But do you see how difficult it is for a people such as ours, such as the Senaarians, who value civilisation above all things, to comprehend a land such as this?'

'I once had a conversation with your Captain,' I said. 'It concerned these children you speak of.'

'The President,' she said, respectfully.

'Is that how he styles himself? Your titles and all that bag-and-baggage of the hierarchy is hard for us to follow. Even Mister, which you call me, although I take it that Mister ranks lower in your hierarchy than President?'

'I apologise if you have taken offence,' she said, quickly. This was clearly a matter of importance to her. 'I was unsure how to address you. If you find "Mister" unacceptable, perhaps I could call you "Technician"?'

'I take no offence,' I said, languidly. 'I see no need for any such title. We have none such here.'

'But I must call you *something*.'

'Why?'

'Because you are a man of importance.'

At this I laughed. 'Only to myself, of course.'

'My mission,' she said, shaking her head, uncomfortable with this topic, 'was given to me by the President himself. I am to build bridges between our two people, to try and come to an agreement about the children, to at the very least allow the fathers access.'

She stopped and looked at me. I shrugged again. 'What do you mean by "access"?' I asked.

'Is the word an unusual one? I am not certain how complete your grasp of common tongue is. It means . . .'

'I know the meaning, but not your interpretation.'

'Oh! I apologise! I had not meant to suggest . . .'

I stood up. 'Rhoda Titus,' I said. 'You are boring with these tics of yours. If I were offended, I would say so. I would not bury my anger or irritation away inside me, as it is the habit of your people to do. If I do not say I am insulted, then I am not insulted.'

She clambered upwards to follow me. 'Again I apologise. But this is my point! How little I understand your ways! But the question of access . . .'

I was walking now, and she was following. 'Yes?'

'It would simply mean that the fathers could, for instance, travel to Als and see their children. That the children would be allowed to know who their parents are, and to meet and speak with them. From time to time.'

'The fathers may by all means visit here,' I said. I said this as a simple statement of fact, there being no Alsist border controls, or indeed borders. But Rhoda Titus took this as a concession: in her mind negotiations, such as the one she considered herself engaged in, were like a war, a battle between speakers.

'Why thank you, Mister – eh, Technician Szerelem. Thank you! I knew that if I made a little gesture towards you, approached you person to person, left my guard, then we would be able to communicate.' I lengthened my stride and she dropped away behind me.

She fished a handkerchief out of her jacket, and called a farewell. 'I must go and report this breakthrough in negotiations to my people!' And away she hurried, with her handkerchief already at her nose, ready for when she went outside.

I did not see her for the rest of the morning; but in the afternoon she returned. Once again, she came alone. Somebody must have told her that I was in the dome, where I had taken to spending many of my afternoons during this period of fixation of Turja. I had spent lunch with my lover; we had taken putty and bread from one of the old ship Fabricants and had eaten together, sitting amongst the long grass of the goose-green. Afterwards Turja went off to talk with some genengineers about adapting certain birds to high chlorine tolerance,

106

with a hope of releasing them wild. The mere thought of birds flying free through the air above us was more exciting than you can imagine! Or perhaps you can. I suppose you have never seen a bird in flight, have never sat amongst them as they twittered about you.

This was how Rhoda Titus found me, sitting cross-legged in the grass, reading a flimsy upon which Turja had printed out some old tract on the origins of money. She had found the text interesting as metaphysics, as a treatise on the sinister power of signs and imagery to dominate real lives, real people. She thought I might find it useful in my talks with Rhoda Titus.

But she did not come wishing to talk, this time. She came grinning, with the after-sex grin that Senaarians adopt when they have gratified the person above them in the hierarchy; the slave's satisfaction at having pleased their master. 'Mister – Technician Szerelem,' she said, sitting down opposite me. 'I have come to thank you! After some difficulties, our negotiations have finally begun well. I will not deny that it has taken me a little time to adapt myself to your ways but I have spoken direct to the President! He is delighted with our agreement.'

I was feeling pleasant disposed towards women, having lunched with Turja, and so I was minded to be agreeable to Rhoda Titus. 'There is no agreement,' I said. 'But your pleasure gives me pleasure.' This was an old saw of my mother's. Simply saying it, feeling the pressure of my lips against one another on the ps and the kick at the back of the throat on the gs brought her memory back to me. I had been drinking vodjaa, and my soul was soft with such thoughts.

'Yes, well, of course we can call it whatever you like. But to allow the fathers visiting rights, this is more than I had hoped for.'

I shrugged. My mother still appeared in my memory and I was not listening very closely.

'I have been instructed,' she said, grandly, 'to locate the children, to speak to them, and to arrange the first of these visits. My President hopes – personally addressed this hope, to you, mind – that this first step will clear the way to a great deal of co-operation between our peoples; and perhaps a scheme of exchange between Als and Senaar would allow the hos . . .' She gulped, stopped, started again, 'Children the chance to visit the land of their fathers.'

I tried to visualise my mother; she was still alive, probably, but on Earth. An impossible distance away. I conjured her face in my mind, and it blurred with the face of Rhoda Titus, looking at me eagerly. Two dissimilar women, one broken from me, existing only on the other side of the profoundest physical rupture. The other's rupture was only ideological. I brought my mind to attention on what Rhoda Titus was saying.

'I cannot say,' I said, thinking how best to express myself, 'I can't say I know what you are talking about.' I smiled, to try and elicit a smile, but her face had clicked into its worried, haunted expression. A great deal of Rhoda Titus's expressions were devilled with that edge of fear. A function of the hierarchy again, I think, for the subordinate must be constantly anxious and trying to please the superordinate, fearful of pain at their displeasure.

'What do you mean?' she said. 'What do you mean by saying such a thing?'

'I always mean what I say,' I said. It seemed an uncontentious statement.

'Perhaps,' said Rhoda Titus, 'perhaps the best thing now would be for me to speak directly to the mothers. If you would just direct me to the place where the hos . . . , the children are being kept, I can speak directly to them.'

'I have no idea.'

'Give me directions,' she said.

'I cannot,' I said.

'You can. I believe you can.'

'Rhoda Titus: these children were conceived thirty years ago. This is the oldest of old history.'

'No,' she said, as if she had been expecting me to make this point, as if this were one of the anticipated moves in the verbal chess game she had been expecting. 'One year for ten in stasis. They will be biologically eleven, at most.'

'In which case,' I said, curling the corners of my mouth downwards in a facial shrug, 'they will still be staying with their mothers in the women's dorm.'

'Then I must ask you to arrange a meeting there.'

'It's the women's dorm,' I said. And then, because this did not seem to be enough for her, 'I am a man.'

But this seemed to strike her only as facetious. 'Technician Szerelem, you are the diplomatic officer for this community, it is your responsibility to arrange this meeting. You told me that the fathers could visit their children.'

'I told you the fathers could come here,' I said. 'And indeed they can, for who would stop them? We have no borders, or border controls, unlike you. But whether the fathers can see these children has nothing to do with me. That is a matter for the mothers concerned.'

'But you *said* . . .'

I stood up, bored with all this now. But she stood up as well, speaking with a loud voice now. 'You cannot *walk away*,' she said. 'You promised me. I spoke to my President on the basis of . . .'

'It is nothing to do with me.' This was a simple truth as well, but it seemed to inflame her. She stood on the grass shouting at me, yelling and abusing me. But I was in a placid mood, so her words did not affect me and I wandered out of the dome.

What happened then is that she attempted to gain entrance to the women's dorm, but was greeted there (as I understand it) with non-comprehension, and then, as she pushed her case, with hostility. Eventually, when she would not stop her strident demands to be taken to see the *hostages* and to be treated with the *respect* and the *dignity* that a diplomatic official from a great nation deserved, a few women grabbed her and threw her into the general hall. She tried to come in again, so they threw her out again. Then she went back to her shuttles, and summoned her men, and tried to force an entry again.

By this stage, the commotion had drawn a fairly large group of people to the entrance of the women's dorm. I had wandered off to swim in one of the eel pools (I liked the slippery sensations of the eels brushing against my body as I swam), so I was not present in person during these events. But reports were widespread, and I heard several eye-witness accounts. It seems that Rhoda Titus returned to the dorm entrance with six armed men. A group of women from the dorm blocked their way, yelling and shouting at her; and she stood there (they say) quivering with her rage, which was chronic in her, impacted like a bad tooth. The soldiers took aim, but the women from the dorm would not back down. They were yelling, and spitting, and somebody brought out a pillow from her bed and began slapping it on the heads of some of the guards. They flinched, but it would not be right (according to the hierarchical code of honour that Senaarian soldiers swear to) to shoot a woman armed with a pillow, only because she would not stop hitting you on the head with it. They say that some of the dorm women were shouting in home tongue, some in common tongue, and that the commotion was deafening. Then Rhoda Titus ordered her men to force their way through and enter the dorm, and the men surged forward; but there was such a crush of women in the entrance space that the soldiers heaved and heaved to no effect. They say that when Rhoda Titus withdrew her men to their shuttles, she was dark red in the face with her shame and embarrassment, and weeping tears copiously.

I did not see her for two days. Then, on the third day, she came and found me during my rota shift.

'It is Sunday,' she said. 'I would like you to take me to one of your churches. I have been dreadfully tested by God this week, and it is time for me to pray in a House of God.'

I was chewing something; leekroot I think. 'Church,' I said, the word mushy with my full mouth. 'This is one of your Senaarian customs.'

She looked blankly at me, and then digested my words. But her reaction was not what I might have expected. She did not rage at me, nor lecture me on the ungodliness of Alsist peoples. Instead she sat down, with a bleak expression, and began sobbing.

'We do not have churches,' I told her, taking another bite of leekroot. 'There are no priests, no establishments, nothing to interfere between the individual soul and God. Why should there be a special room to which people have to go to speak to God? Is any one room on Salt different from any other? As God sees it, does it matter whether a soul is in a certain room, or is somewhere else?'

'I have tried, God knows I have tried,' she whispered hoarsely. Then she sobbed some more. Then she said again, 'I have tried, as God is my witness.'

'Surely,' I continued, 'you can pray where you like? You can pray here, if you like to.'

'I have *tried* to understand you, your people. But I see lawlessness and misery. That's all I see! Lawlessness and misery, and a people with no *point* to their life, no *harmony*.' The sobbing had stopped now. 'My President has instructed me to leave, to abandon the godlessness and return home. But I told him, No! I said, give me one more chance to reach out to these people, to this Szerelem. I said, it is Sunday, the Sabbath, the Lord's day, and on this day I will be able to speak to him in the language we have in common, the language of God. Because we *have* that in common, Senaar and Als. We both worship at the feet of the same God. And it was this God who said, suffer the children to come home to their parents, do not keep them in bondage like the Israelites in Egypt, do not keep them as slaves.'

I was not sure what to say to this, so I observed, 'We keep no Sabbath here. Each day is equally appropriate in our eyes to the business of the individual's connection to the Divine.'

A great sob rose in her throat, and she swallowed it down. 'But it is in the *Bible*,' she said, as if this were a final judgement. 'How can you keep no Sabbath, when it is in the Bible?'

I shrugged. 'The Bible is a book, somebody else's book. If we fit ourselves wholly into that book as you say, then we become slaves to it. The only freedom is to shape one's own relationship with the Divine. To write one's own Bible.'

'Slaves?' she said. 'How can you talk of slavery when you are keeping innocent children in captivity?'

I laughed at this. 'Ask them, and they will not speak of being in captivity. Nobody is captive here.' She seemed to have genuine difficulty comprehending my words so I repeated the sentiment, speaking slowly, 'That is the point of Als.'

'If I ask them, they will say this? But how can I? How *can* I speak to the children when your warrior women will not allow me to see them, meet with them?'

She went away, her face blotchy with crying. But half an hour later she returned, a little more composed. She sat opposite me, cross-legged (to show me how far she had lowered her dignity), and began a long, rambling speech about how she apologised for her behaviour this morning (the *apology* is one of the deference rituals of the hierarchy), and how she had been upset because the President had recalled her mission, and how she had felt she had made progress, and had begun to understand our culture, and more along this line. It was quite dull, listening to her. Then she said:

'But I knew that just as God is Mercy, so I would have another chance to break through the barriers between us. We must reach out, we must connect. For all that you have fallen from the true path, for all that you no longer congregate in churches, no longer observe the Sabbath – nonetheless, we have this bond. I *know* you worship the same God I do, I *know* this as a fact.'

'How can you know the God I worship?' I asked. The question was curious, not aggressive. 'This is difficult for me to comprehend. You do not really know me, so how can you know how I perceive something as numinous as the Divine?'

She stalled at this, but then lurched on. 'The people of Als have' (note the possessive!) 'the same God as the people of Senaar.'

'Rhoda Titus,' I said, pleasantly. 'The people of Als *have* nothing at all. There is nothing possessed in this land, nothing *owned*. The only thing we will talk about *having* is when two people enjoy themselves in sex, and here we only talk about *having* because the experience is, of necessity, so fleeting.' I would have gone on to explain this point a little further. After all, Rhoda Titus had been talking about how difficult she found it understanding the ways of Als, and it is an interesting crux. The only thing we can *have* in the sense a hierarch might understand it is precisely the thing that cannot be *had*. I have sometimes thought that the point of this idiom was to identify the essence of the possessive culture, that the pleasure it takes from its possessions, as great as the pleasures of sex, is in effect evanescent. But Rhoda Titus was not interested in this line of discussion.

'I *know* you worship the same God. This is what binds us together. We were all part of the same fleet, we all travelled through space together in praise of the same deity. You could not have joined the fleet unless you were from the same Earthly congregation.'

I made the gesture, turning one hand palm up, palm down, several times, that used in those days to indicate a half-agreement.

'What you do mean by that?' she said. There were tears in her eyes again.

'The situation on Earth,' I said, 'was difficult. Politics there had coalesced around a stricter and stricter definition of the hierarchy. This made some sorts of religious worship difficult, as I know was the case in Senaar. But it made the position much more difficult for a people such as us. There were establishments on Earth dedicated to destroying us, wholly because of how we lived.'

Blank face; a glittering in the eyes where the tears were accumulating, a curve of salt water swelling, ready to fall. 'Do you mean,' she said, but stopped. I waited a little while, to see if she wished to complete her sentence, before going on.

'There were three fleets planned,' I reminded her. 'And the only one we could have joined was the one we did join. The others would not have accepted us, for all that we had assembled the necessary monies, because ideology, which is the wickedest thing, barred our way. With the fleet as it was set up, all we needed to do was declare our faith to be your faith, and pay our share, and we were allotted a space on the cable.'

'You lied,' she said, in a small voice.

'No. There are many religious people amongst us. I am one. I was present in many negotiations, and whenever I was quizzed about my relationship with the Divinity I spoke simply about just that. Of course, it is the nature of life with us that I could not have spoken about other people's relationship with the Divinity, even had I wished to do this. I could only ever speak for myself.'

The tears had dried away now, and there was a pale edge to her voice. 'I have failed,' she said. 'I shall return to my shuttle, and then I shall return home.'

I shrugged again, because it mattered to me very little either way. Rhoda Titus stood to leave. She did not leave, of course, because it was then that the raid happened.

Barlei

Ms Titus's mission was, as I had always thought, pretty much doomed from the beginning. But her going enabled a number of political manoeuvres. It gave me a set of eyes and ears actually there, on the ground, in Als; able to discover where the hostages were being held, for instance. And, as a woman, it gave me somebody whose honour could very well need protecting from the anarchist advances of a lascivious people. This last eventuality did not come about, unfortunately; but the incident where Ms Titus had attempted, in broad daylight and with law and right on her side, to enter the cave in which the hostages were being kept and speak with them, and where a mad horde of screaming maenads had prevented her, provided the necessary pretext.

I ordered her to leave Als at once, but she stayed behind. Perhaps she was fascinated by the very hypnotic qualities of evil that repulsed her. Perhaps she thought that she could, somehow, save the Alsists from themselves. But whatever the reason, she was still on site when jean-Pierre moved in with his troop.

Petja

They came armed with needleguns. Do you know this weapon? It is built around a butt that contains a reservoir, and the reservoir

114

contains a plasmetal alloy. A solid lump, that fills the butt, gives it weight. And from the butt there is the usual barrel, the sight, the trigger. And this is what happens when the trigger is pulled: the gun melts a little of the reservoir of metal and injects it into the base of the barrel. Then the laser, a powerful little laser, spurts it out. Pushes out the molten metal in a long thin line. The metal is fired very fast, no muzzle friction to slow it down, almost as fast as the laser can propel it (and the laser wants it to go at the speed of light). The metal solidifies in the air, and you have produced a very fast, very thin, very long needle, hurtling through the air at your enemies. Now, this needle can be as long as you like; the gun can be programmed to produce little darts that puncture and injure, or longer strands, half a metre or more, that do more damage. The design admits of a great deal of compactness; the Senaarians have pistols no bigger than a palm; rifles that are aimed from the shoulder and reach no further than the crook of the elbow, which is the prop from which it is fired.

We unearthed the loading of needleguns (and more importantly, the Fabricant software for needleguns and rifles) before the voyage even began, and made a complaint, because all colonists were strictly forbidden from carrying weapons of war. But the Senaarians appealed, claiming that needleguns were not weapons of war but police accessories. They were filed as such on the ship manifests. Their defence of this position was specious (as events proved), but hinged on the fact that needles were not conventional projectiles. The argument stated that needles were thin as a hair, that one fired at you would go right through you. A policeman might fire one at your torso, the needle might go straight through the lung and out the other side. This can collapse the lung, causing immobility and pain, but this damage might be repaired. A projectile, they said, would strike the torso and force out large pieces of flesh, much more likely to be fatal. They said that if a projectile hits your head, then your head will explode; but if a needle strikes the head then the result might be disablement rather than death.

I have faced needleguns in war and I have wielded needleguns. I have been struck by needles. I can vouch from my own experience that the Senaarians lied when they presented their weapons as peacekeepers. And so, when we put ourselves in the position of fabricating these guns, you might say we acceded in this hypocrisy. But such is the necessity of war. We poached the software of this weapon and fitted up a Fabricant to manufacture it; but for a long time we did not actually utilise the machine. Who would want such a weapon circulating in society? But when the war began, we armed ourselves.

But I am getting ahead of myself. The raid.

Barlei

The raid proceeded with a precision worthy of the finest musical composition. Now that the war is over, I sometimes dilate on this analogy; surely the greatest general is indeed a composer, putting men and machinery into the right positions as if each unit, each piece, were the physical manifestation of the musical note. Man-oeuvres are phrases, some short, others longer; the melodies of the battlefield. The analogy bears a further inspection, I think: some wars are symphonic, the bringing together of a great many different forms of warrior, flesh and machine, in a grand and stirring design; other wars are sonatas, the deploying of (in this case) jean-Pierre and his men with their specialist training and ordnance. And, like a sonata, the raid involved action, counter-action, and then a reprise of the original action.

I ordered the intervention at dusk, after the Devil's Whisper had died away. I inspected jean-Pierre and his twenty finest men by floodlight on the airfield. They were a handsome sight to see. Twenty of the strongest warriors of our nation, in their blue combat fatigues; swords at their backs, pieces by their sides, and needlerifles smartly angled against their shoulders. I am not ashamed to say it brought a tear to my eye to see them. To think they were ready to go to their deaths, if necessary, to defend the honour of Senaar. I wept a little, manly tears; I embraced jean-Pierre and sent them away into the sky.

It was jean-Pierre who had the command, of course; his number Two (nowadays this rank would be called 'Point') was carrying one of the two recording chips; the sub-sergeant the other. All these men were the finest. They flew due north in their sound-damped military shuttles, two of them; they could have fitted into one, but redundancy is an important thing, particularly with respect to machines.

They flew directly into the middle of the Alsist camp, and landed within metres of the entrance to their women's dorm, the prison in which the hostages were kept. They landed next to the Senaarian shuttle already present, with its contingent of honour guard for Rhoda Titus. These men, apprised of the shuttle's approach, were ready. Their job was to provide a rearguard, protecting all three shuttles from any attack. jean-Pierre marshalled his men and moved in. Surprise was absolute. The recording chips reveal only a few people gathered about the cave entrance, around a primitive little camp fire. They stare, they stand up. One starts shouting. But jean-Pierre's men have already moved through at the double and are at the entrance of the dorm. There is no door. Three women are standing on the inside.

Silently, jean-Pierre moves through. The chip on Point records the astonishment on the faces of the women. One starts shouting, her fist up, her beautiful face contorted with the hatred and violence that is the disease of every Alsist. But then the soldier carrying the chip moves on, and the face disappears from view.

The room inside is long and low, part carved and part adapted from a natural formation. Glowlamps are bobbing up by the ceiling at intervals; visibility is good. There are beds throughout the space, and at the far end further rooms; presumably kitchens, shower-rooms, child spaces. Each glowlamp carries an echo-breaker to keep the sound intimate and small. There are maybe four hundred women in this huge space, and more than a hundred children. The men fan out, their discipline perfect. Each of them carries a specially designed DNA test button, on the end of a long prod. People are rising from their iniquitous beds, couples (unmarried, of course), children: voices are raised, fists shaken, people start forming angry-looking

117

knots, taking courage from one another's outrage, but there is no discipline, no master-will guiding them. Our boys start to identify children amongst the throng, and move towards them. Sometimes this is a simple matter of one man taking an infant, touching him with the prod and getting a result: if negative then the soldier moves on; if positive, then the hostage is reclaimed. Of course, we had anticipated that so many years of Alsist brainwashing might have disposed the children to stay in their Sodom, and the hostages were mostly sedated, another painless jab with the DNA prod. Then the soldier would pick up the body of the infant and carry it back to the muster point near the door.

The efficiency and purpose with which jean-Pierre's men manage this difficult task is wonderful to watch on the tape made from the recording chips (several versions of this have been circulated; indeed it became something of a bestseller. My favourite is cut to a stirring soundtrack from the final movement of Beethoven's Fifth Piano Concerto – the build up and then the release of action). Within minutes jean-Pierre musters his men, fourteen young bodies carried in their powerful left arms, their right arms aiming their needlerifles. They defend themselves against savage but uncoordinated attacks by several waves of banshee women.

The initial task completed, jean-Pierre gives his orders in a clear voice, and the squad moves as one being towards the exit. The element of surprise has given them the edge, and the Alsists have barely registered what is happening. A few more well-placed needles (*wounding*, I should stress, not killing) mean that the path to the exit is through twin rows of fallen bodies; excellent strategy this, since it provides a barrier to other Alsists wishing to impede the march to the shuttles, and provides a certain degree of cover to jean-Pierre and his men. They move swiftly, despite their burdens, and with few stops to bring fire to bear on attackers they soon make the outside. Light flares in the image we watch, the recording chip takes a moment to adjust to the light outside. The shuttles are visible in the middle distance. The operation inside the Alsist cave has been carried out without a single casualty.

Sadly, the rearguard, left by the shuttles, had not been so favoured by fate. Their job was to hold the shuttles until jean-Pierre and his men could make it back to them. But in the event a small group of Alsists surprised us. We had not reckoned on any of them being able to put together a fighting unit in time, given their well-known hatred of discipline. But whilst jean-Pierre went through the cave with such efficiency, a small band of Alsists attacked the shuttles. To begin with, they were armed only with stones and one or two axes (which they threw; regular barbarian tactics). The rearguard, taking position around the shuttles, and finding their cover mostly by fitting themselves under the curving prows of the shuttles' front ends where they arched down towards the salt, were able to keep these marauders at bay with barrages of long-needles. They retreated, and the men started to pull themselves out of position, standing up. Then two of them were shot through the throat with needles fired from long distance – a remarkable piece of sniper accuracy, it must be said; although the very fact that the Alsists possessed firearms in the first place testified to their theft of Senaarian technology. The number of times they had denied stealing this technology! Still, we can expect little more from the amorality of these people.

The snipers were positioned over the lip of the cave entrance, and it is remarkable that they were able to bring together arms and men so quickly, but then war is about adapting to new situations. The men in the rearguard took what cover they could and concentrated fire on the cave mouth; as they were doing this they were rushed by an ugly-looking mob of Alsists, who came tearing along the strand from down by the water where they had been lurking. Our boys, caught in a primitive pincer movement, were forced to divide their fire. Many Alsists fell groaning, heaped on the salt, filling the air with their foul curses and unrepeatable imprecations (tapes of the raid have had to be edited to remove much of this appalling language: some of it was in the common tongue). But some reached the fallen bodies of the slain soldiers and stole their weapons. Now a real crossfire began, with more and more Alsists swarming in from all over their camp, taking positions behind what cover they could, even behind the fallen bodies of their fellows.

This counter-attack was made with enough vigour, and with such a superiority of numbers, that things looked difficult. But jean-Pierre, emerging from the cavern, took in the scene with a practised eye. What was needed here was speed. He called for the charge, and the advance guard started running, carrying their burdens and firing from the hip with their right hands, pounding the ground between the cave mouth and the shuttles. This sudden infusion of force tipped the balance. The mob surrounding the shuttles was startled, began losing cohesion. The snipers over the cave-mouth began firing again, of course, and several of jean-Pierre's men were wounded. The Alsists (this shows how little they truly cared for those hostages, howsoever much they called them 'their children') even put a needle through the arm of one of the young people being rescued. But with dispatch jean-Pierre was at the shuttles. There was some hand-to-hand fighting now, as our boys pressed their way onto the shuttle bays; and then, with a rush, the recording chip on Point's helmet carries the picture of the ground angling, dropping away, of the lake at the mountain coming into shot, with the light from the setting sun falling beautifully upon it. The raid was over, and it had been a triumph. We carried our own dead and wounded back with us, and we also carried the children, freed from their bondage.

The shuttles landed in secret at the central barracks, the men were debriefed, and the children hospitalised before news was released to the community as a whole. And then, there was such rejoicing! Crowds thronged the streets, singing hosannas and cheering over and over. All newscast channels were given over to reporting the event. It was a moment of tremendous joy for our people, an historic moment. I stood on my veranda before crowds of people so huge that extra police had to be drafted in to control them. I spoke, my words amplified by a dozen newscast microphones, and once again I wept. True tears.

Petja

It was dusk, and Rhoda Titus was about to return to her shuttle for the night, perhaps to order a flight back to Senaar, I do not know. We were in the office assigned for diplomatist duties, and she was saying something to me of a diplomatic nature. But before she could finish her little speech and leave, someone (I no longer remember who) put their head through the door and said, breathlessly, that soldiers were going about the women's cave, shooting people. We went at once; even Rhoda Titus came with us, except that seeing the commotion outside she shrank away from the bloodshed and went back in.

We dashed over the salt towards the women's dorm, but by the time we arrived the raid was well into its progress. Three shuttles stood a hundred metres from the entrance, with a loose company of Senaarian soldiers huddled about them. These soldiers were firing at the growing crowd of Alsists, some of whom were stretched on the ground by the water, some of whom were about the higher ground above the entrance, and some of whom in their rage were making forays towards the shuttles with rocks, and hurling them ineffectually against the bellies of the machines. But news was spreading throughout the immediate vicinity; I could see people in the distance turning, people emerging from tents and buildings

What had happened, we later discovered, was that the Senaarians had carefully planned the raid to arrive in Als shortly before the waking time for night shifts. In the dusklight they had forced their way into the women's dorms where they went from child to child stabbing them with needles to take DNA and straight away test it. The mothers, obviously, fought to prevent them, but were unarmed; many were shot with needles, and eighteen died. Afterwards, impromptu hospitals had to be established to help all the wounded, for there were too many for the two wards that we already had. But this came afterwards.

Shall I tell you what my first reaction was, seeing those soldiers huddling under the curve of their metal hulls, or dropping to one knee to steady their needleguns and fire towards the margins of the water? My thoughts were not for the wounded, although I could see people crumpling as needles penetrated them; nor did I stand idly there, or stunned (although the person I was with seemed dumb-struck, trying to decipher what was happening). I had no care for this. Instead I felt a weird bubbling in my belly, as with excitement; and in my nostrils (even though I was wearing my mask) I had the savour of a weird smell. I felt a spiritual *click*, as if I were suddenly home. And I could see what to do.

The shuttles were between me and the water, and most of the people were on the shore. So I began running, sprinted towards the entrance to the dorm and darted in front of it. There were sounds of screams coming from inside, and the occasional *hish* of a needle fired. Some women were stumbling out in the light, one or two were coming down from the heights above to see what was happening. 'Never mind what is happening in the caves for now,' I said. 'They came in the shuttles, and we must disable the shuttles first of all.'

People around me stopped, turned to me. One woman, I think called Dharc or Dharse, said, 'There were some needleguns fabricated after we arrived. They are in the farm. I think some have gone to fetch them.'

From the darkened cave mouth still the cries, the sounds of battle. But surely they would not stay there long; they would soon be bursting out into the open air.

'Hurry,' I said, gripping this woman by her elbow. 'When they bring the guns, position them along the lip over the dorm entrance. Tell them to concentrate fire on the shuttles.'

It was as if I energised her, as if electricity passed through my hand into her arm. She nodded once, and loped off towards the farm buildings made from the shell of our spaceship. The others were all looking at me. 'What shall we do?' said one of them.

'Come with me,' I said. 'We need numbers by the lake.'

I sprinted off, and these others followed. We made a crocodile of people running over the open land between the dorm and the water, which was not good. Looking back, I should have ordered them to stagger their coming-over but at the time it was pumping in my head that I needed to rally the people by the water. As we ran, some of the guards by the shuttles began firing at the target we represented. One of the women following me was dropped by a needle to the head, another took a needle to her hip: it went through the ball of the joint and lodged deep in her pelvis; only a half-inch sticking out – she fell screaming and lay on the salt, although she had the sense to dig herself into the grains a little, to dig herself a little cover. Afterwards, I found myself in a bed next to her in the hospital.

Needles whished past me. They make a distinctive sound in the air when fired, one not easily forgotten: a sucking sound, and if they pass your field of vision you see them as a sort of instantaneous glowing streak, a retinal flash. And I heard and saw several pass, but none hit me. I was running under fire, for the first time in my life, and yet my sense was of the rightness of what I was doing.

I reached the water, and threw myself forward where the ground dipped down towards the sea; the slope gave us only meagre cover, and so people tried to bury themselves deeper into the dune of salt, paddling with their hands to open the ground by their heads and duck deeper down. People were stretched there, their masks giving them snout-faces, but their rage clearly visible.

It took a moment for my breath to return to me. I crawled on my belly towards a knot of people. 'We must attack,' I said. 'We must do it now. Our chance is to take the shuttles and prevent them from leaving. Only by doing that can we win.' But in the flurry, and with so many people talking and no centre to the group of people, my words were heard only by those immediately next to me.

People were shouting and bickering all at once. Some yelled how they wished for nothing better than to beat out the pigs' brains with a rock; one even started to get to his feet. Others were less coherent, and some seemed frightened. I wriggled forward suddenly, like a striking snake, to grab the leg of the man who was clambering to his feet.

'No, no,' I cried out. 'We must all attack at once, or it will be luckless.' I began calling out to all the people about me, telling them to pass the news along. 'When I stand, we all stand,' I shouted. 'When I rush forward, we all rush.' The men were lodged in close to the shuttles, and our best chance was to draw them out. Then we might pick off one or two, seize their guns, and give ourselves some of their firepower. I could see no other way to success, but I could see that; it was present in my head, complete, like a finished piece of music.

I tried to pass out orders, but none of the people were trained. Most had been brought out in curiosity at the landing of the shuttles; some had come afterwards, when the fighting had started. Few even had weapons, except some saltstone rocks, or the tools they had happened to carry with them. Quickly I slid backwards into the water and ordered some others to help me tear apart one of the osmotic tanks floating in the sea. We broke the spars of the construction from their floats, and passed them among people. This commotion behind them, our shouts and splashes in the water, drew the attention of some more of the crowd gathered.

'We'll rush them,' I cried, trying to ensure the words carried, howsoever muffled by my mask. 'We'll attack! Try to keep to a bunch: if we run as a line they'll have more of a target. But if we all rush at once, we can overpower them with our numbers.' Only numbers were any use in this conflict. But I could not impress the plan upon the furthest of the gathered people. The fear twitched in my belly that when I rose and ran forward only a few would follow, and we would be easily cut down. But note this: my fear was not that I would be killed, but that the plan would fail. Fear in battle is a strange thing. Let nobody tell you they face battle fearlessly, for the greatest of warriors feels that abdominal commotion, that simultaneous tightening and loosening. But the fear becomes displaced, away from personal injury and death, and onto larger questions.

I was prepared to stand up and forward the change towards the shuttles, when I noticed people dropping into positions over the cavemouth. Two snipers had taken position behind the lip of rock, and without pause they began targeting the shuttles. This drew the fire from the Senaarians, and suddenly, my blood pounding so loud it sounded like a great machine in my ears, I stood up. The people rippled upwards beside me until we were all standing. I lifted my spar, and started running.

And a crowd followed. We started over the few hundred yards of salt desert, the grains giving under our heels. It was only the sloppy running that is possible over loose-grained salt, but we were making towards the shuttles.

I was screaming, as we all were. Many brandished their clubs or stones over their heads, and I felt my spar become heavy and deadly with my rage, filled with the power to kill. Ridiculous, in truth, that a man might think a simple lump of plasmetal the equal of armed and armoured soldiery, but this is the way adrenalin takes a fighting man. The men by the shuttles, torn between two targets, reacted without cohesion. Some focused their fire on us, and needles began whipping amongst us. People dropped straight down when hit, or else fell backwards with their legs kicking forwards.

Many people dived to earth in death or injury between the water and the shuttles, but a group of us had almost reached the Senaarians, had come close enough to see the fearful eyes of the enemy. With maybe fifteen metres to go there was a shift in the dynamics of our band. Being untrained, we were, after all, a system governed by chaotic logic, whose courage wavers between killing and self-preservation according to an algorithm difficult to determine, and the evanescent common will that held us together suddenly failed. It is a strange thing to watch, because on the surface there is no change: indeed, if anything, we had surmounted the greatest difficulty. Covering the first stretch of ground was the most dangerous, and now that we were within striking distance the Senaarians would have found needleguns more difficult to wield. But it is not a matter of logic. At one point the adrenalin keeps the soldiers mostly in the fight dynamic; and then at the next, with a mysterious flip down, they find themselves with the overwhelming inner urge towards flight.

We broke and ran; even those few at the front (as I was) sensed it, glanced round, and had to lurch backwards. I could hear whoops of joy from the Senaarians, and the rate of fire increased. More people fell, screaming and crying, or else fell without a cry, never to get up again.

A fury took me. I began screaming, yelling at the loudest pitch. 'To me!' I howled. 'To me! Forward, forward!'

After the initial spurt, the urgency of the retreat diminished. Some, of course, sprinted all the way back to the water but others slowed, turned. Their heads were ducked down, out of the way of the whistling deadly needles, but they saw me. And the switchback started to take hold. Still I was yelling 'To me! To me!' I raised my spar. A needle went through the outer part of my thigh, clean through (as I later discovered) but I did not even notice until afterwards.

'Back! We have them! We *have* them!' I yelled, the odd-sounding phrase sounding perversely right to some deep part of myself (as if we were actually taking ownership of them). And, just as suddenly as we had fled, we found ourselves advancing once more. Again screaming, a more ragged formation.

Several Senaarians had left their cover to chase after us, to provide better firing platforms; and two of those had been picked off by the snipers over the cave mouth. We were on their bodies almost straight away, two women wrenching their guns from them, another man turning one corpse over to pull free the ceremonial sword. The other soldiers were running from us now, scattering back to the shuttles to take cover. And we came down upon them, howling and full of rage.

I was running so hard, I remember, that it was difficult for me to pull up straight when I arrived at the shuttle, and I collided bodily with the metal of the shuttle hull, and was knocked a little backwards. But we were on them now: people falling back with needles in their faces, but others battering the soldiers with our weapons, or pinning them with our captured rifles. I myself took my spar to one man, and the pleasure of striking him with it removed me from myself; there was a timeless period of intensity, unlike anything else I know, and during it, all I was doing was bringing the spar down, and I was yelling, was (the spar seemed to have got itself lost) punching and throttling with my bare hands. Somebody's face was very close to me (the memory itself is a little dissociated, and I can't quite remember how I got to this position), and I was ramming my palm hard against its yielding features, its eyes rolled upwards and white, blood coming from several places.

The next thing I remember, with the conscious deliberation of true memory, is the shuddering as the shuttle began to rise into the air. This, I remember, intensified my rage, to think that we were losing the shuttles. What had happened was that the cave advance party had returned and rushed us, and that the extra bringing-to-bear of firepower had forced a way through. Most of the remaining Senaarian soldiers retreated inside the shuttles, and they pulled away into the sky. Only a few wounded and a single fighting man (except he didn't last long without the shuttles) remained.

And then I was sitting, gasping, on the salt: conscious of blood all over my leg, and blood all down my front, but unsure which blood was mine (and there seemed to be a pain somewhere, I was not sure where) and which was from other people. The area between the cave and the water was a mess of fallen bodies; some cursing and moving, others lying quite still. By now, everybody had heard the commotion, everybody from the settlement was coming, and soon there were people everywhere. A man helped me to my feet, and a woman came by with some water (I was very thirsty, either through my exertions or my loss of blood) which I sipped through the straw in my mask. And the sun went down in a glory of red and gold, and the field was all dark as people limped from it. Somebody brought out trolley lighting and, as I went away towards the hastily inflated medical tent, they were going about the floodlit field, checking the dead.

I spent an hour inside, sitting, letting the sensations drain out of my body. I felt bitter that the shuttles had got away. Eventually a medical-rotation came to me, and I stripped, although my only wound was on my thigh. He bandaged me and I dressed again in the blood-stiff clothes.

I could not face sleeping in the dorm for some reason. And I had no partner to share with, nor did I want to seek somebody out. I intended sleeping in the diplomatists' office, being by myself. And it was there, in that office, that I discovered the whimpering Rhoda

Titus, hiding behind the desk. She shrieked when I turned on the light, and shrieked some more when I came towards her. 'Please don't kill me, don't kill me' she kept saying in the common tongue. I sat watching her until she calmed down and stopped making noise, then I turned off the light and lay on the floor to sleep.

Barlei

I am sometimes asked whether we anticipated retaliation. But you must understand that it is not a leader's job to waste his energies in pointless soothsaying. God orders the future in his own way, and a leader must learn to *respond* to events, not sit about like an old wise woman, attempting to anticipate them in the entrails of animals. Preparedness is everything. And, with our great success building our reputation all about the shores of our sea, we did prepare. I promoted jean-Pierre, and put him in charge of building up our defences. Historians of the counter-patriotic type (the Alsists used to say that I suppressed all public discourse of which I did not approve, but how untrue!) have criticised me for not following the raid on Als through with more thoroughness. I can say, before God and with truth, that I had my suspicions but would it have been lawful to flatten Als? No war existed between us; the only provocation was the children, and they had been removed.

I prayed, and I received my answer, my consciousness of Grace. Make Senaar a strong citadel of God, I heard; and so I did. So I have done.

4

Wandering

Petja

There was a certain sinking of my spirit, a curving reflex action of the soul away from people. I became bitter, angry at the world's people, almost at the world itself. It was as if some part of my being had tasted too much sweetness in the euphoria of battle and now I revolted. It was not that I had killed people, not even that I disgusted myself because I had enjoyed killing, although perhaps a small part of my nameless rage was to do with that. It was that, for an instant, in the belly of the battle, I had wanted the other people who were fighting with me to cease to be people, to become instead automata, to become mere extensions of me. I wanted them to do what I told them to do, whether they wished it or not. I wanted, perverse as it seems, to *own* them, to possess them, to have them. At the time I experienced frustration that they were not doing what I wished, and my frustration took the hierarch's bent of wishing them somehow, metaphysically, *under* me.

At the time I barely noticed that this was happening in my soul; but afterwards, by myself and not wanting a partner, I fell to thinking about it. I dwelt on it, perhaps, and grew revolted with myself. I decided I had the seed within me to become a rigidist, as the common talk styled me; and worse than that, I had the capacity to become a hierarch.

And then there was the issue of Rhoda Titus. I woke on the morning after the raid, and she was still in the diplomatist office. She was sitting like a frightened child in the corner of the room, her hair disarrayed, her blotchy face scrunched up. Her eyes were shut, and she seemed somehow to have fallen asleep in that awkward position, with her knees up in front of her and her hands clenched together resting on her feet. I watched her for a while, with a weird detachment, but then got up and went through to wash without waking her. I think she finally woke to a sense of panic, because I heard a dog's yelp as I rinsed my face. I put my eyes round the doorjamb and saw her curled in the corner with her eyebrows up against her hairline.

My lack of compassion for her should perhaps have alerted me to the change in myself. I had little thought for her, but evidently (with hindsight) she was in a state of terror. She had, as she saw it, been abandoned in the camp of the enemy, with no means of making the trek to the other hemisphere where her own people lived. Perhaps she feared torture or death (many of our people had died in the raid, after all; and she might have feared our rage). Whatever, she was too afraid to come out of the little office. She later told me that she had sometimes shrunk through the door, pressed herself up against the wall, and come a few metres down the corridor, but that the sight of somebody or other had sent her scuttling back where she had come from. She had drunk and relieved herself in the tiny toilet pod attached to the room, drinking the water out of the toilet pan itself (so low she had sunk from her former pride).

I, on the other hand, spent two days in my thoughts. There were angry meetings of people, coming into being and drifting apart all over Als; people were full of high words about the terror that these Senaarian soldiers had inflicted upon us, and people were eager to repay death for death. I took little part in this but instead wandered about places where people were not. I avoided the farm spaces for fear of running across Turja (so absurd had my relationship with her become!), but I spent a while operating the excavation machinery that was opening up new tunnels and smoothing out new caves deep in the mountains. The workers allotted to this had been caught up in the general mood of outrage at Senaar, and so were doing what most people were doing; abandoning their rotas, planning revenge and reprogramming the Fabricants to turn raw materials into weaponry. On the second night there was a large gathering outside, people crowding about a communal fire that burnt green in the chlorine, along with its fiery whites and yellows. Individual after individual spoke up to denounce the murderous actions of the hierarchs. It suited me that everybody gathered in this way, because I was without desire for human company and it made it easy for me to avoid them. I operated the machines, or allowed them to follow their pre-programming, and sat in the cabin in the glow of electric lights, letting the wombish hum of the grinding technology envelope me.

I had never been one of those hermit-people (*soldjosbeyen*) who, from time to time, are seized with a desire to quit humanity and live by themselves in the wilderness. Such people have always been a small part of Als, and usually they will spend a number of years solitary before growing tired and wanting people again: and so will return, and take up work rotas again, and mingle with people, drink, make love, until the urge for solitude becomes strong in them again and they leave again. But this was not me. I was always amongst people, always with a partner, always engaged in work that benefited the whole of the community.

Now, for the first time, I yearned to be absolutely alone, and alone for a long time. I slept in the cab, and woke with a sense of liberation that there was nobody with me. Then I worked some more at grinding away a tunnel, and finished late in the afternoon with a resolution: I was going to spend some time alone. I would take a car and drive into the desert, simply be by myself: perhaps simply stay in the car and drive slowly about the world. Or perhaps find a likely place by a water source and build a hermit-hut.

I could have gone straight then and there, but I did not. For a while I contemplated telling people where I was going and what my plans were (as if people would be interested!), but I realised underneath

131

this strange desire was an attempt to give myself an excuse to get back into the company of Turja; to say, perhaps, that I was leaving. And perhaps (so perverse had I become) to hear her say, 'No, don't go, stay with me.' But once I had identified this lurking desire I was able to sidestep it. Being by myself would do me good in that area as well.

I only returned to the diplomatist office to collect my screenbook and to ensure that there was a car I could take (it occurred to me, as I wandered back through the evening, through knots of people coming together and separating and all talking war, that all cars might be taken in this new enthusiasm). By the time I went back inside the cave it was dark outside, and in the office I turned on the light. There was a squeal, little more. Rhoda Titus, unused to fasting, was in a feeble state.

'Technician,' she wheezed. 'Please, I throw myself upon your mercy. I am your supplicant.'

I replied, but my voice was hoarse with having been silent for days. 'I admit to surprise at still finding you here, Rhoda Titus.'

At this she cried, her tears coming so copiously from her eyes that they scattered and dripped off her face. 'I had no idea that any military action was planned!' she gasped, each word requiring a breath. 'Please, believe me! *Please* believe me!'

I was not paying too much attention in fact, but was busying myself with gathering together a few things from the office and accessing the datastore on the terminal, but she seemed to take my involvement in these things as a snub of her. She came over, her red and blotchy face pressed into my shoulder, her hands taking hold of my arm and repeated her insistence.

'You *must* believe me. Oh please! Please believe me!'

This, of course, is another function of the hierarchy, the need for the person above you in the chain to 'believe you', that is, to accept the assurance of the subordinate that her mind is properly in tune with the requirements of the hierarchy itself. As you can tell from this, it is in the nature of the hierarchy to seek to control even thoughts and beliefs, and it is the way of those who live under it to boast of their openness, as if their minds might be read by telepaths and be proven pure. I did consider trying to explain to Rhoda Titus how alien this was to me (why should it matter to her whether I believed her?), but decided it was not the best time to do this. Instead, I completed my requisition of three months' water and food, with a fuelled car, and stood up to go.

At this Rhoda Titus started keening, an unpleasant sound like an engine slipping out of gear. Her hands slid from my arms and she tried to take a grip at my hips as she collapsed onto her knees. But, as I stepped towards the door to leave, she relinquished me and her wailing broke up into a series of shorter and shorter sobs.

As I stepped through the door into the corridor outside I heard her voice, pitched almost too low for my ears, as she said:

'How you hate me.'

For some reason this snagged in my brain. Hatred. I had managed only a few metres down the corridor before I turned myself back. I came back into the little room and found her in the same position, still kneeling on the floor.

'Rhoda Titus,' I said. 'I am intrigued that you should say such a thing. Why should I hate you? Why should I feel anything about you at all?'

She looked at me with blackened, bleary eyes, and said only, 'What?'

'You said I must hate you, but I assure you I do not. You seem to think that I have some emotional connection to you, to feel one way or another about you.' Having said this, perhaps I should have gone straight away. But still I loitered.

'If you don't hate me,' she said, her voice thick, 'then why don't you help me?'

This was a puzzle. I sat down on one of the chairs. 'I do not understand. You cannot help yourself?'

'Of course not!' she blurted, anger getting past her tiredness and her hierarchy-trained subordination.

'This is strange to me,' I said.

Perhaps the kneeling was uncomfortable to her on the hard floor, because she sat back, and then wriggled her legs out from underneath her to clasp them in front of her, the posture of a frightened child. 'You're mocking me,' she said.

'Not at all.'

'Of *course* I can't help myself,' she said, the warmth of her words seeming to heat her a little. 'I am a woman, all by myself in the middle of the enemy; forgive me, but you are the enemy. I looked outside, I saw your mob: Als is famous for its lawlessness, but it was terrifying to see, that anarchic mob venting its caveman urges, killing and destroying. If I had,' she went on, her words gathering speed as she spoke more of them, 'if I had not hidden myself away in here your people would have torn my limbs from my body, would have mauled me to death. Of course I'm scared; what would you *expect* me to be, except scared?'

At this she paused, as if waiting for my reply. I was shaking my head a little. 'It is genuinely difficult for me to understand you, Rhoda Titus,' I said. 'You talk of *my people* as if I owned them all, every woman, man and child in Als, as some sort of slaves. And you talk about being scared, when I asked whether it was true you could not help yourself. You speak as if being scared and being unable to look after yourself were the same thing.'

Her brows contracted. Anger and despair jerking in combat over her features. Then she started crying again.

'You're a monster, a *monster*,' she said over and again. I tried to speak some more. 'Rhoda Titus, if you were scared of coming to Als why did you come? If you considered coming to Als as putting you in a position where you felt unable to help yourself, why did you come?' But she was not listening to me.

I sat for several minutes whilst Rhoda Titus worked out her crying, and then for a minute or so more in silence. Then I said, in what I hoped was a softer voice (but it was so difficult talking with this strange creature who never said what she wanted or what she did not want, but rather expected you to read the complexities of her alien social relations into her moods), 'Perhaps you would tell me what you want of me?'

But now, having cried, she was surly. She said, 'Nothing, thank you very much. Nothing at all, thank you.'

'Why do you thank me for nothing?' I said.

She stared at me, and then her face fell again. I was afraid she was about to cry, but she managed to hold off against that and instead said, 'In the name of Good God I am so hungry!'

'Well,' I said. 'I can stand friend for you at a Fabricant if you would like that.'

She tried to get to her feet, stumbled and fell down again. Now she was gabbling, speaking so quickly in the common tongue (which I do not speak well) that I could hardly follow her, but talking nonetheless about how she had starved for two days, how she had been reduced to taking water from the toilet and so on. I helped her up and through to the corridor. There was a Fabricant at the junction of the corridor with the main hallway, and I provided her with a little pasta in eel sauce and some water. She stared at it with wide eyes.

'You do not eat it, though,' I observed.

'Not here,' she begged. 'Back to the other room, the one we were in.'

She was beyond being reasoned with on this matter, and soon I agreed to go back with her to the office space. There she gobbled the pasta down, strands of it lying against her chin, and drank the water in a single draft. Afterwards, she said she had stomach cramps, and was compelled to lie on the ground. 'I'll be sick,' she said. Then her speech disintegrated into a series of heaves, as of somebody straining at something: but she managed to keep the food down, and shortly the cramps disappeared. I leaned her against the wall, and wrapped her own cloak about her shoulders. For a while she sat in silence, and soon I became bored.

'Rhoda Titus, it is time for me to go,' I said, standing up. My knees creaked as I rose; I was not a young man.

'Will you return to me later?' she asked, pleadingly.

'No.' Her expression collapsed into misery. 'I am leaving Als for a time that will be at least several months, and may be years.'

'You're going?' she hissed. I thought at first she spoke with contempt, but when she continued it was clear the wind had been taken from her with the shock of my words. 'Can it be true? Has God shown you the truer path, shown you the wickedness of the people you call your own?'

This was so bizarre a thing that I laughed out loud, and Rhoda Titus' expression collapsed again. 'Not at all, Rhoda Titus. Only I wish to be by myself. The reasons are complicated, and I do not care to tell you them. But I suppose this is a goodbye, and I suppose I shall not see you again.'

'No, wait,' she called out, lurching a little forward to clasp me about the knees. 'Wait, wait, wait.'

'You must let me go,' I said.

'How are you going? In a shuttle? Take me with you.'

I sighed. Bending down a little, I disentangled Rhoda Titus' hands and crouched down to bring my face more on a level with hers. 'I am going in a car to roam the desert. I do not believe that you wish to spend three months in the salt desert with me.'

But there was an eagerness about her now. 'You can take me with you, take me where you are going. You can take me south, take me back to Senaar, *you* can take me home, you can be my saviour.'

'No,' I said, and stood up.

At first I think she refused to understand the word I spoke but when I made towards the door she began howling and shouting, mixing imprecations against me with the most abject begging. I could not leave her in such a state; she was a woman, after all. So I returned to her and tried to reason her out of her position.

'I am not going in the direction of Senaar,' I said.

'Then Yared,' she said. 'There is a spinal railtrack from Yared to Senaar, our leader's personal project. Or to any settlement by that sea.'

'I am going east, not south.'

'It would hardly be out of your way. I implore you. I can reward you; I can give you anything you desire, any monies, any goods.'

'Monies and goods do not interest me.'

Now she was crying and laughing at the same time, more than a little unsettling. 'Then tell me what you are interested in, and I'll trade it – or I'll arrange to have it sent to you when I get home again. Oh, home home home. I am begging you, I am imploring you, in *God's* name.'

She went on in this fashion for a while. After a while I became bored of it and went away, wandering about the sunlit settlement for a little while. I sat by the waters of the Aradys, feeling the sun against my naked head, and watching the wriggling currents within the sluggish banks of green fog on the water. I cannot remember thinking about very much. A few images from my time with Turja may have gone past my inner eye, those sorts of memory that give pleasure in solitude. Perhaps some tatters of my perversion still clung about my imagination; perhaps some recalcitrant part of me wanted a better conclusion, a more aesthetic rounding to our time together, but this was doubtless just the old desire to see her again, to be able to hold her and hear her speak to me. The patterns in the fog-bank shifted again. After a while I felt the time had come that I should leave, and so I did.

I went back to the office, and found Rhoda Titus with a strange expression, eyelids risen high and eyeballs convex and straining out of her face, doing nothing I could see other than staring at the wall opposite her. I told her, 'I will take you to Yared, and you can make your own way along the coast to Senaar.'

She stared at me, and I realised (I had already begun to understand the arbitrary conventions of Senaarian behaviour) that, despite having heard my words perfectly well, she wished me to say them again. I am not sure why she wanted this reiteration: perhaps it is another game of the hierarchy, that the subordinate must make show of not comprehending a positive act bestowed by the superordinate, as if she were saying, 'But I am too humble to deserve such a thing.' But I had no desire to play the games, so I shrugged, and turned to go. Then, at my back she began babbling her thanks (another prompting of the hierarchy, I suppose) and struggled noisily to her feet.

I took a twelve-metre car, with enough supplies of food and water to last two people a little under two months, and rolled out of Als. It was dusk by the time we left, and I rolled on through the darkness for a while. Rhoda Titus spent these first few hours of travel nervously flitting from the driving cab into the back of the car; exploring the territory like a spooked mouse. I tried to put her from my mind but her rattling and banging in the back was a small distraction. After a while I called for her to be quiet, and then there was absolute silence. This was oddly extreme in the other direction; because she had neither replied with assent nor denied my request. I believe now she was scared of me; at the time I merely put it from myself.

Eventually she came through and sat in the co-driver seat, but she was still abnormally silent, and sat with her hands in her lap. It did not look comfortable. The darkness thickened around us, and soon all that was visible from the cab was the Venn diagram of the three headlight spots on the salt before us. When a small stone, or a patch of salt-grass, slid across this shape of light it was possible to snatch a sense of movement, but when the path was clear (and I was travelling along a ˙well-travelled path) the lights seemed motionless, silver-white, and the night around us was darkened further in contrast.

After a few hours I began to grow tired of this weirdly dissociated travelling. My mind moved into a near-fugue state, staring at the bubbles of light on the ground ahead, almost to the point where the white circles hallucinatorily lifted upwards and danced in the sky. I was not exactly tired – not sleepy, at any rate – but I decided it would be best if I stopped driving. I pulled the car off the road, and halted it.

Rhoda Titus looked at me, so I looked at her. I realised that she required an explanation (even though it was obvious what I was doing), and I realised at the same time *that it was somehow inappropriate in her conception of the hierarchy to ask for one.* It is a bizarre creed. We sat for a moment, and to attempt to put her at ease I decided to say aloud what I was doing.

'I have stopped,' I said. 'I am not sleepy, but I think it best to stop, to go through to the back, to lie down.'

She did not reply to this, although her eyes opened slightly as if in repressed panic. My vision was weary from the travelling and I found it hard to decipher this, why she might be scared, why she might now be gripping the driver's wheel with unusual force. I could not be bothered to decode these fathomless signals, so instead I rose out of the driver's seat and went to the rear of the car.

I opened the door and stepped through into the airlock chamber, an uncomfortably tight fit, even for a relatively short man such as myself. Then I was outside in the cool darkness, and my mask leapt at my mouth. I went round to the side of the car, and pulled free the car supports so that, should I still be asleep or disinclined to get up at dawn, the Devil's Whisper would not knock the car flat over. I fixed one, then the other, and then wandered right around the car on the outside, just to check if it was all right. The night air was cool on my skin, and the yellow lighting from the inside of the car spilled out. Rhoda Titus was still sitting in the cabin, illuminated vividly in the windscreen: still sitting stiffly gripping the wheel, with her eyes wide. It was impossible, I decided then and there, to reach empathetically and enter her consciousness. It was blank, a blot. I shooed it away from my imagination, climbed back inside the car, and pulled my mask free.

'You're free to spend the night in the driving cabin if you like,' I called through to her. Perhaps I was a little angry with her. 'Or you can come through and pull out your own bunk. It makes no difference to me.' After this I pulled out my own bunk, climbed into its envelope, and turned to face the wall. I spoke out the lights in my portion of the car, but the light in the driver's cabin spilled through, casting out pouring shadows at the back and greying my bunk. After a moment it seemed that Rhoda Titus was not coming through, and so I called to her: 'The light in the driving cabin is distracting me from sleep: I would like you to speak it out.'

For the first time that day her voice came, 'Does it respond to common speech?' It sounded fractured with lines of exhaustion.

'Of course,' I said. 'Did you not hear me speak out the lights here in the back in common speech?'

She said, 'Lights, out' and the whole world went dark. I shuffled in bed to get myself comfortable but there was something, some little grit of irritation that was preventing me from drifting to sleep. Presently, I heard Rhoda Titus rise, with a clicking of joints, from her sitting position, and attempt to come through to the back; but of course in the deep blackness it was not easy. There were several small knocks, bangs, and I could hear her sucking in breath to prevent herself crying out. It was ridiculous.

'Rhoda Titus,' I said, my face to the wall. She froze. 'If you are coming through, why did you not speak on the lights?'

She breathed several times, and then said, in a low, hurried voice, 'I didn't want to disturb you.'

'You disturb me with your banging about. Lights on,' I said. Bright electric light, the colour of condensed orange juice, filled the space. I turned over to look at her standing there, although the light made my eyes wince. She stood like stone halfway through the driving cabin hatch.

'You are a strange woman,' I told her. 'Why do you stand there? If you get into your bunk, we can speak off the lights and both sleep.'

At this she began hurrying, pulling herself through the hatch, stumbling into the back. She could not find the bunk strap, and then she could not unhitch the bunk. I sighed, I think I remember, and offered to get up from my bed and unhitch the bunk for her, but she gabbled no, no, that she would do it herself. And eventually the bunk unhitched itself, and she climbed into the satchel and lay still. I spoke out the lights and soon after I was asleep.

The next morning she seemed a little easier with me. I woke before her, sometime after noon, and got up and washed, and went into the driver's cabin. There I sat and watched the bright landscape around me whilst I ate a breakfast of grain and pasta. I pondered waiting until sunset before driving on but decided against it: the car, after all, was fairly well rem-shielded, and the dark-driving was tedious to me. And so I geared the car and started off.

The tremble of the engines woke Rhoda Titus, and after a little time she came through and sat next to me. Why she should be happier in the morning than she had been in the night was too much for me to understand. Perhaps, I reasoned, she was fearful of the dark.

But she said a good morning to me, and asked how I had slept. This was another cultural difference, I think; for she could hardly have had a genuine interest in my sleeping, and said this only to placate the person she perceived as being higher in the chain.

The afternoon's drive took me through metal-bright sunshine and the white salt desertlands past the last outposts of the Als settlements. The track faded on the ground before us; the few cars that had passed this far south before had left no tracks deep enough to withstand the Devil's Whisper. For as long as the Aradys sea was to our west the ground was rolled smooth by the wind, and the car moved smoothly forward. Soon, though, we passed the southernmost extremity of the waters away to the west: and now, for the wind, there was nothing but planet-belting salt desert: a complete latitudinous stretch of emptiness. The terrain changed: dunes of salt gave our journey rise-and-fall; and the further south we travelled, the larger the dunes became, until we were travelling along the spines, or diagonally up the face and down the slope of the megadunes. This was a landscape that presented a certain bleakness of view and, of course, driving now became a matter of mere monotony; yet I began to find it rather soothing. From the peaks of dunes, rivulets of finest salt scurried down the face, balanced by the wind and then released like Moses' spring by the wind. A thousand scurries of salt so fine as to virtually be a fluid: they glittered. Driving became determined by a slow rhythm, the gradual rise, peak and then the gradual descent as we moved over dune after dune; and this rhythm was a sinal one, almost organic. It was the slow in-breath and out-breath of the flotation tanks. It restructured the circadians of everyday life at a more deeply peaceful level. And as we travelled, the extraordinary beauty of the world through which we moved settled slowly at the bed of my soul, like a rich sediment.

Rhoda Titus, however, did not like it. She became increasingly bored as the day stretched on; she began fidgeting, humming to herself until I told her to stop (and she did stop, although without the abject terror with which she had regarded me the day before). Then, as the sun finally set, there became almost something sullen about her, something as of a child. She began saying things such as, 'How terrible this landscape is, how wasted and terrible' and then she might sigh and say to herself, 'Well, it must be to God's purpose, I suppose.' Then, from memory, she might quote some section from the Bible, some passage about the destruction of Sodom and the sowing of the fields with salt.

After sunset we stopped and ate some food. Abruptly, in the midst of eating, she looked up at me and said 'I don't know if I've said how grateful I am to you for taking me on this drive.'

I was in a peaceful mood after the beauties of the day, so I let this idiocy pass, and continued eating. But she continued with her hierarchy rituals, and thanked me several times. Eventually my patience was eroded, and I started shouting at her to be quiet, not to try and afflict me with her ridiculous rigidist perversions. At this she became very white, pale as the salt itself, and her mouthful of food went unchewed. I, of course, felt better for the expression of my anger, and finished up eating swiftly; but she was too blocked inside to allow the flow of her own angers to come out, and it was easy to see the harm this 'repression' did to her. Her eyes were rheumy, her face began to flash with red blushes. But she said nothing, and I went through to the cab and started the car again. She did not join me. I drove for four or five hours through the darkness, and when I came through to the rear she was in bed, with the lights on, and her back to me. I got into my own bunk and spoke out the lights. Sleep came easily.

The following day Rhoda Titus was cowed, her head sunk so far forward that the back of it was of a level with her shoulders. But the rhythm of our driving was set. We woke at noon, ate, and I drove on until sunset. Then I would batten down, and we would eat again; and after food and the Whisper I would drive through the radiation-quiet darkness. As we moved south it became hotter, although the cabin kept the temperature at a reasonable level. From time to time we would stop and I would step outside and walk around the car, just to stretch my legs and admire the view. The heat was fantastic in the early afternoon; a positive pressure on the skin of heat, and the view of salt dunes sparkling away towards the west. On our fourth day Rhoda Titus came out herself, holding her hand over her mouth to ensure she breathed through her nasal implants. She had not been out for days, and it was, she said, easy to forget the presence of chlorine and take in a choking lungful; after which the body reflex took over and coughing would automatically draw great shuddering breaths after it, which would only make things worse. I winked both my eyes at her over the snout of my mask.

But the world! My heart crumpled and filled like a lung, like a spiritual lung, in the oxygen of its beauty. I had rolled the car to the peak ridge of a megadune, and we stood looking east, where the great ripples of white powder, the standing waves, shrank in their perspective towards the world's-edge. The shadows cast by the reclining sun stood out very black against the silvery-white of the salt itself, a barred range of black haloes about the white peaks. Then, to turn west and to bring up the hand like the peak of a cap to guard the eyes against the brightness of the sun, a white sun, tinted into a pale pink the colour of flesh by the refraction of the approaching horizon. Here the dunes possessed the eye, like the curves and the sockets of a body, swelling and retreating. Where the light caught the billion crystals of the summit of each dune it was shredded into spectra that threw out reds, pale greens, mistral blues, faint traces of all colours scattered in the air.

I dropped to my haunches, and put my bare fingers through the dense salt that made the dune. Up by the mountains, where the land has more shelter from the winds, the grains of salt tend to be much bigger, and to accrete in a variety of micro-shapes. But out here, in the bareness of the deep desert, the wind was the hammer that broke the salt into very fine globular grits. They rolled and trickled over the dunes like water flowing over water, the corners of each grain all worn away from the crystal. The grains rolled so smoothly over one another that putting a finger through the slightly stiff outer crust (which was the creation of the great heat and the slight moisture in the air) it felt like immersing the hand in water. I reached out a handful of the grains and held them in the cup of my palm, and it was fascinating to swirl my fingertip through it. To draw spiral patterns, like shamanic signifiers. A few grains adhered to my index finger after I had done this, and I brought my finger close to my eye to examine it. The grains were so tiny that they fitted inside my fingerprint ridges. I had a sense of the dislocation of scale, as if the megadunes through which we travelled were only the indentations of a titanic fingerprint, and the car but a miniature grain of salt rolling from peak to trough.

I poured the salt from my hand, and the sweat on my palm held a patina of salt, like the dusting of sugar on a doughnut.

I breathed in and lifted the mask with my left hand, so that the salty finger could go into my mouth. Then, the tart tang of salt on the tongue, gritty but giving the sensation of biting down on the grain even as it dissolves in saliva.

But the wind was starting to stir, and the sun was near enough the horizon to presage the Devil's Whisper, so I stood up, and returned to the car to brace it against the coming tempest. Rhoda Titus followed me, puppy-like, with her hand still over her mouth.

After we had retreated back into the car, and as we sat eating, whilst the rising wind outside began its grinding ascent to that world-scarping intensity, Rhoda Titus spoke to me, for the first time in days. She did seem calmer.

'Mr Technician,' she said. 'It is difficult for me to know how to address you.'

I finished my mouthful and looked at her. 'I do not see the difficulty.'

'I seem . . . to anger you.'

This was so straightforward that I said nothing. After the silence had stretched a certain distance, she said, 'So it is true?'

'You say nothing,' I told her. 'Human beings anger human beings. But this is not the point, I think.'

She stuttered, and then said all in a rapid breath, 'Surely you don't think this, and since we must spend time together would it not be better to work a way around this anger, although I confess I do not understand why I anger you.'

I paused after this speech, but it made little sense. 'The point between us, I think,' I said, once I had finished my meal, 'is that you have a spastic reflex that crushes your anger inside you. Why can we not be angry with one another?'

She looked horrified. 'Rage is a sin,' she said.

I snorted through my nose. 'How nonsensical you are, Rhoda Titus,' I said.

'You despise me,' she said in a sorry voice.

'You would have me limit my feelings for you so that only good ones are permitted to emerge,' I said. 'Sometimes I do despise you, sometimes I am angry. Sometimes I feel pleasure to be around you, sometimes I feel desire.'

At this she only narrowed her eyes, and opened her mouth dryly to speak without saying anything. So I continued, 'But it would cripple me to break the bones of my feelings the way you wish.'

She was shaking her head, shallow rapid shakes from side to side, almost a tremor rather than a gesture. 'I'm sorry I spoke at all,' she said. I shrugged, and went through to the front of the car. For the afternoon's drive I was alone, which made me happy. The day shrank towards night, and I drove on through the blackness.

By the following morning things were easier. Perhaps Rhoda Titus had finally begun to believe she was on the path to her home, for she was more blithe with me. 'The part of your society that interests me,' she told me, 'is your fathering. Can it really be true that you do not know who your father is?'

'And why should I know?' I replied. 'Parenting is of the mother. Fathers come and go, but mothers are the connection.'

'You are close to your mother?'

I spat on the floor. 'She is on Earth.'

'Oh. Why did she not come?'

'She is no Alsist. I am sure she does not realise I am no longer on her world.'

At this Rhoda Titus was silent. 'I did not realise,' she said.

'I was born into a religious community in the heart of the Old Continent,' I said. 'But I realised in my youth that unless a person gives birth to their own system, they will become enslaved by another's. I travelled for many years, and for many years after that I was with the Alsists. I have not seen my mother for decades.'

Rhoda Titus had fallen easily into a sombre expression, another skill of the hierarchy. But when I saw it I laughed: 'I cannot believe, Rhoda Titus, that you can genuinely feel concern for myself, or for my mother.'

At this she was jolted. 'What do you mean? Of course, it is very sad, and I feel it.' She was silent for a while. Then she said, 'I miss my father.'

I had little interest in this, and told her so, at which she retreated into the back of the car. I drove until sunset, my mind occupied by the spareness of the landscape. When the evening Devil's Whisper began rattling the car, I drove down the lee of a dune and waited, cursing myself for letting the drive go on so long. It was a stinging business, rushing outside in the semi-dark, battening the car. Back inside I examined my face and hands in the mirror: tiny scratches. But once the wind had died down, I went out again and freed up the car. Getting back into the rhythm of driving soothed me. My heartbeat. Even the stinging of the salt winds became, in memory, a devotional meditation. The caustic emptiness of the desert. I began to feel a fluttering sense of inner dawning. This, my marrow knew, was the true arena for closeness to God. The whiteness of the salt was an emptiness, clear as lymph, reaching out in all directions towards a sky that was the silver presence of God. Reaching in all directions away from me, because all directions away from me was the true path to deity.

Epiphany.

And afterwards, always, the reassertion of the flesh. I was suddenly fiercely hungry. My water bottle, in its dashsocket, was long empty. I pulled the car to a halt and rose from the driver's seat. It is the harmonic of spirituality: the further one retreats into the soul, the more tugging is the backswing, back into flesh. I went through to the back of the car to find Rhoda Titus standing, as if to attention. I believe she used to leap to her feet when she heard me coming through from the cabin, perhaps (who knows) in fear, or in some odd hierarchical game.

I drank a long pull of water from the Fabricant spout, and then ordered up some ersatz-speltmash. Then I settled myself down on the stool at the back of the car and ate it.

'Technician,' Rhoda Titus said. 'I must confess.'

'More hierarchy games,' I said. Pieces of the mash scattered from my mouth. I saw her wince.

'I have been bored,' she said. 'And you make no effort to put your personal belongings away, no effort to hide them from me.'

This caught my attention. 'I have no personal belongings,' I said.

'Your notepad,' she said.

I turned my head. The notepad was on her bunk. I looked back to her face. 'Yes?'

She steeled herself. 'I have been reading your notepad,' she said. And then, when I said nothing, she said, 'You are very cross with me?'

I shook my head and finished off my mash.

'I only wanted to access the Bible,' she said. 'And maybe some poetry. Perhaps a story. You understand how bored I have been?'

My belly was full now, so I replaced the bowl in the Fabricant, and ordered up some vodjaa. I lay on my bunk and started sipping out of the little bottle it provided. My eyes, used to staring at blankness, and emptiness in a visionary fugue, lighted on Rhoda Titus and I was as soaked in the image of her face as I had been of the salt desert.

Rhoda Titus, unsure, sat down herself. Then she picked up the notepad and held it towards me; and when I did not take it, she placed it on top of the Fabricant. Then she said, 'Please, don't stare at me, Technician. It is making me all uneasy.'

'At what shall I stare?' I asked, not taking my eyes from her face. The features seemed bizarre, dissociated from one another in an unsettling manner. Decomposing and recomposing at a level beyond immediate sight. But the unsettling thing was that it was occurring to me that faces were always like this, always radically strange, but that I had never noticed until this moment.

'I don't know,' she said. Her face was blushing to sunset shades. 'But please, this is embarrassing to me.'

'At what shall I stare?' I repeated. 'At the Fabricant?' And I notched my head about to look at the machine in the stern of the car, although the action of moving my head was somehow very hard.

I stared at the Fabricant.

'A Fabricant,' I said, 'can only ever be as good as the raw materials you put into it. It can be worse than them, but it can never add anything to them. All it does is deconstitute and reconstitute, boil and freeze, mix and separate.' I spoke this speech with many pauses and lacunae, and in each silence I sipped more vodjaa. But as I spoke on, I discovered a deeper resonance in myself with my own words, as if I were expressing some tremendous truth. 'A food Fabricant,' I explained, 'takes raw roughage, or the base derived from the shit tanks (perhaps) and mixed it around with other raw materials, spices, textures.' I stopped, drank some more vodjaa. Rhoda Titus was silent, a perfect terror holding her face rigid. 'Drink Fabricants only add flavour to water, or hastily distil to produce the roughest of alcohol. Machine Fabricants mould and plane and tool and work the plastic of their base model; or they melt and reshape metals put into them.' I angled my head, looking carefully about the whole cabin. 'They mat and compress grasses, or whatever their software tells them to do.' My head came slowly back round to look at Rhoda Titus. 'And so it is with people.'

She was goggling at me now, perfectly motionless, perfectly speechless.

'I think that I will never see a person lovely as a tree,' I said. A vivid, almost photo image of a tree came into my inner eye; tall, with the branches sprouting half-way up and supporting a hair of leaves. 'People are made by fools like me. But only God,' and I stopped. Part of me wanted Rhoda Titus to complete the rhyme. But she was a statue. 'Can make,' I prompted. 'A Tree.'

The silence was eerie. I shuffled down further in my bunk, the empty bottle on my chest. 'If I were a tree,' I said, 'I would drink with my feet. I would eat with the top of my head and my hands, held upwards. I would sneeze my sex into the wind.' My slippage into sleep was not something I registered.

The following morning Rhoda Titus was unusually jolly, forcefully jolly. We breakfasted and she made impassioned smalltalk, about the food we were eating, about the journey ahead of us, about the differences between the Aradys and the Galilee. The Devil's Whisper in the morning (whilst we slept) had been very severe, and a large bank of salt had built up against the side of the car. I had to clear some of this away with a shovel. Rhoda Titus came out into the hot air with me, holding her left hand over her mouth. She even offered, with her voice muffled by her hand, to help dig. But she refused to uncover her mouth for fear chlorine would sting her lungs, and there is little a person can do with a shovel held only in one hand.

Afterwards, when we set off driving, Rhoda Titus sat beside me in the second driver's seat. At first she spoke over-brightly, but soon she settled down. Perhaps my conversational responses reassured her that day. She talked for a little while about her father but I have no memory of what she said. Then she began a long debate with me over the necessity of rules. Als, she insisted, had rules, just as did Senaar. It was only that Als expressed its rules differently. I listened to her talking without becoming angry. Indeed, I felt so liberated (it was so pure being in the desert; it was so good being away from Als; it was so much better to be driving in the day than at night) that I found myself becoming involved in the debate.

It continued after we stopped at the reddening of the sky, and after I had battened the car down for the Evening Whisper. We sat in the back of the car, and I drank a little more vodjaa (I was parsimonious, now, because the supply was limited).

'But there are rules,' she insisted. She was very loath to give up on this point. 'You are given a work rota, which you must follow.'

'No,' I said, mildly. 'There is no compulsion to work.'

She gave a little sigh, like someone trying to blow out a candle. 'How ridiculous! Then why does anybody work?'

I shrugged. 'I can speak for myself,' I said. 'And say that it is dull indeed to have no work at all. Work is a good way of filling the time.'

'But there will always be lazy people,' she said. 'That is human nature. Laziness, perhaps you see it as a weakness or a vice, but what of them? What of such people?'

'Lazy,' I said. 'I do not quite understand. Do you mean people medically disinclined to work? They are to be pitied rather than despised, surely, assuming you wish to give them any thought at all.' I thought of Lichnovski with his months of enforced 'laziness' on his back in a hospital bed, waiting for his new lungs to be grown. He would certainly rather have been working than there.

'No, no. I mean, if there is work to be done, and some people do it and others shirk it, then the ones working are carrying the load. The lazy ones are taking advantage of you. They are laughing at you, sucking the fruits of your labour from you. They must be made to work.'

But I could make little sense of this.

'Really,' said Rhoda Titus, leaning forward, as if it was particularly important that I grasp this point. 'You do have rules. What would you do if somebody refused to work their rota?'

'What would I do? Probably nothing.'

'Well, what would any Alsist do?'

'How can I say? You must ask them.'

'Are there no such people, people who ignore their rota, even if it is important work for the good of the whole community?'

'I suppose so,' I said, vaguely.

'Well, what happens to them? Do you see my point? There must be some mechanisms for *making* people work, even if they don't want to.'

'Why would such a person not want to work?' I asked.

'Because,' said Rhoda Titus, a little too loudly, as if she were growing angry. 'Because he prefers sitting about with his friends drinking and eating and talking to doing any work.'

'He has plenty of time to sit around drinking and talking,' I said. 'He has three-quarters of the day to do this.'

'But he wants to spend the *whole* day doing this,' Rhoda Titus insisted.

'Why? It would become very dull.'

'I *don't* know why, that's not the point. Say that there is such a person. Surely you would make him work?'

'No,' I said.

She made an exasperated sound now. 'You are merely saying that to try to win this argument,' she said, hotly. 'But I know you would.'

'Believe me, Rhoda Titus,' I said. 'I have no desire to win this argument, or even to have an argument with you. But if there were such a man as you describe, his boredom would be a sort of punishment I suppose. But it would be his responsibility to deal with that, not the responsibility of the state. I suppose his friends might become cross with him, if he avoided all rota duties and if they suffered as a result; say he had a medical duty, and a friend were hurt and had to wait longer because the medical rota was understaffed.'

'Ah!' said Rhoda Titus. 'Exactly.'

'Well then his friends might shun him, might even beat him up, I suppose. Then he could sit and drink all day, but he would be by himself. Most people who feel that way, who want no friends. Well, they simply leave and set up homes away from habitation.'

She seemed to have had enough talk for the time being, and wordlessly turned about and stretched herself on her bunk, staring at the ceiling centimetres over her face. I took up my notepad and read some matter or other. The Whisper was growing now, rattling the walls of our car and jerking it like a pendant on a chain. For minutes we did nothing but lie in our bunks and listen to the world outside us. Then I got up and poured myself some more vodjaa, sitting on my bunk to sip at it. Suddenly, Rhoda Titus sat up herself, swinging herself out of her alcove to sit on the edge of the bunk.

'I remember,' she said, triumphant, as if the clincher in her argument had occurred to her. 'Out of your own mouth you said it, when I first arrived in Als. When I was prosecuting my diplomatic duties: when I asked you to take me to the women's dormitory you said no, that you could not. So there is a law there, isn't there, a law preventing you from going to that place if you're a man.'

I laughed a little. 'There's no law,' I said. 'There are many women there who would not like to see me, I think. They would beat me up, throw me out. But that does not make it a *law*. And besides,' I said, after a little while. 'Why should I wish to go there?'

Rhoda Titus did not answer this for some time, except with a gentle shaking of her head from side to side. 'There might be many reasons,' she said, eventually.

'Why, though? To meet a woman? I might meet her at any time. Why else?' When there was no reply to this, I said, 'I can tell you why I think you ask, indeed. Because *you* have a law, you naturally immediately think of breaking that law. You squash that desire deep in your heart, perhaps, because you think it wrong, but you feel it anyway. So then you have the law, and then you need police and army to prevent people breaking the law, and you need prisons and executions to punish those who do, and you need something greater than all this; you need the edifice of thought in which you wish every citizen to live, the prison in which thinking the opposite of the law is forbidden. And what we have chanced upon, in Als, is that without the law in the first place you need none of this.'

She shook her head, but said nothing in reply.

'It seems,' I said, slowly, 'that we have different purchases on freedom. From this bunk, the view is of Senaar as a nation of slavery.'

This brought a reaction. 'But it is Als that is enslaved . . . to savagery. To your own primitive lusts and urges. To the ego and monstrousness inside each person.' She was really quite heated. 'None of you comprehend the beauty, the *liberty* of service: of feeling something larger than yourself, of gladly worshipping God. Freedom for you is always freedom *to*, but there are other freedoms, and the freedom from the self is the greatest.'

This was so splendid an idiocy, so passionately voiced, that I tipped my head backwards and laughed with joy. 'Rhoda Titus,' I said. 'There is passion in you after all, for all that your upbringing teaches you to squash it deep inside! For the first time I can see you as a beautiful woman!' I leapt up suddenly, the vodjaa warm in my bowels, and cast myself across the car towards her. Her eyes sprang open with the suddenness (it was a look like fear) as I grabbed the back of her neck and had a lengthy kiss with her mouth.

When I pulled back, her face was absolutely frozen, white with passion, motionless as it struggled to register desire past its own internal censors. Her eyes were very open. I had felt little desire to have sexual intercourse with Rhoda Titus for most of the journey, but there was something now that wrestled my desire upwards, that hauled the snake-charmer's animal from its box. I was still holding my vodjaa glass in my left hand, so I drained it and tossed it away. With the free hand I grabbed Rhoda Titus by her hair, and pressed my body against her, so that she sagged and fell back against her bunk.

She was making little gasping noises, desire sounding almost like sobbing. Perhaps she was trying to say something, to push the words past her internal censor. But all I felt then was the stretch of her flesh, palpable to my own body through the fabric of her clothing. Her breathing was jumpy. I had another kiss, and then raised myself a little to feel the dunes of her breasts. She was managing to say something now, a tiny whispered voice, but the words were less important than the little, raspy texture of the whisper itself. I was complete in my desire.

I started pulling off some of my clothes, but as I did this she started bucking and wriggling beneath me, so I had to pause to hold her down with one of my hands. At first I pressed her face, but she still struggled, so I moved my large hand to her throat. This had the advantage of drawing both of her own hands to my wrist, scrabbling and grabbing at my arm, fruitlessly trying to pull up the deep-rooted tree of my arm, planted against her neck. I pulled off my clothes, except my undershirt, and fumbled left-handed with her hooks and eyes; but Senaarian clothing is strange, and I had to rip some of them to get them loose. Her body was very pale, salt-coloured, a silvery and freckled series of silver arcs, thigh, hip, the loose flesh of her belly and the sides of her body under her arms against the bunk. Her face was red now, but I had seen it red with blushing so often that this did not look out of place. Pale like a candle, with a flame-coloured face. She was trembling, her legs jerking with little spastic motions. The languages of desire that her body speaks were curious, and difficult to decipher. I pulled my hand from her neck, and she convulsed with a huge indrawn breath; then I replaced it with the left hand, the better to enable my right hand access to her thighs, squeezing them apart and placing myself inside her. At this, she went very still, and then as I started thrusting, she ground herself against me, wriggling and struggling with renewed effort.

And then there it happened, the peak, the hiatus, the outside-time moment where you hang for a moment at the top of the dune and then the rapid slide down the other side back towards the trench in which all the rest of our life is conducted. It happened rapidly, but then I had been without sexual intercourse for many days.

They say that the seed of a man has a salty taste.

I was more breathless than the brief exercise might have prompted, so I lay on her as if she were a mattress until my lungs calmed. Then I hauled off, and pulled my trousers back on.

'A release,' I said to her, grinning. 'A release. That is another definition of freedom, that feeling.'

She was looking at me now, without expression, her breasts bulging upwards and sinking down to the rhythm of her own gasps. I refilled my vodjaa glass and drank it. 'The pleasure was less for you, I think,' I said. 'But if we have it again, I will not be so rapid.'

But she was gathering herself, sitting up, clutching her torn shirt about her torso. Then she tumbled from the bunk to her feet and pushed through to the driving cab.

I finished my vodjaa, and pulled on a shirt. The Whisper had now died down, so I decided to set off driving again. I came through to the front, and Rhoda Titus uttered a little groan. She was standing, in a shirt and naked from the waist down, over by the right window. I smiled at her (because the dimples in her thighs where they connected with her knees delighted me) and pulled myself into the driver's seat.

I charged up the drivepole, but Rhoda Titus rushed from the cab. Assuming she had changed her mind and wanted to lie down, I started the car going, but the faint *clack* of the back door alerted me to something else happening. I got to my unshoed feet and dogged through to the back of the car, but Rhoda Titus had gone.

This was ridiculous. She was many days' walk from humanity, and would die. I squeezed through the lock, opened the back door and jumped down myself. My mask snapped into place.

The sun had gone down, with only the thinnest train of inky purple on the western horizon to indicate its passing, but the stars were out. In the unlit wilderness, and without a moon, they shimmered in their millions. Some moved (ships in orbit), most lay like sparkling pips scattered on black soil. The whiteness of the salt desert was ghostly in this meagre light, the shadowy impressions of humps and curves lost in the fuzzy blackness. It was perfectly still, and the only noise was the hum of the car at my back. The salt was cold against the palms of my feet, and the air was very cold against my face. I called out, 'Rhoda Titus!' (it is difficult to shout through a mask) and my eyes became slowly tuned to the extremely low light levels. There was no sight of her. I rounded the car, and came round to the back again. Then I saw her, dark hair and her shirt camouflaged but the double streak of white of her naked legs visible, scissoring as she dashed up the face of the next dune over. It is not easy to run on the fine salt of deep desert, and her footsteps dug into the stuff and laboured her way.

I called after her, and she stopped, turned, looked at me, with her hand over the fork in her legs like an old representation of Eve out of the Garden.

'Where are you going?' I called. 'You can't survive in the desert!'

She said nothing, but sank backwards, and curled herself up like a child on the bare salt ground.

I had been feeling good, but this behaviour introduced a note of irritation into my mood. I clambered back in the car, and went through to the front to turn off the engine. For a few minutes I simply sat there, and waited for Rhoda Titus to come back through, but presently I deduced that she had decided to freeze to death, or thirst to death, or to find some other desolate way of ending herself.

I went back through the car and outside again. Rhoda Titus was still there, crouched and hunkered down against the salt of the next dune. I bellowed across to her, 'I'm going now, but the back door is still open.' Then I got back into the car, started it up, and drove off.

For the first ten minutes I made sure to drive very slowly indeed, below even a walking pace. Still nothing. Then I turned a little, and instead of riding the ridge of the dune I was on I slipped a little over the other way, so as to duck out of sight of Rhoda Titus's vantage point. This had the right effect; within minutes, I heard the door clack open behind me, and then a tempest of coughing in the back of the car. Rhoda Titus, I assumed, had inadvertently sucked in air through her mouth as she scurried to catch up with the retreating car, and so she spent twenty minutes or more hacking up the residue of the chlorine from her lungs.

I concentrated on driving, I remember. Speeding the car a little, drifting down and up dunes at a narrow angle of attack that meant I travelled miles up each mighty dyke and miles down the other side. After a while it was very quiet behind me, with only an occasional ratcheting cough in the dark.

I drove until I was tired, and then went through. I could see, in the light from the cab, that Rhoda Titus had put on her clothes again, and had then put on her overcoat, and had then climbed into the bunk's sac wearing all that. The lapels of her coat were visible over the edge of the sac. But she was asleep, and I did not disturb her: I stepped out of the car to secure it against the morning's Whisper, and then I took myself to bed, to a satisfying sleep.

The next day, Rhoda Titus did not get up, and would not engage in conversation with me, but I did not mind this. I had embarked on the journey for solitude, and in truth I was now weary of her company. I ate in silence, and drove in silence. At dusk, I called through to ask her to secure the car against the Whisper (she had watched me do it often enough, and yet had never offered her help), but she did not reply. So I went through and did it myself. She was sitting, still in her coat (but at least it was unbuttoned), eating strands of pasta with her fingers. Her neck was blotted with inky bruises, like a tattoo necklace. Her chin, just below her mouth, was a little grazed from the rubbing of my new beard. I found these marks of wear queerly attractive.

I fetched myself some food from the Fabricant, and sat opposite her. But she did not meet my eye.

'Another two days, I think,' I said.

Nothing.

'In two days we shall be at Yared, and you can go your way.'

At this her eyes danced up to meet mine, and I could see her glittering with some stifled emotion. But then she dropped her eyes again, and I was tired with talk.

After the Whisper I drove on again, until tired, and then I went through. The lights were still on in the back, and Rhoda Titus was kneeling in prayer by her bunk. The sound of my footsteps startled her out of it, and she rose quickly.

I spent an hour reading at random from my notepad, but now Rhoda Titus seemed to be looking at me.

'Stop staring at me,' I said, when I realised that she was. Her eyes immediately dropped.

At this I fed myself quickly, thinking how tiresome the pasta was; how stringy, and how the saltiness of everything took the savour even from the salt. Then I drove on.

The following day I saw the first signs of Southern habitation. A dumper truck wandered past us, on its way to the deep desert to bury some toxic waste presumably. Rhoda Titus dashed into the cabin when she heard the rumble of its distant engines, and waved at its black, blank side like a child. It was the first time she had come into the cab for many days.

Late in the afternoon we came across some houses, and a compound of some sort. I called through to Rhoda Titus to ask if she wanted to be dropped off here, or taken deeper into Yared itself. She did not reply, and so I trundled on. Eventually, an hour short of the Whisper, I came to a central square. Several cars were parked in a grid in front of a foliate dome, which had the letters spelling out SPINAL RAILWAY hologrammed, standing out from the curving roof. So I pulled the car in backwards, with the door close to the over-arch of the building (we all were in these habits automatically, to minimise being in the pathological sunshine). I stifled the engine.

For a while I was content to simply sit, to stare at the place I was now in. After so many days of nothing but blank white desert, of salt stretching sand-like all around, of the bright sun and the dark night, there was something almost obscene to my eye in the mess of this settlement. So many strewn buildings, so many little shapes. The littleness of humankind. And, from time to time, a person would emerge, bug-like, to dash through the sunshine and disappear into the dark of another building. A train of cars groaned through the square and wandered away. Everything blared the banality of everyday doings; it all seemed painfully small. I realised, with a shudder of my heart, that I could hardly stand it. After sublimity, this. Even the thought of Rhoda Titus in the back of the car struck me as a sort of contamination.

And so I strained forward, peered through the thickened plas of the upper windshield to take in a resuscitating glimpse of the open sky, just visible squeezed between the bloc-shaped tops of the Yared clutter. It was breath to me.

And so I was quick in wanting to get away from there. I went through to the back of the car, and Rhoda Titus was sitting on the bunk. The bruises on her neck had tanned to a paler blackcurrant colour, as if drifting inwards and fading. I sat opposite her. 'You wanted to come to Yared, and I have brought you. Here is the Spinal Railway terminus, and it will take you to Senaar.'

She moved her mouth as if to say something, then stopped. Then, as if dragging the words from a very deep place, she whispered: 'Thank you.'

I scoffed. 'I have no desire for the "thank" of the hierarchy,' I told her.

She flinched tinily at this, but said nothing. There was a pause, and it swelled into a silence. Then she stood up, pulling her overcoat tightly about her body, perhaps to be sure of covering the rip in the undershirt. She went through the lock and opened the back door. The chlorine scrubs whined into action. With her right hand bunched at her breast, and her left hand over her mouth, she hopped outside. I followed her and stepped out of the car. My mask clicked up into place.

She stood in front of me for a while, breathing visibly through her nostrils. The corners of her nose bulged and sucked in with the effort. Then she dropped her hand from her mouth.

'I put salt there, afterwards,' she said, in a hurry. 'After you did it and I was outside, I scooped salt inside myself. I did it.'

Then her hand clapped back over her mouth, and her nose registered the effort of taking in a lungful.

I turned from her and climbed back inside the car. The door shut, the chlorine scrubs briefly whined on, finishing their jobs. I went through to the cab, warmed up the drivepole, started the engine, and drove away.

There was some difficulty in obtaining the water that I needed to continue my wanderings in Yared. I stopped and went into a few buildings, talked to a few people; but monies were wanted, and when they realised that I was from Als most of them turned and walked away. I was prepared to deal in barter-monies with people for these necessary things, but few would talk to me for long. Afterwards, I realised that this had to do with the acceleration of events elsewhere, and the first intimations of war between North and South. At the time, I felt only anger. I spent the night parked in the suburbs of Yared, and in the predawn (in the half-hour before the Morning Whisper, when I assumed people would be battened down) I drove to a water tank and tapped it. In fact, as I discovered, the Morning Whisper is weak in Yared, partly because of the earthworks (salt-works?) constructed east of Senaar, partly because of the lie of the land around the sea on that coast. But nobody noticed me taking the water, and I left it splashing onto the hardened salt of the road, puddling and slowly drinking in the baked salt underneath. By midday I was driving in the emptiness north of the place.

5

Warmaking

Barlei

And so my little narrative comes to the war. Historians of conflict are often snagged up in trying to trace back through events to the first cause, the *casus belli*. But we all know, we the people, that there is only one point at which our attention needs to be fixed. War is a terrible thing though glorious, and it is a thing of many deaths. As with any death, the just thing for a society to do is to allocate blame. This is why societies have courts of justice; I speak as the Supreme Justice of Senaar. I understand justice.

And there can be no doubt that whichsoever way they are cut, the trail of events leading to war implicates Als as the criminals. It was they who wickedly imprisoned the children, they who resisted a lawful operation of seizure (supported by the courts) with murderous force, and they who exacted a terrorist revenge on the civilians of our nation. At each stage we, the nation of Senaar (of whom you can feel genuine pride) responded with strength and restraint. After we had rescued our children, there was a national day of celebration. It is still a day kept in our calendar for celebration, although I rejected a motion to have it as a holiday, because I considered the loss in work revenues unjustified. But now I shudder a little to think of that day; to think of the spiderlike Alsists squatting in their camp, watching our joy with bitterness and bile.

It was barely a week later that the first device was detonated in Senaar.

The precise sequence of events remains unclear, but certainly at least two, and possibly more, Alsist planes flew down under cover of darkness, landed in the desert east of the dyke and buried themselves under the salt. Then they sent single backpacked individuals amongst the streets. Critics have attacked me for not sealing the city to prevent such retaliation, but how can you seal a city as great and populous as Senaar? To put a seal upon our mouth is also to seal our eyes, our ears; it is the seal of death. We are, after all, a trading nation; trade is the blood in our bodies. People come and go from all over the Galilean basin, and even occasionally from the North, although it was true, even before the war, that relations were strained. Anyway, when these infiltrators first trod our pressed-salt roads, nobody took notice of them. They looked like any one of five hundred solitary traders; people who made their way by boat or car, or along the Spinal, with goods strapped to their backs, to try and sell in the more lucrative Senaarian market. For the price of a half-day licence they would set themselves up in the secondary Market Square, sell at their best price, and make their way out of the city as soon as the Whisper died down. (The law was that they had to be beyond the original borderline; although this was changed as the city grew. By early evening there would be hundreds of people bedding down under plastic sheets wherever they could pad down the salt to make themselves comfortable.)

It was into this harmless band that the Alsists infiltrated themselves; going so far as to purchase licences, to hawk their goods all morning, and then to rubberneck their way about the sights of the city in the afternoon, as if they were real one-day traders. I find it hard to imagine myself into their heads, their duplicity, their knowledge that the innocents they wandered amongst would, soon after their departure, be lying wounded, bleeding, dead.

They planted about a dozen devices in public buildings; the courtroom, Parliament, the major concert hall. The first explosion happened in the late evening, giving the cowards time to slink out of the city under the cover of our own laws and to rejoin their planes out east. They were doubtless airborne under the confusion as more explosions burst amongst us and our attention was diverted.

How well I remember the brutal chaos of that night. By fortune, or God's Grace, there was no concert in the hall although most nights saw some recital or other. But in the event the only person killed was a janitor, an Eleupolisian as it happens, who kept the venue clean and slept under the stage (he was killed, I seem to remember, by a slab of stone being forced down by the explosion and squashing him). But the enormity of the sound is something difficult to convey using only words. It woke me, and I was asleep half a mile from the building. I was shelled from my sleep like a pea from a pod, and within minutes I was fully dressed and talking with under-Captains and civilian ministers by screen whilst my valet was getting the car ready to take me over town.

To begin with, it was not clear exactly what had happened. Flames were leaping from the roof of the concert hall, sucking up our precious oxygen, burning in exotic colours in the chlorine and oxygen. People had been drawn from their beds, or from their work (half the population had settled into routines of working in the dark hours to avoid the higher levels of radiation, especially if their work involved being outdoors). My imperial car and its troop worked through the crowd to confront the rubble of the entrance hall, the ghastly snake-flames, the black clouds of smoke blotting out the starlight and lit only by their own flames from below; a hellish scene.

There was no doubt, of course, as to who had perpetrated this atrocity, although it is worth noting that the Alsists did not claim responsibility. Indeed, although no historian doubts their guilt, I believe that they never have. It is not their way, of course, to admit that actions have consequences, or that the manly thing is to take responsibility. Perhaps they deny it still. And, of course, the particular villain, the person who actually trespassed and planted the bomb, has never been caught or even identified. Although we can gain some small satisfaction from knowing that, given the high level of Alsist casualties, particularly in the early portion of the war, these criminals almost certainly were killed. Some day I too will go to greet my Maker, and then I shall ask him to grant me the whole sight, to see how His justice was enacted.

Emergency services in those last few pre-war days were in the same state of unpreparedness they had been ever since foundation day. What else? We had not needed them before. And so it was a minor division of army soldiers who were drafted in to put out the fire and to start to set the rubble to rights. But no sooner had I stepped out of the imperial car to address an impromptu speech to the hastily assembled Visualcast cameras, than there was another sound: a mighty *smack* noise followed by a deep bass rumble that hung on the air for a very long time. This was the second device exploding outside the secondary barracks, knocking in the outer wall and murdering nearly a dozen people.

After that they came with a sickening rapidity. The courthouse bomb did little more than break the triple windows and allow a deal of mess from outside in over the floor (there was a minor case being prosecuted in the cheaper court-hours, and a lawyer was killed; it was lucky there was no more damage). The Parliament bomb did more structural damage; most of the windows were smashed, and one of the two towers was so badly cracked that it had to be demolished. Another bomb pulled out a hole in a main clean-water tank, and weeks of precious desalination was wasted. Another broke walls in a dormitory where only half the sleepers inside were fitted with nasal filters; many choked to death, and even some of those with the filters panicked and mouth-breathed to their deaths.

By now, everybody in Senaar was awake, and the streets thronged. I had fallen back on my private dwelling (I reasoned that no public building was safe – although my under-Captains were adamant that my home be thoroughly checked by military experts in bombmaking before I was even allowed out of the car), and from there I made a series of Visualcasts to calm the population. Despite my anger at the atrocity, I was fiercely proud of my people also. The army never lacked for willing volunteer helpers; volunteers, mark you! People happy to work without any form of recompense, to clear away rubble,

164

to pull people out of the damage. The hospitals introduced a standardised billing system as a mark of respect, even though hospital profits were severely limited as a result.

By the morning, the will of the Senaarians had crystallised. Justice. This assault upon our city, this rape of our prize buildings (erections that symbolised the civic purpose and pride of our nation) had to be answered. I called a dawn meeting of all higher officers, and the meeting stretched throughout the day. In the corner we had several netscreens relaying the shock of Senaarian netprogrammes and news-keepers; but also the alarm that these attacks spread throughout the whole of our world. Galilean nations, broadly speaking, were as thoroughly outraged by the Alsist terrorism as were we; our alliances in the South could be depended upon, because they were built on sturdy foundations. But responses to the news from the North were less sure. Newscasts reported the atrocities, of course, but wove webs of uncertainty about the facts, and gave the impression that all this was remote from Perse concerns. When we contacted diplomatic officers in these northern states – and I spoke personally to the Agent for Convento – we were met with the blank wall of suspicion that the success of Senaar had built up. They said many things, mostly to do with the unproved nature of Als's guilt in these crimes; but the truth of the matter was that the Northern states were fearful of Senaarian imperium, and would do anything to try and break our increasing power. It is hard, I know, for us to comprehend the fear that our success, our closeness to the Will of God, sets in the hearts of less successful, less devout nations. A bitter lesson to learn in the ways of politics. But this was the point: Convento and Smith were less interested in the rights and wrongs of the matter (and which wrong could be more clearly elaborated than terrorist atrocity against the innocent?), and more interested in political manoeuvrings.

Very well, then, I resolved. Alone. It seemed to me that both Convento and Smith underestimated the strength of our will, but this was a problem to which we could return later. I breakfasted, and changed into dress uniform, before returning to the meeting of the senior staff. It is important to create the right impression. Indeed, I caught a glimpse of myself in the polished stone of the corridor outside the meeting room: my buttons shone bright as torch-heads, the dark blue of the uniform swam in the gleaming stone mirror of that wall. My soul took a little electric jolt of pride and confidence. And so I went into the war meeting. Perhaps this seems a little vain to you, but believe me. As a man who has devoted his life to the Prince of Peace, it is no small thing to me to commit men to war; men who have families, children, who worship God, and some of whom will surely die. It is essential, vital, that this be done, but the leader who does this is only a man, a man with compassion. At these times we judge the leader by the strength of his will, under God, but everybody is human.

Not (I flatter myself) that anybody in that meeting room realised that I was anything other than simply and clearly resolute. The time was for action, and I was ready for that time.

The meeting was hot-tempered. Most of the people in that room had been awake all night, many of them commanding troops to deal with fire and try to save lives. I myself had slept poorly. The first reaction of warriors is to action, and the mood of the group was that we should counterattack Als at once. The reasoning behind this was most eloquently expressed by a young officer called Ets. He reasoned that Als had perpetrated a deliberate act of war against us, and that they would do so again if we did nothing. The best course of action, he said, was an immediate strike at the heart of their power to disable them. This proposal was hurrayed with loud cheers.

I waited for the tumult to settle down, and then spoke. What my braves were ignoring, I said, was the nature of Als. This was not a people who were capable of acting in concert. The bombs planted in our city were certainly the action of individual fanatics, not of a planned military exercise. Of course we must retaliate, but our retaliation must be carefully planned. The point, of course (and it may seem obvious in hindsight, but it requires a good eye to spy this out in advance), is that the larger power structures must be taken into account. Acting against Als now, after so shocking a terrorist outrage, would win approval from the South, and it might be thought only justice by many inhabitants in the northern cities. But any large-scale military assault on a city on the shores of the Perse would also certainly arouse the unease of the other northern states, who might (they would reason) be next to fall to the military strength of our great nation. Perhaps (I spoke loudly to quell an approving clamour that arose at this thought), perhaps this was indeed the Senaarian destiny, the manifest Will of God for this world. But in this, as in all political matters, timing is everything. If we attack Als and we draw in the military responses of Convento and Smith, then we have straight away declared war on the whole of the Perse, and not just on renegade anarchists. If this is what is to be, then so be it and amen: but we must be prepared for this. We must send in a force large enough to deal with all three nations, and not just the one. Conversely, if we could achieve our immediate end (bringing justice to Als) without involving Convento or Smith, then we would have cut by a third the power of the northern basin; any future development in that area would consequently be one third easier.

Viewed in this fashion, it was clear that how we acted now carried tremendous implications for the future. Haste was not wanted.

We discussed the matter all morning, until lunch was brought in, and after lunch we called up projections of netscreen models. The first alternative was, briefly, to attack Als swiftly from the air and then retreat, such that the other nations of the Perse would not fear invasion, but would instead acknowledge that justice had been meted out. This would reduce the northern threat, and leave us unblooded: but it would also surely provoke retaliation from Als, and possibly from other northern states hoping to use the occasion as a pretext, and to reduce the glory of Senaar a little.

A second alternative was a full invasion, pinpointing Als from above with barrage, and then occupying the broken city with a large force of men. The advantage of this was that we could deal once and for all with Als, and also reduce the chances of their retaliation. Perhaps, indeed, we could civilise these people, bring them discipline and order and take them closer to God. But so aggressive an action would be much more likely to draw out Convento and Smith in what they would term a defensive war. Some of my juniors were less worried than others by this possibility. Their reasoning was that war was inevitable anyway, and it would be better to get it out of the way sooner rather than later. It is true that we would be fighting a war far from home, but so long as we maintained a supremacy in the air our supply lines would be easily maintained.

We argued back and forth between these options, and eventually it fell to me to make a decision. Inescapable power of command. My solution to the problem was, I think, elegant: history has acquitted me of the charges sometimes made by the jealous, that in compromising I weakened the force of both alternatives and gained nothing. Indeed, little could be further from the truth. In fact, my command gave us perfect ground, although I will concede that a certain ineffectiveness on the ground watered down my plan. I was easier in myself, knowing that jean-Pierre – who was present throughout the briefing – backed me throughout. His faith in me never wavered.

This, then, was the action I ordered: Als would be attacked from the air, her major buildings pulped, her will destroyed. Simultaneously we would send (unarmed) ambassadors to the other Perse nations to hold them at bay with intensive negotiations. We would vigorously present the attack as just retribution, and we would explain the presence of a (relatively small) group of armed men on the ground in terms of policing the area, and providing humanitarian aid. This way, I reasoned, we would break Als, and be able to place a force of men on the site to keep them down, without seeming to pose a threat to Convento and Smith. If all went according to plan, we would eliminate Als as a military threat, and simultaneously create a base for further military operations, without antagonising the neighbouring states.

The rest of the day (and I won't labour this narrative with all the tedious details of discussion) were to do with ordnance, numbers, statistics. It is no easy task to organise a large-scale operation, to bring all the hundreds of separate components together (and each individual soldier is a component as well) and achieve the desired consummation. It took us three days.

That afternoon I made another speech for the Visuals; the speech which perhaps you have read in your schoolbooks. I would like (each of us has a little kernel of pride, I think) to claim each of those words as my own, but the truth is that I wrote the speech very rapidly with three or four aides. I even did without help from Preminger. The smell of that room – the salt-polish on the black wooden table (wood that had flown all the way from Earth with us), the close smell of men together – I think that smell will stay with me until my dying day. The words were well chosen, though (or else why would you be studying them in your schoolbooks?): the point of that speech (and perhaps you will forgive me from making comment upon it) is that each of the words I spoke in it was about *action*, was about bringing all the atoms of state together in a unified effort of will. Strike at Senaar, I said, and you will hurt your hand; because her breast is stony with resolve and God's justice. Our enemies had sowed the seeds of fire and death, but this was a crop we would not harvest on our own.

After the words had been recorded for netcast and for use on all Visuals at basic fee (jean-Pierre thought I should have charged artists' rates, so powerful was the effect of my words): after this I toured the city. The speech was injuncted to be broadcast only in the after-Whisper of evening. People, outside now, trying to rebuild wrecked lives, would go indoors for the Whisper, and the audience would be that much larger. Moreover, my words would be followed by news reports of the retaliatory strike against the Alsists. My afternoon tour was partly to allow me to survey the damage at close quarters, but also an opportunity for my people to see me. Rumours had circulated, shortly after the bombs, that I had been wounded, or even killed. Rumour, as many military historians have noted, is a dangerous pathogen, a virus that rattles through the body politic. Visuals, denials of my death might be considered merely politic, but my actual presence in the city was a different matter. A tonic for my people. It was for this reason that, much later, I instituted the anti-rumour legislation, my personal project, paid through the Senate with my own personal votes, because other politicos were too timid to see the wisdom in this legislation. But you, you live amongst a nation shaped by the outlawing of spreading vicious or malicious rumour that might damage the Senaarian polity. You know how much more wholesome our nation is since that day.

But I am getting ahead of myself. On that day, I selected my open car, with only a web of perfectly transparent woven-fibre covering between myself and the world at large (we had been attacked so recently, it would not do to be careless), and drove down the main street, the one that had recently been renamed in my honour. It was late in the afternoon, and the crowds were coming out from their midday-sun rest period. The cheering! It brought tears to my eyes, to think that the spine of Senaar was so strong. Steel, not to be snapped. By the time I reached the central square, word had spread of my progress, and a great mass had gathered to wave and cheer me. The canopy did not permit me to say any words, but I was able to stand and to wave at the crowd. The courtesy guard had to hold some of the crowd back (excess of enthusiasm; not what my enemies have sometimes called it. I know it was merely an excess of enthusiasm; I was there, after all).

Afterwards, I toured the concert hall, the barracks, the justice centre. The guards cleared me a space, and I got out of the car to actually go amongst the rubble with some of the military workers, the life-savers. A huge crane had been erected over the mess of broken concrete and some sappers were constructing an industrial-scale Fabricant to take the broken stone and rework it into usable rebuilding slabs. I was so overcome I bear-hugged the under-Lieutenant, a moment captured on several Visuals for later display. I am a large man, and I entirely obscured the little fellow from the camera eye.

I was frankly exhausted by so much gadding about, and I retired to my second home; my official residence was now deemed too liable to attack, and I had moved to a secret second residence. Afterwards, scurrilous news-reporting suggested that I had ordered the family out of this second domicile under pain of imprisonment. But there is no truth in this piece of anti-propaganda. The family were too happy to move from their home. Of course they were. Try to understand the mood that gripped Senaar now. Young boys presented themselves to army offices, eager to serve the nation in war despite their youth. Women organised spontaneous support groups recording net-messages to be sent to single soldiers. There were mass rallies in support of the campaign. People donated some of their votes – entirely free of charge, mark you! – to the military treasury to ensure that certain of the less obvious military legislation be passed without eating into military vote budgets.

Of course, I am going forward a little here in my narrative, and on this particular afternoon war had yet to be declared. But we were eager, we were eager. When news of other Alsist atrocities became common knowledge (and some of these had to be censored before being put out on widely viewed Visual services), they met a resolve already firm. When Rhoda Titus, for instance, made her way back to her home – after imprisonment and torture by the Alsists (and she an accredited diplomat!), and following a daring escape – her trials were greeted with a resolute determination to avenge her suffering that was very different from the hysterical mob action of a less disciplined people. And, after my sleep, I was roused by my aides shortly before the Whisper, and I went through to a room decked out hastily with the necessary surveillance equipment, to watch the seven ships set out on their mission.

Petja

I was in the wilderness for a number of days, driving north-east. The land rises from the Southern Ocean for about two hundred miles, the tip of each dune marching inches upwards from its predecessor. I drove and drove, as if escaping something, and by the third day I began to feel the echo in my own soul that presaged a sort of emptiness. I woke, ate, slept, drove, and each activity was as full of nothing as the other. I achieved a genuine hollowing out; a paradox, at once a fragile state, since any self-reflection would have polluted the internal emptiness I was experiencing, and yet a strong state of mind, because in it there was the profoundest sort of escape. It is difficult to put into words, twice as difficult into foreign words, but perhaps it approached the state the soul feels as it exits the body, with a rustling sound like dead leaves, or the sprinkle of water at the little waterfall. As it leaves the hubbub of sensual noise for the calm static of the spiritual world. Words abandon their post. It was a mystical something.

Travelling forever in the edenic nothingness. Driving slowly, the wheels slipping a little, up the face of the dune; in shadow, perhaps, with the car lights (always on) punching holes of light through the shadow-grey salt bank ahead of me. And then, with a tremendous sense as of a blossoming, a coming-up to the top, so that the whole landscape sweeps into view, lit white-golden by the low-slung sun.

Sometimes salt gusts in the distance, or perhaps the retreating Whisper would hang like a strip of semi-transparent tape along the horizon. It was beautiful. Beautiful. It is still beautiful, here, here in my memory. A memory cannot be accessed, cannot be churned out by a Fabricant.

The next thing to come to my memory, as I try to stitch together a sequential narrative, is battening down, prior to the Evening Whisper. I could not say how many days into my travels this was, because the essence of the salt desert had become a part of my perceptions. A wilderness inside matching the wilderness out: perhaps that balance, that spiritually osmotic neutrality, gave me the windy inner freedom. I imagined my brain white as salt, each of the ructions in its surface a bonsai dune of heaped salt, blown to perfect curvature by the winds. A white world of dryness, barrenness. Freedom from thought, from the parasites of doubting, hurting, hating, that infest the healthiest of minds.

So I battened down, with no sense of portentousness. I had no knowledge of where I was; although it might be better saying no conscious knowledge, because my fugue state had brought me back, and how can we say this was without reason? I climbed inside, and prepared food. I could not tell you what manner of food, or how I received it, whether it spoke to my tongue as tasty, or whether I even noticed I was eating. Maybe I drank some vodjaa; certainly my Fabricant records suggest I made up a great deal of this over my travels. Maybe I sat, blank, or took out my notepad to read, or do some work. I cannot say.

But I remember the first sounds of the bombardment. The banging, crumbling sounds of detonation in the distance. One followed another, and then another, and another, on and on. I remember thinking, initially, that it was some freak sudden pulse in my own chest. Then I focused, listened again. There is no mistaking the sound of heavy-duty ordnance. It is a sub-grumbling roll, punctuated by booming, thudding folds of sound. I sat hypnotised by this sound, I really did. It was like an enormous door being repeatedly slammed far, far away, in hell.

Then some shameful part of myself kicked upwards through the ice with its adrenaline. Yes, there can be no doubt that the sound of this pounding, grisly thumping excited me. The prospect of war excited me. That must have been it. Some part of me lit and ignited with the thrill of war. That must have been it. A war-eros. I scrambled out of the back of the car and ran to the top of the dune in whose lee I had battened down.

The horizon to the west was red, but not with the south-north-reaching span of actual sunset. It was a localised ellipse of colour, and more orangey, and with a filtered sense of green as the chlorine spouted from its salt. Fire over the horizon. Out of the car, the air cold on my skin, the sound of the barrage was thrillingly louder, registering in a more visceral manner. I stood watching the display for perhaps half an hour, at least until the ground-trembling detonations had ceased, and there was only the sight of vivid fiery colour leaching into its little patch of sky.

I got back into the car and squeezed my way through to the driving cabin. For the first time in however many days I called up the satposition on the dashboard for I wanted to know where it was that had been so bombed. I suppose I suspected it might have been Als, but I did not know. But the satposition was blank. I checked the other programs of the dashboard, but they all worked, and when I called up a diagnostic on the satposition it told me that no satellite was responding. This was something. I reasoned that, had there been an attack on Als, the first action of the attacking power would be to disable our two satellites. But this was more than mere raiding; this was warmaking.

Even without satposition, of course, there could be little doubt where I was. I had travelled north by north-east for days; the sun had risen to the right and back of me. There could be no settlement apart from Als. Unless some unknown enemy had decided to bomb empty desert for an hour, for no reason, it could only be an attack on the east bank of the Aradys.

I started up the car, and turned her about, heading towards the still glowing piece of the horizon sky. And the worst of it, if you press me to say it, is my sense, looking backwards, that my time of spiritual purity in the desert was nothing but anticipation: that I was doing nothing except unknowingly marking the time before war claimed me. That is the worst of it, and the memory takes on an unpleasant sensation because of it. That my life before I began killing was no life, only the antechamber of a life. Because that hints that killing has been my whole life.

Barlei

The essence of warfare (allow me to pass on this secret of soldiering) is *height*. With this we find ourselves drawn back to the very roots of the business of war. In its earliest forms, warriors would seek to raise themselves above their enemy by mounting a horse [*intertext has no index-connection for a%x'48000horse' suggest consult alternate database, e.g. orig.historiograph*]. The strange mythos that used to attach itself to this beast back in my old country was, I am sure, purely to do with the added height it gave. Since then warriors have concentrated on raising themselves: by occupying the higher ground; by castles, and then by siege-engines larger than the castles; by air-machines, and then jets, spacecraft, and so through to modern warfare. If you command the space above your enemy you command your enemy.

Consequently, there was little doubt in my mind as to the way to proceed in this new-minted war with Als. When we first raided Als, we were able to inflict the devastating blow that we did because we commanded the air. Whilst the Whisper hid all ground communications, one of our satellites – it had been secretly fitted with bolt weaponry, although its warmaking capabilities had been successfully hidden from the other ships during transport (it is important to keep some things hidden, even from friends) – swung into position and collapsed both Alsist sats. Within seconds of the wind dying down we were airborne, our brave pilots flying supersonic at superatmosphere, into the darkening north. The first planes sighted and fixed targets within minutes of leaving the atmosphere, and dived back into the air like swimmers in a pool of clear dark water. Detonations were delivered to precisely the marked places. One of the hardest tasks I faced (I can confess now) was knowing exactly which targets to specify in Als. This was made more difficult by the fact that Alsists do not, exactly, have public buildings: which is to say, each building is equally public, or equally private. Moreover, there has been no concerted public planning in Als, only the obvious use made of larger natural phenomena (mountains and so on) and then a higgledy-piggledy accumulation of little buildings and little greenhouses and little desalination facilities and so on. It makes the ethical choice of bombing sites harder, but leadership is about hard decisions and it achieves nothing to be womanly about these sorts of decisions. I took a lightpick to the screen and marked crosses against the sites I wanted. It did strike me at the time (perhaps the rhetoric of my own speeches had inflated my mind with a more exalted manner of thinking) that crosses were actually neatly appropriate to the matter in hand. Some Alsists would die, but theirs would be a sacrifice for the greater good: theirs would be lives placed down to pave the road to Peace. I did not think – and still do not think – that the Prince of Peace himself would find my analogy at all out of place. And besides – have *we* not suffered in this war? Have we not lost loved ones, ones loved more dearly than anybody, than self? Have I not suffered?

The barrage took a little under twenty minutes. One sweep of planes would come down, bundle out their detonations and then sweep away on prearranged avoidance flightpaths, although the counter-attack was so unexpected that the Alsists had no defensive planes in the air, and the intensity so devastating that they were unable to mount any sort of anti-offensive. Still, it was good practice for our pilots to go through these motions of avoiding imaginary counter-attackers, swooping low, then springing up and regrouping. Each set of planes emptied their loads over the town, and then flew back, leaving it blazing. We did not lose a single plane, a single man. No operation in military history has been so swift, so crushing, and so without loss to the operating side.

I watched the whole thing, sat-relayed, from the newly constructed Captain's bunker (the stone was still fresh with paint; the smell of that not-unpleasant ethyl odour). I felt such pleasure, such pride pushing outward from my breast! I remember thinking then that our language ought to have a single word meaning joy-to-be-Senaarian.

Petja

I covered most of the distance towards Als in that night, but tiredness came upon me and I stopped, battened down and slept. In the morning I continued, and reached the first signs of devastation in the early afternoon.

Indeed, to begin with I came across a series of wilderness houses which were untouched, and I wondered if I had dreamt the night before. I did not stop, nor disturb the inhabitants (I had no desire to talk to hermit-people, as I suppose they had no desire to talk to me). But the little saltstone or treated-fabric huts, some no more than pits in the ground roofed over, and all with crude walls east of them with trailing trapezoid banks of salt leaning against them (none of these people would be bothered with clearance); these sparse huts with the desert salt pressed to a road between them, at least looked like normality. I might have thought nothing was wrong, that the hellfire and curtain of flame from the night before had been a sort of dream, were it not for the great block of dark smoke that stood out sharply from the white sky. This was where my eye was, most of the time; and towards it I drove. A huge plume of smoke, kinked massively two-thirds of the way up, bowing down in middle air as if in prayer.

And so I pressed on. By early afternoon I drove into the ruins of Als.

The road that led down to the water had been broken up, and was now landscaped with a series of craters. Large pieces of saltstone had been danced by the blast into tumbled shapes. I pulled the car off the road, and made my way past greenhouses, all of them popped like balloons. I was able to travel perhaps five hundred metres before the passage became unworkable. I had still not seen anybody.

I climbed out of the car, and the first thing I noticed was the smell. Even though I was wearing a mask, the smell made its way to my nose. There was no quelling it. A stench of carbon, a fireworky smell. I stepped past the shelled greenhouses, stopping from time to time to look inside; but the picture was always the same. If a pool, parched and cracked stone; if a growing space, churned earth-and-salt, with perhaps the occasional plant wilted in the chlorine.

And the chlorine was everywhere, roiling about my feet, serpenting amongst the fragmented buildings. There was, I realised after a little while, something of a drift to the aimless flowing of the yellowy gas; it was more liable to flow down the incline towards the water than anything else. So much poison liberated by the bombing. The detonations must have broken up the sodium and oxidised it but at ground level the oxygen was thin, and even after chlorates there was much of the gas left to meander. It was foul stuff.

I made my way to the open space by the water, and saw that precision detonation had collapsed the mouth to the women's dorm. That shocked me. I hurried there, and tried to move some of the blocks, but (I noticed) people had been there before me, and all the smaller stones had been shifted several metres away. But why had they not brought in cranes or larger machines to move the larger blocks? I shouted through what few cracks there were, but my voice was muffled by my mask and the cracks were black as hopelessness.

I stood away from the rubble, and turned to look about. An entire city (I was thinking – and this I remember absolutely) destroyed, and all its people. It seemed a thing to spark a rage that would never die, but the space where the rage should have been was a suffocating kind of sadness. I fought myself, struggled to let my anger come out. The lake, blanketed wholly in the dead yellow of the chlorine gas, was too ugly to be a symbol of mourning.

And then I felt a jab in my back-ribs. I reasoned it was a Senaarian soldier, come to finish the job of killing Alsists (and, I remember thinking, it was foolish of me not to expect that there would be enemy patrols working through the ruins). And my mind went cold. What I mean when I say that is cold in the superconducting sense. Thoughts slotted into place, switches flickered. I would clearly have to pretend to surrender, or he would shoot me then and there. But surrendering – say, raising my arms – would precede turning around, and once I faced him, I would be able to assault him. Imprisonment would be the same as death, evidently; so death was no counter-incentive. But the hierarchical mind is that imprisonment is to be preferred to death (and why not when life is already an imprisonment?); and this fact alone would give me an edge. And so, my hands were in front of me, and I pulled the only thing to hand – my vodjaa bottle, tucked into my belt – and hid it as best I could behind my hand. I raised my arms half-cock, and turned around.

It was no Senaarian facing me, but a man called Bosjin. I recognised him despite his mask, because he had little hair and a rubywine-mark on his forehead in the shape of a puppy. He was holding a needlerifle at my guts. I felt a sudden relief and then, when the gun wasn't removed, an equally sudden veering towards panic. Then he angled the rifle away, and nodded, and my panic drained away.

'We'll be moving out of the open now,' he said. 'It's not easy here, not free.'

'Senaarian patrols,' I said.

'Yes.'

And so we moved back, clambered up the rubble that was now the mouth of the women's dorm (stopped as a corpse's throat in asphyxiation), and along the ridge. We were soon behind a wrinkle of the mountain, out of view. Here we stopped.

'It is Bosjin,' I said.

He grunted. His snout-face jerked up and down in a nod. 'Petja' he said.

'Yes.'

'I watched you come on. I nearly shot your life away, from here.' He gestured with the rifle through a tiny cleft. 'Only the mask dissuaded me. Of course, the enemy wear masks also, but theirs are a military make and cover the whole face.'

'Why have you not brought in lifting equipment?' I asked him. 'To clear away the entrance to the women's dorm?' Bosjin stared at me. 'I was in the deep desert last night,' I said. 'I heard the bombardment, and I have just come. But if the Senaarians sealed in the women, then they may still be alive. Surely we should attempt to take them out?'

He nodded. 'So you were not here. I was surprised to see you wandering about. There is a camp of the enemy to the south, and sometimes they come up here to look at the water, or do whatever it is that they do. And you do not know about the women's dorm. Come.'

He beckoned me to follow with the rifle's long tongue, wagged it away to the left, and we climbed higher up the outcrop. Over a ridge, and I saw that further detonation had utterly broken the crown of the women's dorm. We pulled ourselves low over the rock to the very lip of the place. 'Some people saw the mouth of the cave collapse, the entrance down there,' Bosjin said. 'They rushed to try and pull away the rocks. But we saw them; in the nighttime, we saw them from the curtain of fire away behind them.' He stopped, nodding his head. 'Anyway, we saw them and called for them to stop, to come up here.'

I peered into the gloom. There had been much fire in that place,

179

and everything inside was blackened; the black of the fire damage, and the yellow-brown of burnt salt in long swathes. 'How many died?' I asked.

'Many died,' he replied. 'It was hard to contain the fire. There was little we could do. It was . . . frustrating' (he paused for a long time before choosing the word: *prödjejen*) 'that we were so close to the sea and yet could not put out the fire. Some tried rushing about, tried to get pumps that could spew out a stream of water, but the stream would not reach in at the gap here.' He stopped for a while. 'I was in the water. Then there was another wave of attack from above, and the detonation struck the same place, and the fire was put out. Such is the chance of it; our good chance, their bad one.'

He glanced about suddenly, as if afraid of enemy patrols. But he was speaking in very low tones, and surely they could not hear us.

'Then we scrambled back up here, those of us about the place. We let down a ladder that Lichnovski had brought down from further north in a hurry. You know Lichnovski?'

'Yes.'

'So we went down. There was little air, and it was bitterly hot, hot as hell is hot. Little fires were burning off the floor, off the stumps where cots had been, and off bodies. But further in the depth of the place were some people alive; amazing, I suppose. Some ran to the showers, or were in store rooms, or whatever. We hurried them out. But the noise! All the time, the detonations were continuing, excepting only that the Senaarians had moved their targets progressively south and east. Anyway, we got them out, those still alive. Then we hurried north, as the air caught fire further south.'

I peered into the hole for a while.

'Do you know Turja?' I asked.

'Hmm,' he said.

'Alive?'

'Dead. I think so. I think she is.'

I nodded.

'She had a baby, you know,' said Bosjin. 'Did you know? Quite a new baby. And so she was in the dorm. I spoke with Etenja, who had a cot close to her, and she said Turja was there, feeding, just as she – as Etenja – went off to the showers.'

I nodded again.

'Many died,' said Bosjin. 'We hauled back to a machinery store further north in the Sebestyens, north of Istenem. It's seven, eight minutes from here.'

We sat for a while. There was a buzzing far away, that grew in the silence between us. Bosjin cooped his head upwards, peered between two of the closer stretches of smoke-into-the-sky. I followed his stare. The hull of the old ship, the *Als* that had carried us all through space in her belly like a mother, was all slashed and wrenched. The thickest climbing pillar of smoke came from there. Other smaller sites smouldered nearer to us. Between two of these uprights I saw a black spot, like a bird in the distance.

'They come again,' said Bosjin. 'The smoke renders their sats inaccurate for detail, so they must fly planes. But even from a plane, surveillance is hard. Infra-red is useless to them closer to the burning, but out on the rock here they'll spot us. Best inside the cave.'

Swiftly, he hauled himself over the lip and disappeared. It took me a moment longer to understand that there was a spinal ladder lodged just under the metre lip of stone. I scrambled for it, leaning forward, reaching with my hand, almost tumbling into the darkness (with a lurch in my belly), but then caught it, swung my body round, and scrambled my foot onto the topmost rung. Then I was down.

Five metres down my foot struck Bosjin. 'Beware yourself,' he growled. 'You'll kick me off the ladder, you rigidist.'

'Aren't we going down?' I asked.

'We need not. This will keep us out of his Senaarian eye, and from here we can hear if he passes or stays in the air above us. Besides,' he said after a long pause, 'you will not want to go to the ground. The fire has not eaten everything. What remains is . . . unsightly.'

So I hung there, suspended under the stone roof, with the sunlight above throwing a bright block of whiteness just behind me. The dazzle of this prevented me from acclimatising my eyes to the dark, and I had only a sense of immensity. I quietened my breathing, and was able to hear the gnats-wing sound of the craft somewhere over us. It flew, circled, flew back. After a lengthy silence Bosjin said, 'And now let me climb out.' There was a lurching moment at the top of the ladder, when I reached out and had to scrabble on the bare rock, but my fingers-ends somehow gave me the purchase to haul myself up.

'I've done what I wanted to do here,' Bosjin said after pulling himself out, with more alacrity than myself. 'Come back to the rest of us.'

And so we set off at a pace over the rock, skirting the great maw in the spread of this lower part of Sebestyen, and moving on up and down again over the curled rock ridges. After a few minutes of this, we dropped back onto the salt running alongside the Aradys, and jogged north for a while. Then we turned east, and ran down a gully with a compacted salt floor. This, I recognised, was a narrower cave with a proliferation of salt stalactites, some of which had been cleared to make way for industrial Fabricants and some of their output: cars, planes, suchlike. There were no guards posted.

Inside were people, many with burns and other wounds, scattered variously over the floor. The worst cases (I discovered) were kept inside the few cars and planes; everybody else huddled around one of the two ordinary Fabricants that had been dragged up from the wreckage. Somebody was feeding the raw gruel into the back of this machine, whilst a crowd jostled uneasily in front of it, waiting for the breakfast they had yet to eat. The other was standing solitary. I pointed to it. 'What is wrong with that Fabricant?' I asked.

Bosjin shrugged. 'Broken. Perhaps somebody will get around to fixing, but at the moment people are too much worn-out and hungry.'

'We can hardly feed every person in Als with only one Fabricant,' I said.

Bosjin shrugged again. 'There are many fewer people in Als this day than the last. Besides,' he added, 'there are Fabricants in the four cars, and in the two planes. But those are being used to feed the most sick. Sometimes the nurse-rotas come out with surplus and pass it about.'

'This,' I observed, 'is chaotic.'

Bosjin stared at me.

'We must strike back at Senaar at once,' I said. 'That is the only way.'

Bosjin seemed to be sucking his own tongue for a long time. Then he said, 'Strike back?'

I left him then, because of the tone of his voice, and spent an hour going amongst the hardware of the cavern. We had Fabricated seven planes from materials mostly brought with us, or adapted from driveparts of the *Als* itself. Of these, four had been destroyed on the ground by the Senaarian raid, and one was away along the northern shore of the Aradys (we could not communicate with the mines up in the north because equipment had been destroyed, as had the two satellites, so we could bounce no message into the deep crags of the mountain terrain). But eventually, clearly we would be able to use three planes. Planes possess a self-evident importance in war, but a fleet of three would hardly be a match for the Senaarian Air Strike Force. If we put them in the air together the three Alsist planes would be destroyed.

This put me into a negative set of mind. The Senaarian army was almost two thousand strong; small numbers in the historial annals of war, but in the context of Salt more than many other nations combined. These men (though no women, which was a quirk of the hierarchy) were soldiers all the day and all the night; they were trained and expert. They had a large body of equipment and ordnance. It was no easy thing for the mind to take in the prospect of going against them in war. And yet my mind was eagerly thinking in that direction. I remember, tart as the taste of salt on the tongue, how that eagerness felt. It was not a thing to be proud of but I felt it. I wanted to begin turning Senaar into a place of corpses.

I thought of my car, still left somewhere in the ruins of Als. There were a great number of cars, of course; for we had Fabricated many to do the work of building a city, and ferrying materials from and to the northern mountains. But cars make poor weapons of war; they are easy targets from above, easily tracked and targeted, and can be picked off. So my mind began turning to how to modify them. Dressing them with armour was possible, but not practical: there were the metals in the Sebestyens, particularly silver, but it would surely make them cumbersome, and any such armour would not be of use against the higher-detonation weapons of airborne craft. Better, I thought, was to heat-shield them to dampen their infra-red, then half-bury them in the salt. I was thinking then of placing them in the desert, as bases for small groups of men: little undersalt caves with Fabricants for food and drink, and a space to hide and dress wounds. And I begin to think of how smaller bands of people might strike out aspects of Senaar, how groups of a few could perpetrate the greatest damage.

I met Csooris, wandering amongst the people that were there, and we fell to talking. She now had lost much of her hair to fire, and some of her face was bandaged up. 'I could regrow the skin, or start to,' she said, 'only the Senaarians destroyed the hospital.'

I offered her some vodjaa, and she drank this.

'I was in the women's dorm,' she told me. 'I had been working, and was in the showers, washing with the saltwater. I still have some brine on my body,' she said, laughing chokingly, 'because they attacked before I could finish off with clean water. I think the water on my body saved me, though, because when the pipes stopped sprinkling and I went to the mouth of the showers there was fire all about me. If only I had washed my hair as well as my body, I might still have that. Such a strange sensation,' she said, 'to be moving in fire as a medium. I did not try to breathe, or it would have burnt my lungs; and I did not stay long or it would have consumed me, for all that my skin was wet. I went backwards on an impulse, with my head alight like a firestick, and I fell backwards, and like a miracle of God I fell under the fire. It was there as a flaming roof. I was panicked, I think, because I thrashed about, and the pooling water on the shower floor put out my burning hair.'

I leant forward and kissed her on a part where her skin was clear. She cackled. 'Will you have sex with me?' she asked.

'You are too burnt,' I said.

She nodded. 'Too burnt, too tender. Too ugly.'

'Yes,' I agreed. 'Perhaps you will heal soon though.'

After that I went amongst more of the people, greeting those I knew well and talking with those I knew less well. Then I took a needlegun and went back out. It was dark now, and the Evening Whisper had died away, and I went by starlight and the still smouldering embers of Als, back to my car. No Senaar patrol had claimed it, which was a lucky chance. I set about driving the car back, and round, and eventually to the seashore, where I went north and finally parked in the cave where the survivors were.

Barlei

There was more difficulty with Convento than I had anticipated. Whether they were merely overcautious, or whether the wickedness in Als had somehow infected them, it is difficult to say. But they were certainly strong in their feigned outrage at our retaliation on Als. Clearly, they felt threatened. The Conventon diplomat, who lived in meagre accommodation in Senaar (his government could have afforded better, of course, but chose not to spend enough), was a real irritation to me during those first few days of the war.

For instance, the Conventon delegation flew down, and insisted on personal meetings with me. When I refused (and after all, I had a war to prosecute) they started a series of defamatory Visual performances, giving interviews to net companies all over Salt, denouncing the Senaarian attack as aggression, empire-building and even (can you believe it!) genocide. Of course, history has vindicated me on that last charge; and for a people supposedly destroyed, the Alsists were soon enough fighting with deadly urgency. History should ask the widows and children of the Senaarian fighting men who died at the hands of Alsist warmaking whether I had perpetrated genocide upon that wicked nation; should ask the relatives of the civilians they murdered. I confess the situation made me angry then, confess too that it makes

185

me angry now to contemplate it. But you cannot gag people, cannot stop evil tongues writhing.

Matters became worse with a spurious dispute over airspace. Naturally, having subdued the Alsist ability to wage terrorist war, I needed to keep Senaarian planes in the air over Als. I needed to keep an eye on what the Alsists were doing on the ground. More than this, I had positioned a camp of crack soldiers on the ground to the south of the city, by the banks of the Perse, and they needed air cover. But the Conventons turned this into a dispute, and claimed that we were invading their airspace. As if that were even plausible! We were nearly two hundred kilometres from Convento . . . but they merely insisted that there had been a 'Northern Alliance' (no such organisation had been legally constituted, of course) and that any 'invasion' from the South that encroached on any part of the land by the sea was 'illegal'.

By way of challenging our presence, then, Conventon planes began deliberately intruding on our manoeuvres. For three anxious days we were never certain, back in the control base in Senaar, whether our pilots were going to be able to hold back from opening fire on these intruders. They became bolder and bolder, shadowing our planes in their movements, sweeping down at them, flying upside down underneath them. No matter how we complained, we got nowhere.

They were goading us, of course; attempting to buy a war with us by spending the lives of their pilots. In the event, of course, the Alsist attack took events out of our hands anyway.

Petja

The phrase is making war (*uarfabrejejen*); and that is what we did, within a few days. We made war. But little is made in war, and much unmade. It is a stupid phrase; it has no correlation with the real world.

It took days to talk round the people hale enough to make war. Spirits were low, and I needed a deal of energy. But there was always rage underneath the depression, for what is depression but a crushing down of anger? And people found me, as I spoke, a vivid maker of war in myself. They found themselves listening to my plans, whatever their spirits. And my plans were good.

Not all my plans were followed, of course. Ours was not a hierarchy, for all that war gave me command over some people. And so there were some who insisted, stupidly, that we meet the Senaarians in the air. I advised against it, there were even (I remember) fistfights by the evening fires, but enough of a group of others made the case. And so they decided to augment our three planes with more. But, even with industrial Fabricants and the finest software, it is a slow and complicated business building planes, and doubly complicated to modify the components ad hoc to render them tougher, shield-added, weaponed, all the things that distinguish a warcraft from a peacetime one. And we had only a few rescued industrial Fabricants, and poor software. We made another plane, but within a fortnight all our planes were broken in the air and left in black pieces on the deep desert floor. Only a madman forces himself on even though every step injures him. The better way is to come at it in another manner.

So we developed manpacks. We trucked out a series of Fabricants from the position we had occupied (this was before we attacked, but we anticipated clearly that the Senaarians would retaliate more thoroughly after we began making the war), and took them to the mines in the more northerly mountain strongholds, and there we established a Fordist rota, where equipment was produced in continuous cycles. Mostly these machines were manned by the injured or the maimed, although some able-bodied refused to be part of the war, and they either went north or left altogether. There was little of this, though, because the rage was large enough to hold most people.

And to these people I said, 'Forget that you live in a certain place, because you no longer do: now you live in the desert, you eat whatever you find, you drink from whichever source presents itself. Forget that you are alive, because you are only dead, already dead. Forget that the Senaarians are people, because we must kill them and kill great numbers.' We took the needleguns and needlerifles that had already been Fabricated, and we spent three days preparing ourselves as best we could. The needlerifles were advantaged with a spot-laser that aimed down the spine of the gun, and we spent the afternoon target-shooting in the cavern, and out of the cavern also, on the flat and amongst the creases of the hills. (I was worried about this last, because I reasoned Senaarian sats could spot us easily, and that we looked like soldiers training, which would warn the enemy. This did not come to pass, and I only discovered later why: that Convento had disabled them all, claiming accident.) The rifle Fabricant software came with a training fluid, to be spat out of the rifles instead of metal. This fluid, shot out by laser, hurt and bruised the skin when it struck you, but it did not kill, and so we spiced our training by dividing into two bands.

We also prepared camouflage cloaks: these were very capacious, but rolled behind to sit at the base of the spine in a wedge. These cloaks, then, were coated with salt crystals over a polymer of reflective cloth that gave back the same readings as sodium. In the desert, we could unfurl them and throw ourselves on the salt ground, and dig ourselves under, or cast heaps of salt over us if we had time. No sat, no plane, probably no man (except if he were very close) could spot us. It seems now, as I recall it in this place, a primitive piece of technology, but it served us better than machines with ten thousand moving parts; all our planes were destroyed soonest.

We also (this through our ingenuity) made up large balloons of strong but delicate-seeming material – a cloth of large grown crystals that meshed together to form rigid bags, though they had almost no weight. These were fitted tight about our stomachs, hips and thighs until we needed lift, and then a micropump would empty all air from them and the balloons would begin to lift us. Then the manpacks could raise us. The engines in these packs worked with counter-revolving jet pressure, and they would move us upwards. But they were sluggish and sometimes failed with the weight of a person and kit (and so we had the balloons): and even with as little as fifty kilos or so, they were erratic. They grasshoppered us out, upwards so fast our ears sang with pain, usually on a simple ellipse to 2000 metres and then coming down about a kilometre away. A chip in the motor controlled them, angling them slightly to give us lateral movement, but after that always keeping them pointing dead downwards, so we never spiralled or came down on our heads. But it was a rough ride. I vomited during several trips, and clothing tended to become singed. Nonetheless it saved my life many times.

We were no hierarchy but warmaking has its own dynamic. It seemed I was talented with this making, and most were content to follow my advice. Some not, but we all faced the same enemy. So a force of sixty agreed to come with me. Another hundred wanted to stay with the planes, to fly them and fight from them like marines. The rest, and the wounded, were to go north with the cars, to the mines and safety. It was clear that as soon as we attacked the Senaarian base in Als we would have to leave the cave, because the enemy would retaliate with greater air force, and try to eradicate us. Our only defence in this situation, I thought, was to spread ourselves, although the pilots and the marines disagreed and spat at me, saying that they could wrench control of the air from Senaar. Then we ate, set up provisions, and parted. Most drove north; I took three cars and drove south. They were so full of rations that most of the ground troop had to walk beside them.

It was an hour before the Evening Whisper when we moved. I ordered all weapons hidden beneath clothing, or otherwise disposed of (which was easy, because a needleweapon is a light and compact thing). Any sats seeing us might take us for refugees; a needless precaution with hindsight, because the sats were disabled. Our balloons made us seem tubby, like old people on an evening stroll. We drove the cars out east, and parked them in the lee of a dune, with salt-cloth draped over them. Then we made our way through the twilight towards the sea. It was tightly timed. Our attack had to happen at exactly the time of the Whisper, when nobody expected it.

What this meant was that the sixty of us lay against the wind-side of a dune in the purpling light for ten minutes, waiting for the wind to start to rise. I lay nearest the top, and pushed a sight-tube all the way through the pinnacle so that the end glinted a little out of the other side (but dune tops always glint whites, silvers, reds and purples in the sunset, so no sentry would notice it). And there was the camp. Two planes parked, rigid-structured and packed wind-side against the evening winds. Then there were sentry posts, again packed against the wind. I saw also blocks, which must have been supplies, and a portable plant to desalinate the Aradys. There were three sentries, but they would go inside when the wind came. The rest of the force would be inside, taking mess. The other plane (because we knew there were three) was clearly still up in the air; and would either land very soon, or else would climb higher than the storm winds to be out of the way of the corrosive particles. Either way, the time was almost upon us.

So I pulled out the tube and gave a thumb-signal left and right. We would attack when I stood up; and we would end the attack with our manpacks when I fired a yellow flare from my shoulder. Then we would regroup by the cars, and set up a defensive position; although I hoped we would inflict enough damage to avoid counter-attack.

Nearly time. And the wind was starting at our backs. I pulled on my mask, as did we all; to cover all the skin and hair of the head. Even with its protection though, I could begin to feel the prick of bulleting salt crystals as tiny smarts.

So, in those pre-fighting moments, what was it I felt? Because there was a nervousness, of course. And a sudden hot realisation in my head that I could die, that within minutes I could be dead. But this was not a trembly epiphany; and it reasoned like death without *feeling* like it. It felt like being alive. I could feel every component of my body, every finger and every toe. I could feel the pressure of my heart against its nestling membrane as it sucked in and pushed out. As the wind grew at our backs, and the grains of salt began stinging the backs of our heads, or the backs of our calves through our trousers, this feeling grew in my belly. It grew like a pregnancy speeded a hundred times; I grew great with my elation.

It was suddenly very dark, and my ears were consumed with the howl of the wind. The universe had shrunken to this moment, and I stood. I barely noticed the line to my right and left standing, and barely noticed them following me as we stepped over the height of the dune.

Running.

First, down the dune, with the drop in sound and the reduction in the sparkling stabbing of the Whisper: but only a reduction, a fall in pitch like a musical composition. The heels digging into the pliant ground, half sliding, half running with ridiculous, comic exaggeration, lifting the legs very high and planting them much further forward than would be normal.

Then, with a jolt, onto the harder compacted salt of the Aradys beach. Suddenly we were running in earnest, feet whipping through the sparse salt-grass, the ground beneath us seething with a shallow skin of wind-whipped salt. The Whisper was fierce now, and the flurry of salt grains was intense. It swung us as we ran, trying to tug us over (some did fall, although I did not notice it at the time). The stinging was now a fierce pain, striking like needles at every part of the body at once. But in the moment, the pain hardly registered; or it was only a goad. I may have been screaming as I ran. I really cannot remember. It made no difference. No human voice could impact upon the immensity of the Whisper.

And then, my memory of the engagement is similarly precise. I remember points, illuminated as if they were tableaux, rather than the narrative of the whole; that was pieced together afterwards as we compared our stories. So I know that we covered the ground between the last dune and the camp; that the sentries were sheltering from the pain of the Devil's Whisper, and so hardly noticed us: that it was automatic sensors that alerted them; and that (evidently) the sentries refused even to pay attention to these sensors. We assume they often malfunctioned during the Whisper.

So I rounded the first sentry-hut and nobody came to engage me. I had to stop running, which felt wrong when the elation of running had been so intense. But I had to pull at the sentry-box to open it. As the hatch yawned the guard did not even come out, only looked up with a round expression. I shot him with a needle into the face, and his hands went up. As he fell forward, I shot some more needles into the back of his head. The other two sentries were out of their boxes, with their goggles on and their weapons up, but they were killed before they could fire. I waved the laggards up: they were slower because they were carrying heavier ordnance. These we set up using the sentry-boxes for cover, and aimed at the supply machinery and the planes. We would have to lose this ordnance, because we could not carry it with us when we jumped out, but it was crude. Pipes, from construction software, blocked at one end, with old-style detonation explosives in them on firework thrusters. Each was manned, and there were four of them.

Then I waved the remainder forward. We were still undetected, but the setting up of the equipment had taken time, and the Whisper had passed its worst point. We started over the ground of the camp. Some went behind the barracks tenting and towards the water; I stayed this side of the buildings, and veered a little towards the planes. I was bleeding inside my clothing now, from a hundred tiny punctures. The pain did not bother me greatly but, oddly, I remember feeling discomforted by the sensation of slick wetness inside my suit.

The planes, though, were manned at all times, and as the Whisper began to die, and the air started to clear, somebody must have seen us from one of them. Whatever, there was some warning, and suddenly armed and suited enemy troops were coming out of the two mess tents.

We engaged, but here I remember only snapshots. The fighting was dreamlike, soundless in the roar of the wind. I did not fall to the ground, although some of us did for cover, but I crouched a little over my weapon and started shooting needles at the targets. I remember these shots, because they had the fluid connectivity of music: my finger on the button, the silent lash of metal visible only liminally, the target dropping as if deflated. Needles flashed by me. Then I remember being on one knee, firing my rifle rapidly, cursing, realising too late that the cartridge was empty. Then (this sounds idiotic when I relate it, but this is what I did) I stood up, and slowly (because my fingers were numb and bleeding through the fabric of their gloves) pulled out the old cartridge and dropped it to the ground. Then I fumbled for a new cartridge, a palm-sized circle, in a belt pouch. This took many, many seconds. Then I slotted it into position, and dropped again to my knee to start firing.

The wind was almost passed away now, just a last few fragments of salt whirling through the air. To the west the sky was clearing (the worst the wind could do over the Aradys was to scoop up some large waves), and the light was getting better. I got up to both feet and sprinted over towards a knot of Alsists.

This was when the mortars were set off, and there was an instant *whoom* and a spectacular bellying-out of light, of flame, and then the shockwave reached us and knocked us over with a flick. We all fell to the ground but I struggled round to look up, and saw the planes and the desalination machinery trapped in fire. One mortar had struck the tent, but the fabric (though strong against winds) was too thin to block it and the charge had flown right through both walls and landed in the water.

Because we had been expecting it, we were the first to get to our feet, and then there were some easy targets as the Senaarians struggled up again. I put needles into three or four of them, and then rushed in to claim their guns. The firelight glared hellishly. One of the men, with needles through both lungs, clutched spastically at my ankle; I shook him off.

Somewhere at this point I remember feeling a pinching sensation in my foot, which was nothing. But, later, it revealed itself as a needle wound to my heel. One of the Senaarians, flat on the salt, had taken advantage of the situation to fire low, and the needle had pierced my boot completely. But at the time I did not even register that I had been wounded. I crammed a bundle of weapons into a pouch under my arm, and ran back. I remember tripping over a body, falling, and clambering up again; but I do not know whose body, whether Alsist or Senaarian.

The third plane was back, its belly black as it reared up over the fire: it had swooped low from the sea and then climbed sharply over the battlefield. For a moment it stood there over the flames, frozen, and then it was away above us with a roar that sounded like rage. At close quarters the plane could do nothing without injuring its own men, but if we pulled back or tried to regroup it would punish us.

It was then I shot up the flare, and it howled in my left ear as it rocketed up. Time to jump away. This was the worst moment, because the manpacks had not been tested, and none of us knew really if they would work. We knew the theory: that we should lean in the direction we wanted to go (and lean away from the water if we didn't want to be dropped in the sea), and hold our hands in front of us to avoid having them burnt by the blast behind. But after I tugged my balloons into life, and whilst I waited for them to pump out the air and take away some of my weight, there were three or four seconds when a terror came over me. Somehow, dying in battle did not seem so terrible as dying in a botched flight, as tumbling from the sky and squashing on the ground. The terror froze me, but the system was automatic. Tugging the balloon motors set the manpack into timed life, and there was nothing I could do. I felt the balloons lighten me; I remember distinctly the pressure of my feet against the soles of my shoes diminishing.

Then, there was a shrieking, howling, and I started to scream. My stomach compressed within itself, and I felt like vomiting. My head whined and I gulped. But only then did I realise that the ground was far away, that the air was hissing past my head. I looked down and saw my feet, curled a little in towards each other. And between them I saw the battlefield, laid out like a general's toy. The line drawn by the water at one end, and the corrugations of the dunes at the other. And between, all the damage we had done: the blotches of black smoke edged with the fire, just visible underneath; the scattered bodies like rabbit droppings, littering the ground. A few of the dots were still running. But then I looked up at the still-glowing horizon and the luminous sky above it, and then sideways at the darkening air, and I saw that it was dotted with other flying soldiers.

I cheered with a sudden overwhelming elation; cheered aloud.

Coming down was a more deflating experience. By the time I started dropping, it was quite dark; several kilometres further east with the force scattered over many places. But we checked the compass, and made our way towards the cars. For me, this was the hardest part of the operation, because my foot was now hurting badly. Perhaps the flight had made it worse; perhaps I had simply not noticed how bad it was in the adrenalin of battle. I limped, and made slow progress, and by the time I was back at the cars almost everybody had arrived.

I remember that walk through the dark very well; because even with my painful foot, and even with an uncertainty in my breast about how many of us had survived, and whether Senaar was even now gathering themselves to strike at us with a counter-attack; despite all this, I was aware of a wonderful, near-religious sensation in my belly, a growing feeling that I could best describe, I suppose, with a word I have used little with respect to myself and my feelings: *peace*. There was something alien about this contentment, but it grew there anyway; and when I arrived back at the car, and was challenged, I felt it swell and blossom inside me.

We had lost seven people, killed or wounded. Or, to be precise, killed and wounded-then-killed, because anybody wounded too greatly to jump with their manpacks would certainly have been killed eventually. Whichever, we never saw those seven again. But, although we prepared for it, there was no counter-attack that night.

I pulled off my boot, and treated my own wound with simple wadding. There was no question of regenerating the flesh, and we had gladly put the habits of civilisation behind us. Instead I wadded my foot and put the boot back on it. I took off my jacket, and my topclothing, to see if there was anything I could do for my skin. But it was grazed all over by the Whisper, all red and looking rather inflamed. I decided the best thing was to leave it, and so I replaced my clothing. My warsuit had been rendered a little ragged by the wind but was wearable. I toured the cars for a bit, and everybody talked to me in excited, low tones.

Eventually, I went inside one of the cars and lay on a bunk. Despite the painful tingling of my body on the side I lay upon, I fell asleep easily. What I remember of that sleep is that I dreamt. I dreamt of the

Devil. He was a tall thin man, with a nose so small as to be little more than a crease, but with great eyes, and thick eyelids like blankets of cloth that slid down over his eyes. He was dressed in a scarlet coat and scarlet kilt, and was as white as salt. In the dream I was knelt at his back, pinning up the hem of his skirt, and I was struck by how powerful his calves were, and how the hair on his legs ran in perfect lines, like iron filings caught in the lines of force of a magnet. When I stood up, I found myself (although I did not move round him, and he did not turn about) face to face with him, and he smiled. It was a fearful smile. I said to him, 'Now I must ask you for my payment,' as if I were a hierarch, and he laughed and said that in his utopia there was only exchange, barter, monies. 'And you understand this already,' he said, 'because it is who you have become. You understand that I pay you in pleasure, and that you return the exchange and pay me with your pain. This way we are both satisfied.'

It was an unsettling dream.

In the morning, after the Morning Whisper, we moved the cars east.

Barlei

We were, there can be no sort of doubt around this, unlucky at the start of the war. The Alsists struck during the Evening Whisper which, I freely concede, I did not expect. Theirs was an ill-disciplined but large force, and it caused a great deal of damage in an initial ground attack. But an indication of how ill-discliplined the Alsists were in all military affairs is the time-lag before they deployed their air forces. Instead of co-ordinating these with their attack, they waited several hours before bringing them in. I sometimes think that their error here was the result of shoddy thinking; the ground forces wanted to use the cover provided by the Devil's Whisper (which was good thinking), but the air force could not fly low in such conditions. But, instead of coming in as soon as the Whisper died down, the Alsists decided to wait until it was fully dark, as if they were afraid of attacking during even the merest twilight! Given the ease with which any large flying craft can be detected, during day or night, this was poor thinking indeed. And it cost them dearly.

There are no Visuals of the initial attack, but the footage of the air battle is justly famous. I have been praised for my foresight in putting the full force of Senaar in the air, but the truth of the matter has less to do with my foresight and more to do with the Will of God. I remember the first reports coming through, garbled (because transmission through the Whisper is always difficult) but decipherable. At first it was not certain who was attacking us, whether Convento had launched an assault or whether it was Als, but either way we needed air support for the beleaguered.

Senaar is some sixty kilometres east of Als, and the Whisper dies out of our air minutes before it happens there, so I was able to order our planes into the air before the assault was completed. I knew that some of our planes had been destroyed on the ground, although not how many; but I acted as if we had lost all air support, and acted with dispatch. The planes flew north, skirting the retreating edge of the Whisper, and making difficult turbulent progress (our pilots are the best) at supersonic speeds.

What happened on the battlefield during this time was that the ground troops, encountering greater resistance than perhaps they had anticipated, withdrew as soon as the Whisper died away. For over an hour there was quiet, and our troops regrouped, putting the fires under control, and sorted out their casualties. Then the Alsists attacked again, this time from the air.

Their superior numbers initially overwhelmed the one surviving Senaarian craft, even though they were poorly weaponed and their pilots had no experience of war. The truth, in fact (and perhaps this will put an end to the pointless arguments that circle around this issue) is that our pilots were not initially certain whose the planes were. The first assumption was that they belonged to Convento: not a reason to drop guard, of course, but an explanation.

The planes I sent up there came on the scene shortly after the base plane had been severely damaged (it landed and all but one of the

197

crew escaped with their lives). The sight of a superior force filling the air gave the Alsist crews the terrors. They fled, flying south over the night desert, and our pilots pursued. You will certainly have seen the Visual-enhanced footage of this battle, a glorious one. But try to picture it as it was seen by the pilots. Thrown into battle from nowhere, flying halfway round the planet at speeds many times that of sound, and then immediately engaging the enemy. Seeing them disappear from the orange-lit air over the still-burning camp, where the spotlights played on them, into the utter darkness of the south.

And you give chase! Of course you do, because you are noble warriors for the spirit of Senaar! You follow them on your instruments . . . the same instruments that are recording everything for Visual companies back home. They dodge and scatter, but there are more of you and you are better pilots. And so you press home the inevitability of the situation: that is one definition of war, I suppose. You pull up towards the rear of one of the enemy, the acceleration weighing you against the back of your pilot's seat; and you feel the beautiful click as the weapons fix themselves, and the spiritual roar of them firing. Twin spires of light reaching through the darkness towards the blot of darkness, hidden in darkness, that is the enemy. Perhaps you close your eyes in prayer.

And there is light. And a tumbling of wreckage, falling to the endless levels of Salt below.

Some historians call the engagement the first battle of the air; but why must we name these things? I commend you: unload the Visuals on your netscreen and watch them again. Never forget your history!

Petja

I was wary of using the cars, thinking that they could be easily followed from sats, but luck preserved us. The Senaarian satellites had been disabled by the Convento build-up to war and by the time they were operating again, we had safely buried the cars in the desert, north-east of Senaar.

We deduced the disabling of these satellites on the second day of driving south. There was a lot of traffic in the air for us to monitor, indeed. Most of it was Conventon, as they reported increasing Senaarian build-up on the east bank of the Aradys. They reported the battle over and over again, and it was from them we learnt of the destruction of the few Alsist aircraft. But this we could have deduced anyway, because towards the end of the afternoon of the second day we came across a gigantic spoor of blackened metal, stretching like a God's smudge over the pure white of the deep desert salt. It did not require much time to find that this was the wreckage of one of these planes. Parts of it had been melted and reformed in bizarre, artistic shapes: the work of a blind chance sculptor that I nevertheless found exquisite. Beautiful and pregnant with death. Other parts of the wreckage were almost untouched, except that they had been ripped into uneven shreds and fluttered over the ground from a height. We found some bodies that were only charred skeletons. Another body had had her skin tanned as if from the sun, but she had no chin, and her brown teeth seemed forever biting the empty air. We found nobody we recognised.

Some said to bury these dead, but I insisted we hurry on. My original plan had been to move south until we attracted the air forces, and then to try and meet them with missiles, but it had been a thin plan, and would most likely have resulted in our death. I now reasoned that we would have some days before the Senaarians could fix their sats, and that we could use that time to move the cars south, and base them under the salt. Now, I reasoned, Convento would enter the war, and we would be able to act as guerrillas and attack the Senaarian hometown and the chain of supplies. This seemed to me an excellent way to make war, because we would be able to damage a great deal of Senaar, and to kill many Senaarians. Beyond that, I had little thought.

And so we moved on, passively monitoring the sometimes contra-dictory but generally clear reports of war developing between Senaar and Convento. From time to time we heard the boom of jets passing away to the west, moving south to north or north to south. But we never saw them, nor they us.

And so we moved on, and mostly our wounds healed, and we were ready to fight again. Some abrasions stayed stubborn, open and bleeding. There were patches of my skin that were forever itchy, it seemed; and I was sunburnt; as were we all. Stretches of over-skin (*hörerparm*) would come away, as transparent and ghostly as lizard castings. One night, I remember, I discovered a mole on the back of my neck that I had not noticed before, and that had never troubled me before; but once I started scratching at it, it became more and more itchy, and it spread blood all down the back of my shirt. I slept little that night.

Eventually, we parked the cars in the lee of a long dune, twenty kilometres north of the Senaarian dyke, and we dug them into the great dune by hand. We wedged ceiling boards into the body of the dune, and then we cleared the salt away underneath with power shovels, to make a tunnel. We forced the cars in, and then filled them about with salt again. When we were finished, it was nearly time for the Whisper, so we retreated to the cars and the Whisper finished our work for us, by smoothing down the rough edges we had left on the dune, and licking the shape about us.

Barlei

War with Convento finally broke out, with the official withdrawal of Conventon diplomatic staff from Senaar. Now, some people have accused me of being ruthless in war, but understand this: in all the war we prosecuted with Convento, we acted with honour, because our enemy did. Convento is a religious nation, and it obeyed the rules of war. We fought, we killed theirs, they killed ours, but at all times we knew that we could respect our opponent. Not so Als: Als was never a nation at war, but a rabble of bloodthirsty terrorists. And perhaps you think I use the word *terrorist* lightly, but of course not.

Convento fought us on battlefields, usually the barren salt. Als fought us in our own streets and homes, killed civilians and soldiers without discrimination. Convento fought a war because their government debated and declared a war. Alsists fought simply because it was their bestial nature to fight. There never was any debate in the Alsist government, or declaration of war from the Alsist authorities, because Als never had government, authorities or civilisation of any kind. Now, surely you would agree that I cannot call the Alsists soldiers; or I would be compelled to call every madman individual with a grudge a 'soldier'; every murderer and criminal would claim that they were at war. Of course, an individual cannot declare war; only a government can. It is of the greatest importance to law, to order, that we distinguish these two things.

First, Convento fought us in the air, and I am man enough to admit they fought us well. We lost all our craft save two, and those two returned home with severe damage, such that it was a miracle, or a testament to the skill of the pilots, that they made it back at all. There were grumblings amongst the people at this; the word went round that I had been fooled by the ease of our first battle into complacency in the air. But the truth is that Convento suffered losses almost as great as ours, and that air supremacy was granted to neither of us. There were some ground scuffles as well, with the reinforced base at Als.

But the war with Convento lasted the length a war should last: within three weeks I was meeting the President of Convento in Yared, and signing protocols that ended hostilities between us. We were both honourable peoples. Convento agreed to allow us a military base on the site of former Als (necessary partly to deal with repeated terrorist attacks from the mountains to the north, and partly to facilitate the harvesting of salt eels and other crops: there was quite a scarcity of food at this time). In return we agreed not to fly west of the seventh longitude, not to conduct any military operations in Conventon territory and so on.

The vice-President confided in me (because, indeed, these great statesmen are ordinary people as well, and we chat and gossip as

201

much as any housewife) that many in Convento were anxious about the spread of Alsists in the mountains north of the Perse. They were now nothing more than bandits; they had taken to stealing food, raiding travellers, and generally aggressing the area. Indeed, I harboured the hope that at some future date Convento might join forces with us in flushing them out of their mountains. Without air cover (and the few planes we had left were mostly occupied in supplying the base with necessaries) it was a low, tortuous and dangerous mission.

Things were not helped by the fact that a second cadre of terrorists had established themselves somewhere in the south. With the negotiation of peace with Convento, and the occupation of the ruins of Als, the war was effectively over. It was a matter of great frustration that there were so many Alsists who refused to digest that fact. Of course, they could have signed a treaty and rebuilt their city (probably with a policing force of Senaarians, but the enforcement of law and order could only have benefited them). Instead they chose to carry their grudge.

I remember calling jean-Pierre into my office. He had led men with distinction in the short-lived hostilities against Convento, but now I had a more onerous task for him. 'My friend,' I said. 'We have won the war; it is merely that the enemy have refused to accept the fact. We must make them accept it.'

I remember his smile – his smile! Oh, bear with me, if I become a little emotional. The very memory of him is enough to wet my eyes. I place in the record links to images of him, standing attention in full uniform. Connect with these links, and you will see what I saw on that day.

'Great Leader,' he said. 'These anarchists must understand the Will of God, and if they do not understand it I shall make them understand.'

'I can depend upon you,' I said, clasping his hand. 'Senaar can depend upon you.'

He went north the following day, flying with four planes and a complement of fresh troops, with a mission statement to keep the eastern seaboard of the Perse pacified. Did I think of him as my son? The comparison with another holy relationship between Father and Son is surely not blasphemous. Sometimes I am awake in the small hours, and once I was in a chapel during the Morning Whisper, having spent the night there, and I actually spoke the words aloud, hoping to reach my Creator. Sacrifice! Sacrifice! Why *must* this be the principle of the spiritual in this universe? But the silence, the pure clean silence of the crypt, is answer to me. If I falter, as flesh sometimes trembles, then in my soul I know that only in sacrifice is there truth.

I remember standing in an office overlooking the airfield, as Jean-Pierre made his way, his handsome face rictusing with grins as he laughed with his comrades, striding over the field towards his plane. I watched as the plane swept in the air and ferried him north.

I never saw him again.

Petja

We operated at night to begin with, stealing south and mining the Great Dyke that bore the brunt of the Whisper. That Senaar had left the great stretch of this dyke unguarded surprised me, but then again it was a lengthy construction indeed and perhaps it would have required too many soldiers to guard it all. We left the explosives buried in the structure, like maggots sleeping in meat.

North of the dyke there were scrubbier lands, where saltdomes poked through the topsalt, and were slowly worn to strange shapes. Since our cloaks stood out in this terrain I did not stay long.

We pulled back to the cars and took our daily meal. Listening to ether traffic, we reasoned that the Alsist sats were still not operating as they might. I took our squad of fifty-four, with double rations, and marched south-west. When the Whisper started at our back, we hurried to the next dune and dug ourselves into the lee side, with our cloaks wrapped about us. We were like animals, natives of the planet. In a day we reached a broad press of hardened salt, where many wheels had squashed the grains together into a road. There was little cover hard by the road, so we were forced to pull back thirty metres or so. Still, we only waited half an hour before a convoy of three grumbled over the horizon and started up the road.

I ordered the first truck stopped with a sodium-grenade, fired from a pole (so simple yet so ingenious). Its cab windows broke with the explosion, and let the fire in. Somebody toppled out of the side doorway, but they were burning so fiercely they merely fell to the ground. One of the trucks behind stopped, and its complement piled out with their needleweapons firing. The other pulled off the road, and made slower progress in the unmarked salt, grains spewing out from its spinning back wheels. I ordered the grenade to stop that truck, although the launcher missed with her second and third strike; meanwhile I ordered everybody to charge. We covered the ground quickly, firing needles in continuous bursts. My left-hand cover fell, simply doubled forward with a *nugh* sound and collapsed on the salt. In the silence of the day I could hear the needles swish past; and they glinted in the sun, like rays of light in an optical diagram. One hit my hand, and carved a way in along the length of my little finger: it hurt a great deal more than the more serious wound I had received at Als.

Why am I telling you about this raid in such detail? There was something about it; the sunshine so bright and pure, perhaps. The vision (I can shut my eyes and the image will come to me as if newly fished from bright water) of the great trucks stalled, jolting and swelling with perspective as I ran towards them. Of the maskless Senaarians ducking their heads back out of the way, round the snout of the car, trying to stay behind cover. But they were a small force, and we were forty-four. Three of us died, and one (a man called Sebestyen, like the mountains) received two needle wounds to the lower abdomen. His pain was bad, and there was little we could do. Two offered to drag him on his cloak back to the car, where he could lie and recuperate; which was no small offer, since they dragged him for a day and a half, stopping at every Whisper to bury him and themselves, and then starting again, and on one occasion being buzzed from the air, and having to turn him over (his shouts of pain, they said, were severe) and themselves to hide under their cloaks. They dragged him all that way and finally he died anyway. Afterwards, I spoke to one of them, and he said he was most worried by the way the blood from Sebestyen's wounds kept spilling on the salt, bright red on bright white, and the two of them kept kicking salt over this trail and hoping it didn't show from the air.

One truck got away, revving noisily, rejoining the track and speeding over the northern horizon; and one truck was wrecked. But we took the third, and a group of twelve of us turned it about, and drove south; the rest fell back. Surely, after ten minutes, we saw two dots in the air to the south, and voices coming croaky over the com ordering us to stop and surrender. So we jammed a seat-brace against the acceleration foot-button, and tumbled out of the car. Then we rushed to the nearest western dunes, and threw ourselves down with our cloaks as camouflage to watch as the enemy destroyed their own car. The explosion was magnificent.

The plane made a pass over us, but could not locate us against the salt, and turned away. From here we marched our force to the west, and came to the spinal railway track that connects Senaar and Yared. This was the point of our attack, to destroy the railway terminus in Senaar, and to this end we placed our trays of explosive carefully, so that they hovered over the track itself (we had to tear down the windshield covering), and then sent them scooting down the track at two hundred kilometres per hour, to detonate in the centre of the city.

Freed of our packages, we made swift time heading west. By ill fortune we were spotted from the air. Again, we lay down in camouflage, but the plane flew low anyway and began strafing our positions, and so we were forced to clamber up and deflate our balloons, and jump to the east.

The plane followed us, of course, but our various jumps were scattered so that it could not target a group. Of the twelve who had driven with me in the car, three were killed, and one died when his manpack malfunctioned and dropped him down head first. I found his body; his head was flopped over on his shoulder as if he were asleep. We were concerned, of course we were, at the implications of this but our manpacks were too vital to our method of making war to give up using them.

We regrouped, and broke into several groups. The first, the one I joined, skirted east of the Great North Road, coming down the way until we reached outbuildings and northern suburbs of Senaar itself. Here we deployed the most curious-looking of our weapons of war, devices that had been modified from child-toy software in our car Fabricants. Small fusion detonators, suspended from balloons and fitted with tiny fan-motors. When we inflated the balloons, the things would hover three metres from the ground and begin slowly to drift along. These surely do not sound like very practical weapons of war: how slowly they travelled, how easy they would be to dispose of, to dismantle. But we set a fuse of thirty minutes and let them drift away, buzzing like insects. Then we hid, crouched behind a large storage shed. At exactly twelve minutes we detonated the charges we had planted days before in the Great Dyke itself. We were many kilo-metres from the dyke, and on the northern outskirts, but we heard the billowing *whump-whump* of the detonations clearly. Then we waited. I closed my eyes, imagined a rushing of military services to the east, thinking the dyke was under attack. I imagined planes whirling through the air.

It was minutes before the Evening Whisper was to start, and we hurried away, dashing north-east from the roads and into the dunes to bury ourselves into the lee side. The slipping, abrasive eddies of trillions of salt grains as I wriggled my way under the soil, and safety. And then?

Then, our balloons floating down streets, over parks, perhaps knocking against the walls of buildings, and skidding along with the fan-blades rattling ineffectually against the blocks. But then the Whisper, the air scurrying with jewel-sharp tiny salt grains, the breached dyke letting through a more vigorous scouring wind than normal, and people cowering inside. Nature bursting our fragile balloons, filling the rigid structures with tiny holes and letting the ordinary air suck inside. Dozens of devices settling to the ground, tossed and kicked by the wind perhaps, rolling into gutters, or setting up in the ground-jambs of walls.

The explosions coincided with the height of the Whisper. I heard nothing, buried away in the body of the salt itself, but even had I been outside, I would have heard nothing against the rage of the Whisper itself anyway. And, in the dark, we stole away until the horizon to our south only glimmered with red from the damage we had done.

Four months, nearly. How many engagements did we fight? I cannot number them. How many hundred Senaarians killed? Was it as many as a thousand? I cannot number them.

I think back and try to arrange these memories into a dry account, but the events speak so indistinctly, and my associations so powerfully. It is not what I did, I sometimes think, but what I felt these doings *meant* in my life. Though there is no reason why you should have the same sense of significance, unless I can put it out to you, and even then, there is no passage into another's head. That is a sober observation, and not one I feel a happiness about. But I say it from a certain position. I try to reach you, perhaps, and at the same time I can never reach you. I will tell you, for instance, about the surprise raid. We lay in wait, south of the city, to fall upon a trade car bound for the south coast settlements, to fall on it as eagles. And then we were detonating the underlying saltstone in great blocks to block the way of the car, and suddenly Senaarian soldiers were pouring out from the back, and taking cover in the nearer dunes. That was a fierce needlefight. It was dusk, shortly before the Whisper (and we had reasoned that the driver would be tired and thinking about battening down). In the end, I ordered us to pull back. I decided not to jump straight away, and I am not sure why; perhaps I feared a trap. So we fell back over the dunes, a dozen firing from positions, a dozen scurrying back with their heads below their shoulders, those dozen squirming about as soon as they cleared the peak of the back dune and taking up the fire to cover their colleagues. We went back a good kilometre that way, with fierce fire. I think I assumed that we would fight until the Whisper started, and then the enemy would give up. But they foreclosed that, and instead sent up a shrapnel device, that lit up like a firework, except that the blades of the explosion were needles also, and they rained down over us. People were deflating their own balloons then, and I need give no order; I pulled my own cord and heard my own engine whine to pump the air out of my bladders, and then the jet fired and I was lurched sickeningly skywards. We saw a second shrapnel device explode, but beneath us, and they are designed only to shower downwards upon the place beneath; it was such that from above the burst had some extraordinary beauty. It littered the carpet beneath with fragments of light itself, except that the carpet was the air, and then the salt, and the embers died slowly. We came down slowly, as if being dragged through some torpid element, as a ship's anchor through a treacly sea. By the time we hit the ground again the Whisper was beginning, so that we fell into a cloud of buzzing salt, and had to struggle to bury ourselves. I was badly grazed by that Whisper, I remember.

But how does this transfer the experience from my mind so that it rests upon yours? I could say that we lost four people; that I received my most severe wound, a needle that lodged in my pelvis, the puncture at the top of my leg. That making my way north after that engagement was the most painful thing I have ever done, with every step a wrench of pain. That we had to stop and fight our way through the salt domes north of the dyke, and that I fought although every breath was now a whole world to me, that the pain had contracted about me like shrink-wrap. That I fired my weapon without being able to connect what I was doing with action in the outside world, and only fired it to scream, and only screamed to try and vent the pain. That we finally arrived back at the cars, and that Olega took out the needle with pliers; that the pain of this was almost a relief, because it took the background suffering and focused it into something I was permitted to scream about. That I lay for a week before I could even stand. I could say all this, but then the narrative is focusing on something else. All the pain, which is only expected since war is painful (I understate the severity, but the words are plain). But that is not the experience inside my head. All this happened, but that is not now my experience.

My experience now is back at the road, south of the city. It is the first swim of the battle. It is a certain precision of focus in my senses as the needles start to be propelled between us. It is very hard to nestle the meaning in these words. It was the smell of the evening air, the salty ozone smell of the cooling air before the Whisper. But it was not only that smell, it was the realisation that I had not been noticing the smell of the air before that, and only with the launching of the combat did the smell strike me. But it was not even that, because realisation (*keristalsen*) misrepresents the sensation. It was merely a way of being, as if being were something other than thinking. It was because the occasion hurried me out of thought, perhaps. Or the excitement of it, and the beautiful clenching of muscles in the abdomen, as beautiful as the clenching of a woman around a man in lovemaking. It was the most fleeting of senses, the imaginary connection with the white desert stretching away behind the attackers, greying in the sinking light; and stretching that way forever, stretching all the way about the abdomen of the world itself until it reached us, positioned on the other side of the road (actually this was not the case for this engagement, because the road ran within half a kilometre of the intervening sea, but now I am not speaking of facts, but of a certain hard-to-define something in the memory of war, of this war, of my war). Needles, fired, make only a very shrunken hissing sound, like the draw of fabric upon fabric. They slip through the air invisible, unless they catch the light, in which case they gleam like fish in water. But if you see one it is too late to dodge it; it has already fastened itself into your innards: into your leg, your arm, foot, wherever you may be injured. But there it is, the beauty, and the beauty strikes you quicker than the wound is made. And the beauty is what lasts. That is what I take away. The scurrying, as ballet; the falling into position, with the thrilling in every part of my body. The recoil-less spurting of my weapon, with a dotted line of metal going towards the enemy. The smell in the air. The beauty of Salt.

But I am wasting my time, here. Perhaps you would be more

interested in my injuries. I brought up a bruise on my knee from landing badly after the jump. I scored my skin against the Whisper as I struggled to the lee of the dune, and tried to scrabble myself into the salt with only my hands; and I dug poorly because my mind was completely filled with the pain from my hip. Afterwards, I could barely pull myself out, and I could not muster, so I was forced to call out until somebody noticed me, and the muster happened about me. Gornij tried to pull the needle out but could not obtain purchase and so (agony) tried to push it through, but it was lodged in the marrow. On impact the metal sometimes deforms, so as to lodge itself in flesh. I know all of this, and remember it.

But I cannot call the feelings of pain into my mind by putting this here. And I can call the feelings of beauty merely by shutting my eyes.

This is what I remember now, as my eyes fall shut. I remember the group of faces about mine, as I briefed them. Also, there is the colour of the sky, the headiness of the paling from white to blue at dusk. These people, these soldiers. My people. This moment, before battle, when I was with my people in the salt wilderness under a jewellery sky, was the happiest in my life. I remember it now, and salt-and-water (*kratchadys*) dribbles from my eyes, through my shut lids.

Ah, but I am becoming a sentimentalist.

My troop, my warriors. And so they are running now, into the darkness; they disappear over the cupolas of the dunes.

And the darkness has them.

Is it night now? I am heavy with the tiredness of this task. My friends are mostly dead, and we killed many Senaarians during those months, and afterwards. Those words say enough, I feel. Those words, that have appeared on the screen; they speak. Their *o*s and *a*s open and close as human mouths do, full of air or full of blood that surprises you with its redness. Their *e*s flap their lower lips, seen in profile, up and down. I am bitter, but I will say this: that I am not unhappy because of the deaths of people, since people all die. I mourn instead the passing of this beauty. It is intangible, but the soul is intangible, and God preserves that in the deep freeze of heaven.

Well, well. What else is there for me to tell you about the war? We were in the field, there in the southern hemisphere, for four months. We killed many Senaarians, and a few from other nations. We destroyed much equipment. We fed off the food being shipped into Senaar for their hierarchical 'trading', and drank that water. We broke the spinal railway in four places with detonations, and forced a great deal of traffic onto the road. We knew, because we monitored the various transmissions, that there was a deal of debate in Senaar about the removal of transportation of goods onto the water, but the design for a boat large enough and stable enough to survive the storm-winds at Whisper was beyond the capabilities of wartime Fabrication. All efforts were being put into rebuilding the Senaarian airforce.

We engaged Senaarian soldiers on more occasions than I can remember. Towards the end, they were arming themselves with heavier calibre weapons, and more from Als died. But the heavy-calibre guns and rifles were very weighty, compared with the lightness of needleguns, which meant that they were too cumbersome to take on patrols unless there was truck backup.

On one occasion, we hijacked a multitrailer from Babulonis. The trailer team fought, and we killed them; then we drove the trailer into Senaar itself, and parked it in the main square. The explosives we had Fabricated were not especially effective, but they were able to spread radioactive matter from the drivepole a fair distance. The band that drove the car, four people, simply walked out of the city and were free.

Of a band of sixty, we were seventeen left alive when I decided we should pull back. Why did I decide to pull back? I will tell you the wholeness of the truth: my eyes were fogging. I could see, but only through a pearl mist. All the fighting in the sunshine, all the moving around in the daytime, was poisoning my eyes. Mine were not the only cataracts, either. Of our soldiers, two died of the environment (Mechta developed sores on his face and skin, and they spread quickly into his blood system. He shot a needle through the roof of his mouth when the pain was too much. And a good soldier, a good killer-of-Senaarians called Prizrak, suddenly collapsed into sickness. His skin came up rowdy, red, scurfed with eczema, and his hair dislodged itself from his scalp. These radiation burns came from nowhere, it seemed, but they made him scream, for any pressure on his skin was unbearable. Within days (this happened outside of the cars, of course; when we were in the field, killing the enemy) his skin began sloughing off, great plates of skin simply falling from the body. He was dead by the time we got him back to the car. His body has been buried in the desert salt, where it will be preserved for thousands of years.

Do we ever think of how we are stocking up the research of the future archaeologists? This salt that is our world will let nothing decay, unless we put the bodies in our fertile fields, as is common practice in the cities. But even then, what? We eat our friends, our lovers, as compost in our food. And so they are preserved. But the arena for war is the salt desert, and the warriors that become buried are kept forever. There is something appropriate about it, perhaps; something tribal and primitive about our societies setting the bodies of its warriors aside and preserving them. But then I think again, of the thousands who died and were not buried, because any corpse left on the surface of the salt will be deteriorated by the Whisper within months.

Well. These two died, suddenly, of the radiation; and most of us had sunburn, or had new freckles, new moles that itched and that oozed blood when scratched, but these were not things to worry about in the middle of the battle. My problems were the cataracts, and they were not the only cataracts. As many as a third of our people suffered this same pearling of vision, this same drowning of the particularities of sight in a brine of greyness. For some it was only a fogginess of seeing, for others the world was only dazzle and blocky shapes of darkness. There was little we could do with only the medical facilities of the car.

And so we dug the cars out of the salt and drove north. At all times we remained battle-ready, at all times expecting the sats to pinpoint us, and to send in aircraft to intercept. We thought we were about to be bothered with some aircraft, too: two low sorties in the distance, but nothing more.

Of course, we were cautious. It was not practical to dig ourselves in every time we stopped, but we wrapped the cars in salt-cloths, and we kept no heating to minimise infra-red. All of us knew, we were as exposed on the salt plain as mosquitoes on a white tablecloth; and the eye of the sat was as relentless, as unblinking as the eye of God. And yet we found ways to move around. Sometimes the air, in the very zenith, would blur, a smearing of salty winds in the upper air. This, we reasoned, gave us some small chance of hiding from the eye of the sats, and we tried to use this time to move quickly. Perhaps I was reckless, because my own sight was now incapable of picking out the details, and so some part of my soul rendered it difficult for me to imagine some machine doing so. Still, luck, God, favoured us.

And then, in the night, a plane landed ahead of us. Of course we emptied from our cars, and took up positions; the seventeen of us one body, sprawled along a single dune. I could see next to nothing.

There was a single person (said Salja, who was next to me on the dune) who emerged from the plane and approached us. We held our fire. And it was only when he was close enough for me to hear his voice, and to touch his face with my questing fingers, that I knew it was Eredics. A friend of mine.

Barlei

Hopes for a swift victory over this terrorism were broken by the elusiveness of the southern terrorist force. I sent troops against them time and again, but they had developed a random jet-jumping device that scattered them and took them away. Every engagement cost us men, but cost them men as well; and we had more men to spend. Perhaps you consider it heartless to talk of human lives in this way, as if they were monies that we could easily deploy but everything in this universe has a cost: God has told us that. In this case the cost was high, but the product being purchased was liberty. Our soldiers died bravely, and each of them took another of the enemy with them. And the alternative was to allow the enemy their evil. The destruction they created, the buildings in Senaar they destroyed with loss of innocent blood, the number of soldiers and associated workers they killed: all these things.

I was tempted to pull jean-Pierre back from his important work in the north. But he was having a hard time of it, securing the necessary base at Als. Indeed, I tell no lie (as indeed I should not) when I reveal that for a whole month we spent more public money on Als than we did on Senaar itself, even though (and my enemies have made enough capital with this) some people were hungry in the streets of our great city. But my responsibilities were clear! To end the war as quickly as possible, so that we could refocus energies on producing food again, so that the price might drop down again. Food production on our world is precarious enough, even in peacetime: and with the wanton destruction of carefully-composted growing-fields and the breakage of farming machinery, production teetered. Growing still went on in the west, of course, but they have always been less efficient, and their prices were extortionate. More than this, of course, we lost a great deal of lawful supplies to banditry from Als. Some lawsuits are still, I believe, working their way through the courts on this matter. Foreign traders trying to take money from Senaarians on alleged contracts interrupted by piracy.

Still, jean-Pierre made a number of suggestions, and I agreed to them. He had taken a large body of broken-spirited Alsists into effective imprisonment but this took a large manpower to guard, and cost us dearly in supplies. So we rebuilt their town, and fenced it about to stop the terrorists in the area from infiltrating it. We told people to get on with their ordinary lives. Told them that the war was over, and that they should grow food because Senaar could not be their bread-basket forever. In a way, this action was the most selfless act one nation ever bestowed on another: for the victor nation to rebuild the damaged parts of the losing city, to provide that defeated people with laws which they never had before, to place the means for their own livelihood back in their own hands. Many have called me too generous, but I know how people are.

Once the protected portions of Als were completed, jean-Pierre was able to go amongst the northern hills flushing out recalcitrant rebels, and (of course) offering sanctuary in the new town for all who accepted that the war was over.

Petja

The enemy had built a number of large camps, and fully enclosed them in wire. Criss-cross wire fencing twenty metres high surrounded them, and the wire was heat-releasing, such that a light touch would only scorch but with prolonged touch the heat would build until your flesh cooked. And from the wire fences, they had hung wire ceilings, presumably because they had encountered our manpacks in the south and thought of Alsists as grasshopper folk who might spring away if unprevented (even though only my troop had possessed the packs). Inside the camps were built parodies of towns: barrack-like living grounds, warehouse blocks where work was required for eight hours a day. Hundreds of Alsists lived there now. It was a mere prison and was patrolled by a tight force of soldiers as guards: but each (there were five when I returned to Als) was enormous, covering many hectares. The effort and labour that had gone into this exercise was astonishing. That Senaar would do so much, in order to achieve so little (they shipped away a harvest of salt eels to feed their increasingly hungry peoples in the south, I know, but these must have been our world's most expensive salt eels), it amazed me. Of course, there was more here: they wished to isolate and tame the people of Als, and thence to turn Als into a portion of the body of Senaar by the northern sea. Perhaps, some day, they might hope to turn the whole of our world into a limb or a portion of the body of Senaar.

Eredics flew the worst wounded of us straight into the mountains north-west of Als. There my cataracted lenses were cut away, and new plastic lenses inserted. Skin was cut away too, but there was less that could be done about it and my radiation-induced cancers. It was Csooris who was on the rota to perform this medicine upon me, but she told me that the old way of rotas was changed now. The War meant it had to be.

'It is a shame,' I said. 'Rotas are a fair way. They are free.'

We were in a portion of a deep mountain crevasse, ceilinged with rubble fallen from above and wedged. Lighting was industrial, with great cables about the floor, but the medical area had been cleaned and sterilised, and there were rooms caddied up against the naked rock.

Csooris fussed about my face, and finished post-op swabbing. She was so close that I could examine her wounds in great detail. Her face was healed now from its burns, and some of the front had been patched with new skin, although there was no hiding the novelty of this part of her face. To the sides, where it mattered less, her skin was marked and puckered by the old burning, so that along her neck and under her ear, onto her cheek and up to where the artificial hair started seemed made not of face-skin but of anus-skin. Still, as long as she faced me, and with the tug of old acquaintance, I did feel some sexual urge for her. In the field, I had mostly been having sex with Salja but I had grown weary in the latter days, with the cataract and the whole sickness of fighting.

'Do you have many offers for sex now?' I asked.

She snorted. 'Few enough.'

'I would offer, when my wounds have healed.'

She was washing her hands in a medical soda-wash, away in the corner of our little booth. 'Some of your wounds will never heal,' she said. 'The cancers are not only floating on your surface now, but have sunk into your depths.'

I was silent for a while, contemplating this. 'At least I have lived,' I said.

She came over to me again, as if not having heard what I said. 'Yours is no uncommon thing,' she said. 'Perhaps there is some comfort in that. Most of us will die this way.'

'And most Senaarians too,' I said.

She nodded. 'It is our world. Still, we live for a while. We have children. Perhaps that is the point.'

I blinked my eyes, slowly, but the scars were already healing. I could feel them as slight ridges on my cornea. 'At least some radiation sickness can be cured,' I said, blinking again. 'Although I am sorry to discover that my chlorine-lenses did not protect me from the cataracts.'

'Nor are they supposed to,' she said. 'Nor could they, I think. They only keep the chlorine from stinging your eyes.'

'Must I still wear lenses outside?' I asked.

'Oh, yes, of course. Your eye is the same; it will still be irritated by the chlorine.'

I lay down again, sleepy, but she slapped my torso. 'You cannot sleep there, Petja,' she said. 'If you are tired, go sleep on the cave floor outside. This is needed for some other patient.'

Grinning, I got up and pestered her for a kiss, but she was stronger than I, and I was sore with my operation. 'Still,' I said, as I pulled on my clothes, 'it is good to see you again.'

'I am glad you are not dead,' she said. But she did not smile.

'Do you remember what your Lucretius said?' I asked. 'Dust falling forever. I think of that, from time to time. It is a way of explaining the universe. Did he have much to say on the matter of war, your Lucretius?'

But Csooris was not to be drawn. 'I have no time for reading these days,' she said, curt.

Then, as I was readying myself to go, she said, in a lower voice.

'There have been rumours, about you.' Then, after a pause: 'You talk about the people you fought with as "yours".'

At this I was silent.

'Many say that you always were a hierarch and a rigidist. That you were this way even on the voyage, and that now you dream of setting yourself in power at the top of a ladder of hierarchy. That you order people about in war as if they were slaves, as if they were belongings.'

I breathed slowly in.

'War,' I said, 'is a weird prism, through which all is distorted, I think. I say things in war that would revolt me in peace. I never was a rigidist, all those times before the war.'

'Oh yes,' said Csooris, turning from me. 'Nobody doubts that. Of course, during the war you will be praised. Nobody doubts that this is an efficient way of making war.'

'But,' I said, 'you will never have sex with me?'

'No,' she said simply, as she busied herself with something out of my sight.

I left then, and slept for several hours. But later that day I discovered that what she said was true. Many people disdained me, some even spat at me or rushed up to strike me. But many also clustered round me, offered me rations (it was a kind of money, because rations were so scarce; they were 'buying' the right to talk to me, but I was so hungry I did not even recoil at this perversity). And all these people thought of me as somebody with the talismanic power to strike a blow against the Senaarians.

I was a sort of god. A war idol.

And it made me feel sick-tired, a depression in my bones. Or perhaps all I felt was a response to the operation, or to my growing inner sickness. It occurred to me that I had been so ready to die, and that this was where my battlefield happiness and purity-of-mind (*vernou*) had come from; and at that same time, with the jarring of a joint going out of socket, it occurred to me that now I was amongst people again, that purity was being polluted. I spent the evening talking with a group of about thirty, many of whom were friends of mine, and I wanted to be able to look forward to more of these in the future. And so my readiness to die diminished, and so my purity-of-mind greyed. That night I slept in a cot in the side of the mountain, matted with a sack filled with soft plastics, and I had some sex with a woman, little older than a child. But the act was no longer the act of release from the body, the prelude to battle: it was the act that tied me to a certain life, a certain living. Three days later I led my (so – possessive) group of

218

guerrillas out to kill Senaarians on the site of old Als; but I did so with a sense of the irritation of having to do this thing. Yet still I did it.

6

The Gift

Barlei

It has been two years. So long? Surely not so long. I have lived, for those years, in the war-room longer than any other room. But our war has been glorious, and God and freedom have prevailed. There were those who doubted, but doubters never thrive.

Ours is the strongest, the proudest of nations. Ours is the strong right hand God has chosen to shape His new world. But war is terrible, and we have all suffered. All have suffered, from the lowest to the highest. All of us must pray to God to have the strength of will to ask that terrible question: was the price worth the payment? Is even as glorious a victory as ours a thing worth buying with so many of our finest pearls?

But this war has been a necessary thing. Nobody can doubt that. I look to the salt now, the salt that surrounds us all, and I pray to God to tell me what the landscape *means*. I used to think that Salt was a place of tears, but now I think differently. If the salt were to lose its savour . . . ? This war has been the savour in our meat. Without it, life would have been the dull round of planting and reaping, of giving in marriage and giving birth, of growing and dying. But the war has given us interest, excitement; it has rendered the meat more palatable. And, like salt to the body, war is essential to the body politic. Then I can again give praise to God, that He has seen fit to so perfectly emblematise our life. Our planet is a rebus in God's text.

It has been a year and a half since my jean-Pierre was taken from me. A sniper's needle took him: how cowardly, the sniper's serpent task! To lie in the shadows, in the distance, and to poison the Eden. I was furious for weeks afterwards. I broke the furniture in the war-room in the rage and fugue of my grief. I howled like an animal. My generals fled from me in terror, and I broke wood from the table's edge with my bare hands. And afterwards (the memory is almost too painful for me to relate) I sat in the bathroom en suite to the war-room proper. I sat on the floor, in the unforgiving strip-lighting, and I stared at myself in the floor-ceiling mirrors on the far side. What a sorry thing I was, how old, how pale, how grotesque: and yet I possessed life, and the young, the beautiful jean-Pierre did not. I think I was not entirely rational. My enemies say that I ordered the immediate poisoning of the whole Perse Sea, the nuclear detonation over multiple sites in the Northern Mountains. If I ever ordered anything so destructive, and so certain to bring damaging retribution from the two other Perse nations, then my generals wisely ignored it. But I cannot believe I would say such things. I did not believe my leadership would be capable of such ill judgement. Instead, I believe that my enemies in Senaar have been spreading poison about me. Of course I would do nothing so foolish as to destroy valuable items in the war-room.

But the grief was real.

I had authorised the construction (at great expense, because new software for the Fabricants had to be carefully devised, and the first attempts revealed terrible flaws in the programming) of some mountain attack craft. The problem this difficult northern terrain provided was extreme: our sats told us little, our cars and trucks could not travel over it, our aircraft provided neither the necessary reconnaissance nor efficient platforms for warfare. This meant that we sent a succession of foot patrols into the area; an area known by the enemy much more accurately than by us. It is not surprising that we suffered heavy casualties. And so I ordered the creation of a craft deft enough to be able to negotiate the ways of the mountain, but sturdy enough to stand up in combat. At great cost, we developed a low hovering craft with heavy lower shielding. It is known as the Senaar Military Craft VII, or SMIC 7. It will finally finish the war – a war we have already won, over and over, but which refuses to die. But the program has not been problem free. We produced four SMIC 7s before we discovered difficulties in the engine that resulted in the distressing explosion I am sure you have seen on the Visuals. And so we redesigned the craft, and brought them into service six months later than we wished.

And this, this ridiculous flaw in Fabricant software, caused the death of my beloved jean-Pierre. Had he possessed the new craft, he would have patrolled with them. Lacking them, because of this flaw, he was forced to continue patrolling on foot.

He set off shortly after the Morning Whisper (I have his subordinates' reports by me at this moment), and marched for three hours through difficult terrain. At fourth hour he encountered a group and exchanged shots, but our fire-power being superior the enemy cadre withdrew. Of course, my jean-Pierre followed (was he tricked? Did these devils deliberately lead him on? Entice him into a deeper, darker part of the mountains? We can put nothing from our minds, no suspicion is too tenuous). He brought up his men in quick time, and they chased the enemy through awkward-lying land. Then jean-Pierre (recklessly, according to one under-lieutenant, reasonably according to the other; but neither of them understand the bravery of jean-Pierre as do I, the perfect bravery, the perfect purity), then jean-Pierre followed the enemy into a rock culvert, and came into heavy crossfire. The reports do not specify whether the men on the ground assumed it to be an ambush. Nor do they give any sense of the immediacy of the moment, the sudden hot realisation of danger, the silent flash of needles through the sunny air.

I feel myself closer to his Soul when I relive it.

So, jean-Pierre tried to pull back, but found that by chance or skill a cadre of the enemy had made their way behind him. Many of our men were cut down by enemy needles. The reports speak of them falling stuck with many needles, and firing back as they fell.

With jean-Pierre's skills, the troop was able to regroup, and fight back out of the engagement. They then fell back, but under fire at all times and being pursued by a much larger force. They retreated in good order, and finally broke through to the more open ground that slanted down towards the sea-plain on which the New Towns were visible. Three-quarters of the band were lost, and not a man free of injury, but my jean-Pierre had survived, and was able to lead his men down the final stretch with dignity. And this is the bitterness. Within sight of the sanctuaries, a few moments away from the heroic welcome for his good work, a needle felled my mighty warrior. The reports manage some of the banality of it, the way tragedy sometimes masks itself as comedy. They say they had dropped from the rock to the salt plain, that they were within a few hundred metres of the first gate, with their comrades' faces clearly visible on guard duty, when jean-Pierre (not that they call him that, of course; but I cannot chill this narrative by referring to him only by his rank), jean-Pierre suddenly tripped and sprawled, like a child. There was even some laughter, I believe (soldiers are hearty laughers). But he did not rise. Then an ensign stooped to help him to his feet, and he stood up and danced backwards, crying with pain. Some of the others laughed at him too, but this was no matter for laughing. The ensign had been shot through the shoulder, and my beloved jean-Pierre was dead, shot through the back of his neck, with the needle sticking a half-metre out of his Adam's apple. And this is where I leave him, as his comrades dive for cover in the salt and try to return fire (but where?); as his fellows, with whom he had fought so valiantly, scatter away from him in all directions. How could the sniper have chosen jean-Pierre? He was not to be distinguished from his subordinates by dress, for that would be to give the enemy the chance to slice off the head of the military unit. He wore the same deep blue combat fatigues, the same whole-mask. How did the serpent in the wilderness know whom to bite to cause such hurt? Satan has luck; God's people are luckless, because only then can their faith be tested. So said a religious man of my acquaintance. Do I believe him? Do I believe? He is still dead, my boy.

But a war must go on, Freedom cannot go without its champion for the death of one man, even if he be the greatest. I ordered the body flown home, and a magnificent state funeral was paid for from my personal fortune. I had him interred in a saltstone tomb (he was a hero! A hero's body cannot be simply dumped into the compost bins, to help grow the meanest vegetables! My enemies in Senaar seem unable to grasp this distinction: one law for all! Ironic! Who was it that protected that law, that upheld it? It was him). I visited his tomb this very morning, prior to writing this.

But there is a bitterness even here. When I think of the crowds of cheering Senaarians who gathered at the founding ceremonies of our great nation, I was shocked and personally hurt at the meagreness of the popular show. My enemies tell me that many stayed away in protest at my handling of the war, at the fact of the war at all! Mendacity. How easily cancer breaks into the body politic. But I can still see that littering of thin pale bodies along the route, an insult to a great man. There were so few of them bothered to turn up, and those that did wore such ragged clothing, and seemed to be protesting and preaching sedition with the very boniness of their arms and legs, the very drawn and skull-visible faces. The people are the limb of my body. I will not have it.

But he was so fine.

Petja

I am dying, now. The pain is fiery in me, and vodjaa helps little. But I have fought and fought. I have become what I despised and I am content that I have done good, because it has brought death to so many. Now the habit of command is second-nature to me, and I think in terms of having and owning. In this fashion does the war go on. The last of the birds died last week. Only a handful had survived the attack, and those few were in small cages. They did not prosper. The last of them, a linnet, lost its feathers and finally refused feeding.

Many people have made their way right around the northern coast and have settled, to some degree, in Smith. This is no concern of mine. Some stay in the mountains with us. But people are different from the way they were before. They have been infected with the ways of the hierarchy, or so it seems to me. Couples cohabit, couples stay with one another during childbirth. It seems somehow wrong.

I have fought and fought. More recently, my legs have been disused. My cancers poisoned my lymphatic veins and channels, and the treatment was not as successful as possible. My arms still function but my legs are withered and blackened, as much with the treatment as with the sickness. It is little loss. For months before the operation it was agony to walk on my legs, as if my joints were filled with acid; and they were swollen and ugly. Now, after it, I have them strapped up against my chest, and make of myself a tiny parcel; and then I go on the back of Hamar, an old friend. Hamar is a large man, although he has lost much of his hair to the effects of radiation. But he still has much of his strength, and he carries me like a backpack. The voodoo of war is such that I am now talismanic; people are happy to think of themselves as my people, as my beings.

Hamar is dead, of course, but you knew that. He was bearing me through a skirmish, and I was waving people round the flank of one of the new Senaarian hovercars. They deploy them poorly. They fly up, but then they park and the machine is left stationary: and so we can go round it and destroy it. It had happened once, and then again it happened days ago. We held the attention of the enemy from the large scree and an agile force slipped away and behind. We destroyed the car, it was easy work because the hover-skirt is a weak place. But Hamar fell, still carrying me. A needle went through his lung, which is not a fatal wound in itself, but he bled into his lungs and up to his mouth, until his mask was filled with blood and he drowned.

Normally, high in the mountains as I was, I would have pulled away his mask for him and allowed him to spit out the blood and breathe, because usually the mountains are relatively free of chlorine. But this war has liberated a deal of chlorine: and the enemy bring dischargers that pump it into the battlefield. Their masks are better than ours, and even if they lose them they have sinus-filters, so they use the gas as a weapon of war. We do lose people to chlorine, if their masks are knocked off, or if like Hamar they bleed from their mouths or vomit into them. It is a stupid way to die.

But we have destroyed the car and killed the soldiers, so it was a good day. And Hamar is dead, but I will soon be with him. Every day I kill some Senaarians I thank my private God that I have lived another day, that I survived long enough to kill more of them. And when I die I know that it will be in my heart to rage that I have not been granted one more day to kill some more.

We were able to retrieve three more needlerifles and some heavier projectile guns from the engagement in which Hamar and Capal and three others died.

Textualising these memories has had one curious effect. I have recalled the time before we made war. It has made me realise how war becomes a simple way of living, how it seems to provide all that a human needs as material and spiritual membrane, wrapped tightly around them. It is the reason to go on living; it is what to do, how to do it; it is how to arrange the priorities; it is the end of the day and the beginning of wisdom; it is the left hand and the right hand. I might almost say I am glad to be dying before the war comes to the end, for what would I do afterwards?

Mostly I feel the pain in my bones themselves. My arms do swell a little, and sometimes my teeth come away from their sockets and wiggle. Several teeth have dropped away altogether, but mostly now I eat well-cooked salt eels, where the flesh can be broken off only with the gums, and soft pasta, and some soups. I still have my hair, unlike many of us. But for much of my time since the cancer, I have found the pain a help to war-making. There is a step, a shelf, from feeling unhappy and unmotivated with misery, to suddenly leaping up to energy and killing-fury, where the pain is a goad. Hopping up this step gets harder with each sortie, but I manage it.

I must sleep now. That is the thing. Sleep.

I have dreamt, much more than I used to do. I would say it is my mind putting the events in an ordered sequence, tidying before closing down. Who can say? Sometimes I sleep only to jerk awake. The sensation is as of the world tipping, angling; and I lurch spastically awake. My dreams are of needles, of people dying beside me, of all the stench and pain of war. But if the pain has rooted in the bed of sleep, then the beauty is in a purer place, in my waking imagination.

But then I find myself thinking: is this war? Sometimes the memories arrange themselves as strange, as comical; a circus-war, a war with balloons and strange colours; a war set in a landscape of white, whipped up like peaks of cream. I find myself shrinking, collapsing in on myself so rapidly it feels like falling: and then I am a speck, a pollen-grain-sized man. Here, then: amongst the grains of salt, in all their geometric precision. The universe is filled with them, choked and cluttered with the cubes, the spheres, the rhomboids and the pyramids, all in their bridal white, all in their funeral white. And still I shrink, until my world is only the world between the shapes. I run along the ledge of a grain of salt, and hop from it onto a great ball of salt. White shapes looming huge, and all the rest a blackness.

Rhoda Titus

It was Ruby who told me about the drowned boy. He and his friends had been playing (she said) on one of the hulks, climbing onto the derelict structure, diving off into the water. They liked the hulk, of course, because it was well away from the shore, and well away from the scums of hard salt that accumulate there. But it was the depth out there that did for him. He dived and the mask he was wearing came

227

off, and because there was so much chlorine on the water's surface he choked and went under.

At first I felt an awful, physical sense of horror at the story, as if a fist were clutching at my heart with its nails inwards. Partly this was Ruby's manner of telling it. Her wide face was red with the effort of hurrying up the main plaza and coming to the office, and she looked flushed and excited. Of course she was horrified too, but the impression she gave was of somebody over-delighted to have this piece of gossip. I remember thinking: some small boy's death has this value, that it can be exchanged for an afternoon's chatter in an office. But perhaps I felt bad because, despite myself, the news sucked me in, started my heart rapping. It was the news, and also the environment, the bustling of women about me. I was caught up, and along with the rest of them I hurried out of the office and down the main road to the seashore to watch the army diver bring the body ashore.

I had a hemp handkerchief, and I was blotting my eyes continually; the faint sting of the air simply swelling the sense of how utterly appropriate tears were, of how everybody was crying. I am not saying I cried because everybody was crying; that's not exactly it. It was rather as if some shadowy permission had been granted, and a faucet turned, so that a great pressure of salty water could be relieved. Once, on Earth (how fine those words are! How they captivate the younger people when I talk to them) . . . once, on Earth, at my father's farm, I had seen a vet deal with sheep. The sheep had some sort of intestinal complaint. The complaint seems exactly the right word, because that was what the sheep did: bleated querulously with the discomfort and the fixity of it. They were all lying on their sides, and every one of their sheep bellies was horribly distended, swelled as if with an enormous, monstrous pregnancy. Except that when I went to touch them (I was nine or ten) these bellies felt nothing like the comfortable yielding of my mother's tummy, in which my brother was still hidden. The sheep felt hot and hard, with no give at all, and only a painful-looking sense of absolute bloat. I remember feeling scared that the sheep were going to explode; not so far-fetched an idea, said the vet. And when he arrived, flying over the hills, he said there was no time to lose. With the mixture of open fascination and inscrutable horror of the nine-year-old child I clung to my father's knees and watched the vet go about his work. This is what he did: he took a large hypodermic from his bag, and then he pulled away the plunger and got rid of it, so that he had only the needle and the open phial at the end of it. Then he went from sheep to sheep, rubbing at a place on the wide pressurised belly, and sliding the needle in swiftly. And as he did this, there was *hush* sound, the trapped air inside came out, and the belly sagged and subsided, until it was only a loose sag of skin under the wool. He went from sheep to sheep doing this, and the miracle was as soon as the belly had been deflated, each sheep hopped to his feet and began again at his endless task of munching the grass over the hillside. There was something wonderful in this, to the eyes of a child. Afterwards, the vet took me from sheep to sheep as he fed each one some pill, to help clear the blockage that had caused the problem in the first place, and talked to me kindly. I think now that perhaps he was a little in awe of my father, and that this chatting with the little girl was a way of approaching the great man without having actually to address him. He was an intimidating man, my father; at least he was to other men.

But the memory of the sheep came to me that day, by the waters' edge, because in a sense that was how the tears felt. There was that same mingling of physical necessity combined with a slightly shameful, even absurd and vulgar, voiding. My tears were releasing an intolerable internal compression, and so I could simultaneously hate them for the indignity, for the display, as if they were some appalling escape of wind: and yet at the same time feel so thankful for them that I almost offered up a silent prayer. The day was waning, and the sun was starting to blush slightly as it approached the horizon. Quite a crowd had gathered down by the seashore, and us at the forefront.

'They ought to sink those hulks,' said Ruby.

Clare, who was standing next to me, hummed her agreement. 'They're a danger. Kids will always go out to them, because the shore is always so blocked off with salt crust.'

'And because they're kids,' said Ruby. 'They'll go for that reason alone.'

'They can't sink them,' said somebody else. This was a woman who didn't work in our office, and so who (perhaps) hadn't got into the habits of public cynicism that were the patter with us. 'They will still maybe develop them. They'll be the first boats in the Senaarian Navy.' The hulks had started out as the hulls for the great Galilean barges, ways of taking trade from Senaar to the other southern nations, at a time when the roads weren't safe from the terrorists. But they had not been well built, and they had been extremely expensive, and when the terrorists were got rid of, the need to continue the project had faded away. I think it was true that the official version saw the hulks as a future investment, to be completed one day; but I suppose few enough believed that. Just to look at them, to see how much damage they had endured from the repeated Whispers and the corrosion of the chlorine and salt, belied the idea that they would ever be anything other than floating platforms of decay.

But once this other person had spoken the official line, about the Great Senaarian Navy, the mood to carp at officialdom was dissipated. It gave the occasion a nervous edge, and we felt like the children we were, bickering and bitching about parental rules.

'Still,' said Ruby, voicing one of the few comments that could be offered without being gainsaid by anybody. 'Still, it's a wicked shame about the boy being drowned.'

'Oh, it is,' said Clare. And she started crying again, and so did Ruby. And so did I, with that same half-ashamed, half-grateful sense of public release.

I think I had a particular vision of the drowned boy, one that came to me spontaneously as soon as Ruby had come panting into the office with the news. I saw him as I remembered my brother, Zed, when he was perhaps six or seven. I saw him as that sort of creature, with skin the colour of pale whiskey in the sunshine, and limbs narrow as ropes; I saw him dancing in the yellow sunlight of earth, laughing and rushing. There was always something fluid about Zed. Father was stern with him, because he was a boy, to exactly the degree he was yielding with me because I was a girl. Sometimes Zed would take refuge behind me, as if my frail femaleness could perhaps shield him. He was a fluid boy, always laughing, in motion, always flowing; but my father was as strong and as rigid as a rock. As strong as the hill about which the farm seemed to rest by sufferance; as tall as the town house in which we spent winter, six storeys high, dominating the street. I suppose that was why I thought of Zed, because the collocation of *boy* and *drowned* made me connect with my memories of the fluidity of my brother.

But then the crowd went silent, and the outboat started towards the shore, bringing with it only a hollow disappointment. The diver, tugged along behind the outboat, found his footing on the beach and started up through the water to the dry land, carrying the body, salt breaking like ice about his steps. He was no boy, to my eyes, but rather a man. I later discovered he was fourteen, a week shy of his fifteenth birthday. The tears dried up. He was not a boy, he was a man. They carried his lazily drooping body from the water's edge, with strings of water dribbling from his flaccid arms and head. And suddenly the sight of him revolted me, and I had to turn away.

It seems strange to have experienced that sort of reaction at the thought of a man, of a man dead. I always valued men, felt most comfortable with men. Loved men, their company, their conversation, and simultaneously despised the banality of female companionship. But now I feel banished from the world of men. Now my world is the office, and the women I work with. There are few enough men around anyway, with the war taking the best of them. But after what happened to me, my reactions to men have been broken, like a long bone; the wound's edge still bright with pain. From time to time, I might be struck with the sheer beauty of a squad of men marching down the road, their legs moving with such precise rhythm. But at other times, as with the drowned boy, the fact that I can mentally shuffle a human being from the 'boy' pigeonhole to the 'man' pigeonhole can lead to profound upset. Ruby didn't notice me turn away, or at least if she did I suppose she assumed it was because I was so upset at the thought of a young man drowned. Ruby has never understood how friable I am, or even that a personality can be taken that way, with self-contradictory moods. Ruby sees the world as a straightforward thing.

Afterwards, back in the office, Ruby said, 'I was speaking with somebody in the crowd. They say he was only weeks away from an army commission.'

'I heard that,' said Clare. 'He was only a few days from turning fifteen.'

'It's a shame,' I said, although I didn't really feel it was. But Ruby and Clare exchanged significant glances. If ever I comment on a man they consider it significant, be the comment ever so conventional. They expect me to announce a sudden marriage, I suppose; and they think it odd that I have left it so long. It's been years since hibernation, they say. A good-looking woman like you shouldn't wait around for ever. I know, of course, without it needing to be spelled out, that when they say *good-looking* they actually mean *not as good-looking as you used to be*. I am broad now, and my midriff droops. I have started playing absently with my arms and neck in the shower, tugging at the skin there, pulling it into a flap and letting go. It slinks back into position, but only slowly. It's nothing more than age, of course; nothing but Old Adam as Ruby puts it (when referring to herself, of course; she'd never talk about me in those terms). Ruby is biologically sixty-something and I am only just past forty, so there is more Old Adam about her. But she has a husband, a man younger than her, about whom malicious stories sometimes circulate. He is a supply officer in the army, which keeps him away from the front line. 'Good thing too,' Ruby says, and then blushes for thinking so unpatriotic a thing. I wonder what Ander would have done, had he survived. Would he have insisted on going to the front line? I think he would, because he would have feared the stigma of not doing so. And, more than this, I think he would have been a good front-line soldier.

When Father introduced me to Ander I assumed he was one of Father's 'people'. This nebulous crowd had never really coalesced in my imagination beyond an indistinct vision of interchangeable men in uniforms, or in suits, who sometimes called by the city house. What they did, or precisely how they related to my father, was not something I could easily have put into words. Nonetheless, it seemed to me utterly in the way of things that my father had 'people', just as it seemed logical to assume that all such people were smaller than he was. Father was a tall man, and not bulky about the body, but he held himself so taut he gave the impression of greater muscle than he had; and most of the people I saw him with were indeed shorter than he. Ander certainly was, a tubby little man with a swirl of hair on a bald head that even I could look down on, and which put me in mind of a pattern of debris left dry on the bottom of the sink after the water had curled away down the plughole. Perhaps, on that first day, it struck me as odd that Father went out of his way to introduce me to Ander, when he never usually bothered introducing other of his people. But it was only a full day later when I even began thinking about him properly, only when the realisation came over me (and, of course, Father would never say something like this in so many words) that Ander was intended as my future husband.

I was twenty-five. I had never really thought of myself marrying. Or, to be more precise, I suppose I had *thought* of marrying; I suppose I had always assumed that one day I would be married, as most women were, but I had never *felt* marrying. The emotion had never twisted in my solar plexus. The thinking, accordingly, had an almost abstract quality to it. I suppose I daydreamed about big weddings, about a house of my own, all those girl-things, but in these fantasies the role of the groom was always taken by some imaginary and indistinct man-figure. He was probably of the conventional sort, slim, tall, dark, blue-uniformed, I don't know (it is hard to think back to pre-Ander and actually remember), but by the same token he was absolutely not real. I never, for instance, daydreamed of marrying anybody I actually knew. And when Ander said his first stuttering hellos, my mind was as ignorant and blithe as if he had been an old woman. I said 'hello' back, and we walked in the garden for a while. I thought I was making polite conversation.

Indeed, I *was* making polite conversation; it was just that Ander heard more than politeness in it.

When it occurred to me belatedly, the following day, after a number of carefully non-specific hints from Father, that Ander was going to return and ask for my hand, I did feel panic. There was an instinct to rebel against this future; but that meant rebelling against Father, something I had not thought of doing since I had been a very little girl, and the grounds for rebellion had been accordingly petty. But to deny my father? This was so removed from possibility that I could only conceptualise it in oblique, symbolic ways. I thought of all the things that Ander might do to offend Father, and then I dwelt on imagining Father spouting his fearsome rage at Ander. But this was getting me nowhere.

And so I took myself to my room, at the top of the house, and lay on my bed, and tried to re-imagine Ander minutely. He was so plain that I had barely registered him, and it was hard to conjure up the precise order of his features. He was short, his flesh arranged itself in rolls, but not the loose, flabby rolls of the obese; rather, a series of tight, packed rolls at forehead, chin, neck. He was mostly bald, and his head was speckled like a red-pink egg. His lips bulged. I had never really contemplated kissing a man before, but as I struggled to recall his lips it seemed to me revolting to have to put my *own* thin lips against two such thick ones. A man shorter than myself! All the ridiculous girlhood fantasies, the dreams that most girls have at a younger age, pressed for entry to my mind: surely I deserved a soap opera husband? A man *taller* than me, as *young* as me? A handsome man? I thought how grateful I was that Zed was off on another training camp, because he would certainly have mocked me with theatrical and comical expressions of disgust at the prospect of Ander, and I daresay he would have made me cry.

But the thought of that somehow brought me a certain calm. I was able to discipline myself. When Ander returned two days later, he was even more nervous than before. We went into the garden again, as he hummed and coughed his way towards the question. And as I sat there I was struck by something about him. He was, as Zed would hootingly have pointed out, quite ugly; and even his ugliness was without distinction, for there were any number of men out in the city whose faces and figures were equally squat and coarse. But, for all this, he was a man, and a person. I stared at his eyes (it made him nervous, I recall), and I thought to myself, perhaps he was handsome once. He was forty-four when he asked me to marry him, but I thought of him at seventeen, or eighteen. And his eyes were a glowing blue colour. Indeed the flurry of his complexion, that redness, only served to make the blue eyes stand out all the more powerfully. I thought of him young, slim (maybe), with a full head of hair, and then I thought of those same eyes beaming out of his face. Why do eyes age not at all? Why can't human beings be made out of eye-stuff, so that we might maintain our glow into old age? I thought to myself that Ander's features connoted not 'handsomeness' but 'man-ness', and that as such they were perfectly fine.

After the wedding, we went away for a honeymoon cruise, on a thirty-metre yacht that another friend of my father's loaned us. It was Ander and myself, with two crewmen and a chef. But, as we sailed round and about, through Hercules' Pillars and down the coast of Africa, I got to see another side of my new husband. Where before he had always been stumbling shy, physically awkward and stiff around me, or else tripping over garden weeds, or dropping cutlery from the dinner table, in the bright yellow honeymoon sunshine he clambered about the yacht like a monkey. He stripped to the waist, revealing the same patchy, swirly hair on his body as head, and sprinted up and down the rigging. I was quietly upset by this, for reasons I wasn't entirely able to articulate to myself. It was, somehow, unseemly; as if my husband had revealed himself a fraud, as if his gaucherie had been nothing but an act and now he was taunting me with his true agility. Perhaps I was angry because a part of me had hoped I had been marrying a man who would always be less than me, and this display jarred with that expectation. Certainly I was rather angry, and the anger came out in high-pitched shouts of concern up the rigging. 'Be careful, dear! You'd better come down now.' Or, 'Don't, don't, you'll fall in. There are sharks in these waters, you know.'

After the honeymoon I did indeed get a house of my own, two hundred metres down the avenue from Father's town house. And with nothing to do, and the housework attended to by servants, I spent much time strolling up the way and simply being in my old and more familiar place. Father would sometimes come across me, and joke that I had run away from home. That was a fantasy that sometimes occurred to me, in fact. Not that my husband was a bad husband. He was not. I think he was a fine husband. But there was a certain awkwardness that never wilted between us, a certain kind of wrapping that he was never able quite to pull off me.

Part of it was ill-timing, of course. The first three years of our marriage coincided with the coming to fruition of the plans for the Voyage, the voyage here, to Salt. Ander's own anxieties about going, about liquidating enough capital to see us clear on the new world, about arranging all his affairs on Earth, all that was rather over-shadowed for me by the ructions in the family that was no longer, strictly or completely, mine. Zed refused to go to the new world, absolutely refused. Father absolutely insisted that he would, that we all would. There were horrible arguments, in which Father shouted about how the army had taught Zed no discipline, and in which Zed howled, positively howled, a series of incoherences. And these were only the fights that I witnessed; there must have been many more, when I was down the road in my own home. Through all of them the one strand that kept us as a family together was that Zed never once contemplated actually leaving Father's house and making a life for himself. Father seemed so absolutely a fact of nature with us that we could no more conceive of an alternative to his will than we could an alternative to our hearts' beating.

Eventually Zed agreed, gave way before Father's will. The yelling he had done, the shouting down of so inviolable an icon as Father, seemed to leave him listless and drained. And so we were all prepared. It was Father's great project, the culmination of his connections with the high-powered military people. And for a while after Father's death, Zed became tearfully obsessed with going to the new planet. He was going, he said, so that he could devote his life to building a new world, a monument to Father's memory. 'He showed us the way,' I remember him saying. 'Father showed us the Promised Land, but he was a Moses and God has taken him from us.' My own sort of grieving was so different from Zed's that all this display merely bounced off me. After two weeks of melodrama, bluster and weeping, Zed cooled, calmed, even seemed to stiffen a little. He was not going, he said. He could not go. Why should he throw away a perfectly good life on this distant alien world? Why should he subject himself to the frontier hardships of some unformed wilderness? He never suggested I not go, of course, because he knew my husband was going, and clearly I would do what my husband did.

And, recently, I have begun to wonder if I did the right thing in coming to Salt. Putting the question like that seems to invite a negative answer, but I really mean the question open-endedly. When I think of Zed, still alive (I suppose) on Earth now, as we speak, I can grow homesick. Zed is the closest thing left in the universe to Father. But then I think of that old world and I can only envision it in terms of its closure.

Ander died in the hibernation tank. I wept more publicly for him than I had done for Father, but again that was partly because many people died in hibernation and there was a public mood of tears. The infectious quality of social grief, like laughter. And, hand on heart, the truth was I wasn't exactly crying for him. I was crying for Father, for the strength that he breathed and moved, the strength that defined him. And for a heart that couldn't flex, and so burst, in a catastrophic attack that knocked him clear out of his chair and into the bookshelf and left him lying on the floor of his study with hardbacks littered on top of him.

I have only slowly emerged, then, from the grieving for my father, although that grieving has been a hidden thing. One of the ways it came out was in my establishing the Women's League of Senaar, which kept my hands free from the Devil's mischief on the voyage out. It pleased out Leader to regard me as something of a spokes-woman for the female opinion, as if such a thing could be easily condensed. And I worked hard at the League, keeping locked deep away in my breast the fact that I didn't really like women, and that I certainly did not respect them. Looking back on it (and the League was more or less wound up when we finally established Senaar on Salt), I think of it as an elaborate device for placing me in the company of men, of winning approval from men in power. The day I met the Leader for the first time was one of the proudest of my life. But if that was all the Women's League of Senaar was, then I was in some sense lying to everybody. I prayed about this, and asked guidance from God. Perhaps God was taking the issue out of my hands by the turn of events. Because, once the war began, there really was no further need for a League of Women. It is rather paradoxical, in fact. Nowadays, it is possible to walk down Barlei Parade and get the impression that Senaar is nothing but women. Even the few men who loiter around the city have a feminine air to them. Old and bent with the vanity of old men, all expensive fabrics and overstated neckties rather than the plain blue of the uniform of the young men. Or a few sick men, wounded or lame, and they too tend to preen like women; forever stopping to examine their reflection in a shop window, to see whether their empty sleeve is tucked neatly enough into their jacket pocket. Oh, I shouldn't have such thoughts about heroes of Senaar, men who have given up parts of their body, but increasingly the urge comes upon me. Women are wounded too, but because the wounds are not so blatantly displayed they go unremarked, ignored.

Last week Ruby came into the office full of joy. 'It's all over the street Visuals,' she said. 'The war is over!'

It almost came out of me, like an ill-controlled belch, to sneer at this and say, 'What, again?' But if I had been sarcastic, Ruby would either have misunderstood, thinking me sincere, or – if she had actually caught the sense behind my words – would have been deeply hurt. And because she believes in the Leader, it was no contradiction to her that the war could be announced as over, as won, and yet still carry on being prosecuted. Each victory announcement filled her with a real joy.

Actually, I see I am painting Ruby as a sort of fool, an idiot, and she

238

is not. I suppose she is able to swallow the official line on the war with so much ease because most of her thoughts are away from official things. Perhaps most people are this way. She thinks of the day's work, of what to cook for her husband when she goes home, of what Visuals to watch over the weekend. She is most comfortable with gossip about people (women, inevitably, because there are only women around) which has nothing to do with the official life of Senaar. And perhaps this provides her with comfort, with a shield against the brutalities of the larger picture.

After the incident with the drowned boy, for instance, we were back in the office, all three of us talking about it. 'It is such a tragic event,' Clare was saying. 'He would have been fitted with a sinus-filter after his fifteenth birthday, wouldn't he?'

'Yes,' said Ruby. 'That might have saved him.'

'Fourteen,' said Clare. 'Such a tragic age at which to die. So much ahead of him.'

I felt like saying: the army ahead of him, and his body stuck like a porcupine by the enemy until he bled his life onto the salt. But of course, I said no such thing. And, anyway, this was not the line Ruby and Clare's thoughts were following.

'There are so few eligible young men,' said Ruby.

'And now one less.'

'The young men in their uniforms . . .' said Ruby, her voice wandering a bit. It was not a sentence, just a random piece of speaking, but it communicated enough to Clare, who nodded and said, 'Hmm.' Then they both looked at me.

I am sure they find me odd. They are unsettled by the way I sometimes seem dissociated from life in Senaar, from the war. I might sound snide in what I say about Ruby, but if I were ever to challenge her banality she would flush with controlled rage, and tell me (as she has done several times in a more indirect way) that I was not in the city on that terrible night when the enemy first bombed Senaar. That I did not experience the horror of it, and that therefore I have no grounds to speak. Perhaps she is right. Certainly there have been other bombings, one of which broke all the windows in our office, and threw us to the ground with our hands over our mouths. But I still feel the war is something that happened whilst I have been away.

After Ander died, I found I had plenty of money to live a comfortable life. And for a while, this was what I did. Most of my time was connected with the church; at first, actually helping finance and build a church, with a big end window quintiglazed and overlooking the Galilee. And then there were many duties associated with the church. I spent a lot of time praying. But after I came back from my ill-fated diplomatic expedition to the enemy, I did nothing at all. I sat in my house, and literally stared at the wall. Or I waited outside, heedless of the radiation danger, and watched people hurry by. Money can buy that level of depression as well as that level of indolence.

But, as the war heated up, my money became diminished. There were three devaluations of money savings in as many weeks, and then a devaluation of vote savings (where a deal of my fortune was tied up). At the same time, food began to go up in price to an astonishing degree. Prices would increase between morning and evening, so that people took to eating breakfast as the main meal of the day to save a little money. Standing in the street opened up a new display, of thin and ragged people, particularly Eleupolisian wastrels, workmen and women whose fixed wages after tax meant they could no longer afford to buy food. A few of these tried begging, but that was an expulsion offence. Most they just hung about outside, as if daring the sun to give them cancer and so end their misery.

It was not that I was rendered exactly destitute by the devaluations or the price increases, although things certainly became tight. But it seemed a hint from Fate, from the Divine, and I took it as such. I found work in the office of the Vote Treasury: not one of those brokerage houses, where all is spent haggling and shouting with people on the phone. That was too disruptive for me. No, I work in the Official Vote Treasury. The work is light enough, and I was high-profile enough to be a plausible applicant for the post as Chief Secretary. But there is actually little to do, apart from occasional meetings of the Senate or Parliament where Official votes are required in a hurry. And the pay is small: Ruby and Clare have husbands who provide most of the money for their lives; and I have my savings. My inheritance. I certainly couldn't exist on a basic official salary.

But that is exactly what I am talking about: the attitude of my last sentence. I work at the heart of one of the crucial institutions of our democracy, the very process by which the ballot operates. But do I feel engaged in the political world? No. I feel I sit in an office all day with Ruby and Clare and listen to them gossip. I feel I bite down comments that would be inappropriate, and that would only cause them pain. I feel I go home at night to an empty flat, unless it is a church service evening. Some days I come in especially early, because I have nothing to do at home. On these occasions, I find myself talking to the cleaning-man, a polite young Eleupolisian who speaks the common tongue only poorly. He comes in before dawn, and scrubs and rinses the entire office with cleaning equipment he had to buy himself. But whenever he sees me he drops his eyes, fearful that I might have him deported. I can't believe he earns enough to afford even the most meagre meal, and yet I suppose it is better for him in Senaar than in the chaos of Eleupolis. He is in his mid-twenties, I suppose: a thin, bearded young fellow. Yet I think of him as a boy, even though he is a man. It does matter to me, this awkward mental shuffling of definitions, boy, man, man-boy, boy-man. Sometimes, talking to this young boy, whose name I do not even know, I will watch him slowly emerge from his shell, his smile spreading to reveal his teeth, as his shattered language pieces together some or other comical observation. But then I will hear the door open downstairs, and Ruby's voice cooing hello up the stairwell, and I will frown and wave the boy away with my hand. It would not do to be caught talking with an Eleupolisian. Ruby would be shocked. And, just before he turns to carry his bucket away, down the stairs, into his cupboard, I see his face fall back into its usual miserable lines. When I write about it now, I find a certain watery sense of sadness coming into me. But at the time, if I am honest, underlying it all is a sort of smouldering glee that I can raise him up only to crush him again.

The other day, the wife of a senior officer called by the Treasury. She had some spurious reason for calling, I suppose; preparing the ground for some official military requisition of votes. But in fact she came to display herself before the three of us. She knew Ruby from an Officers' Wives club, and she had been in the area (she said) buying a new stole.

Her name was Pel. She was a bulky woman, with a creaky skeleton that groaned under the weight of her flesh as she moved. Her skin had a strange woody look to it, not grained exactly but with a salmon-coloured mottling that might have been her make-up. She was dressed in a bulging dark brown dress-suit that rustled like dead leaves when she gestured with her arms, or when she crossed her legs after sitting down. The stole was very fine: a carefully manufactured ersatz mink. 'Go on,' she urged, breathily. 'Feel the hairs.'

We all of us felt the hairs.

She stood before us, and stretched out both arms like a crucifix, with the stole draped from left hand to right hand and round the back of her neck. 'Isn't it magnificent?' she said. We all made the noises of agreement.

Then she sat down. Before the war, we might have offered her tea, but there had been no tea for over a year.

'It's a beauty, a beauty,' said Ruby. 'But why have you bought it, Pel dear? Is it for some function, or simply to impress your lovely husband?'

'Well,' said Pel, confidential. 'It's not confirmed yet, but my husband tells me that there may well be a special little gathering next week. That the two of us may be in the same room as – whisper it to no one – the Leader!' She sat back, with a 'what-do-you-think-of-that' expression on her face.

I watched Ruby. I could see her beaming, whilst beneath her face her muscles worked. To be at a social gathering with the Leader was an impressive prize within the economy of gossip. Ruby was searching for some way to upstage it, or at least to take some of the glory from her visit.

In fact, it was Clare who spoke. 'Oh, I'm so jealous!' she said, ingenuously. 'I would love to meet our Leader.'

'Rhoda has met our Leader,' Ruby said, a little too quickly. 'Haven't you, dear? Met him more than once.'

Pel paused just long enough before turning to me. 'Have you?' she breathed. 'Have you really?'

I almost sighed, but managed to hold it back. Sighed, because every time I had told this story to a group of women the narrative inevitably led from the glory of talking with the Leader to the dust and ashes of the subsequent events. Indeed, so obvious was the trajectory that my few friends at church took care not to bring it up in public. But Ruby's way was narrow-sighted. At the moment, all she could see was the opportunity for impressing this fine-dressed woman. Later, as the conversation wound its way to the inevitable painfulness, she would gulp and blush and feel stupid. But it was the nature of her short-sightedness that she never learnt circumspection from it.

'Yes,' I said. 'I have.'

'What was he like?' Pel asked. 'I saw him speak once, addressing a whole crowd. I thought then he had real *presence*.'

For a moment I allowed myself to hope that Pel's reminiscences would drown out my own need to retell the story. But she halted with a stutter on the last word that was almost a cough. 'But how did you meet him? Why? Was it Treasury business?'

'No. It was before I worked in the Treasury.'

'She had private audiences with him,' said Ruby.

'*Really?*'

I paused, but then went through with it. 'It was before the War,' I said. 'It was about liaising with the enemy. With Als, and the Leader asked me to represent my people as a diplomatic officer.' There was a silence at this. I could see Pel putting two and two together.

'That was you?' she said, her eyes bulging with astonishment. 'You were the person who went to Als? Well, I had no idea.' I thought that was a stupid thing to say, since she had only met me for the first time a few minutes earlier. But I am too harsh. It was one of the things people say. I might almost have been able to let the whole story slide past, to turn it back to her with some question about her stole, if she hadn't added, 'But weren't you captured? I heard you were tortured.' The last word, *tortured*, came out in a half-stifled breathy tone, as if propriety had at last caught up with the speaker. There was a sudden chill in the room. I felt an appalling desire to outrage this woman, all these women. I wanted her complacent expression of vague pity transformed into bewilderment, as if I could, with a few words, take this stranger and dip her in the pool of pain so that she needn't take it all so lightly. As if this is (I felt like saying) a matter for conversation with a near stranger! But there was a bar that came down internally, and all the blackness and decay, all the bulging evil of it, was blocked back. It had no name, it was only 'it'.

After 'it' had happened, after I had come back from Als, I had been *debriefed*. Several military officers had promised me that I would undergo this process, as they brought me coffee. Their eyes were wide, their mouths a little open, at the torn shirt I was still huddling about my body; and at the bruises. They brought me coffee, and brought me an army-issue chemise that was too large and too scratchy for comfort, but I wore it anyway. And, of course, I knew what 'debriefing' was; I was not so clueless. But in my state, which was a strange one, rigid but liable to shatter, I could not hear the word right. I had been brought up to use the word *briefs* to refer to undergarments, the sort of word that paid a delicate homage to the fact that if such things had to be mentioned at all, it ought to happen and pass quickly. As I sat there, in a tiny military room, holding the huge mug of coffee with both my hands folded around it, my mind vividly pictured my being de-briefed, being violently undressed, and I began to shudder. Another part of my mind was trying to be stern, telling me *don't be ridiculous Rhoda, you are being ridiculous* and saying *these are your people, they will help you*. But in all my time in that army installation, the three days before I was released to my home again in the city, I could only control the shuddering, and the urge to scream out, by actively freezing myself inside. I think, and I am not given to hyperbole, that at no other time in my life have I had to be so strong.

At the debriefing, when it happened, I was quizzed about this and that. Mostly they wanted to know about the capacity of the Alsists to make war (they called them, throughout, 'the anarchists'; it was only later that the habit was formed of calling them 'the enemy'). But there was an awkward five minutes when they asked me to go through the events of the drive south. They had brought in my old ripped shirt and laid it on the table in front of me, almost as if it were a witness against me, and I fixed my gaze upon it so that I wouldn't have to look at the male faces. And I filled my ears with my internal voice; *they are trying to help you, these are your people,* and I tried to work through the story. The most important thing, I felt, was that I not cry. It seemed the most crucial thing in the world that I not cry. When I came to the crux of the matter, though, I faltered. The words would not come. One of the men there asked, in a voice hushed with what he presumably thought was respect, but which sounded in my ears too much like horror, 'Were you . . . interfered with?' That, then, became the expression that captured the event. And because it was so evasive a phrase, it somehow served its purpose. At all the other occasions afterwards when I was asked, I used it: I was interfered with. But that was a word, a polysyllabic bar in itself, that only blocked out the inner turmoil all the more completely. And behind the bar there was a sense of swelling, a growing.

In the office that day, I felt a demoniacal urge to scream at this woman, to use the words I had always been too inhibited to use (even here, in this document). But the urge passed. A part of me knew, you see, that the momentary release would have left a space into which a tempest of guilt and remorse would have swirled. And so I said nothing, only dropped my eyes a little.

Pel said, 'How terrible!' And then again, 'How awful.'

Ruby scowled. I realised then that she felt cheated, as if the credit that would otherwise have reflected on her for having a friend and workmate who had actually met the Leader had been poisoned. It didn't matter that it had been that Alsist man who had done the poisoning; it was somehow, in that context, my fault. I suppose, ideally, Ruby would have wanted a friend who had simply met the Leader, without any of the subsequent unsavoury stuff. But because of who I was, of what happened to me, Ruby was trapped in a circumstance where her spontaneous glowing of pride was always going to be polluted, and polluted by something that we, women together, could not even name.

To try and rescue something of Ruby's credit, then (and certainly not because I felt like speaking further, for I would rather have said nothing) I tried to lift the mood. 'I only met him twice,' I said. 'And once more when there were some other people present, but only twice for personal meetings. He was always extremely courteous.'

Of course, as I said the word, I realised how feeble it was. It was not that it did not describe the Leader, because that was exactly how he was: courteous, with all its connotations of external politeness and chivalry, and a deeper sense of distance, of a man who had no connection with women and was not interested in cultivating one. But the word was hopeless and inadequate to Ruby and Pel's expectations of a description of the Leader. They wanted more.

'So, what was he like?' Pel urged.

I almost gave up, because I really didn't have the energy to go on with it. But the consequences would have been more unpleasant, so I added, 'He's a great man. You can really feel it when you're with him. You have an almost electric sense of a people's destiny resting on him. But he has such vigour, it's a wonder.' Or I said something like this, which I have said any number of times at gatherings of women, or at parties or whatever.

And Pel breathed, her anxiety at my unmentionable suffering, anxiety that it might intrude its ugly self into the conversation, finally relieved. 'I always said,' she said. 'I always said that he had a real *presence*.'

There have been several dreams about the drowned boy-man. In some of them it is I who do the drowning, stuffing a shirt into his mouth so that he chokes and gags. I wake up from these dreams feeling dreadful, sweating and asthmatic, gasping for breath myself. I go through a litany of panics in my head (has the window broken, am I choking on chlorine? Is the house burning?) before I am able to settle myself. But the dreams keep coming back. My only remedy, I think, is prayer. Maybe it is only inside a church that I can step away from the world of men, the world of war, and speak a bubble of peace that can wrap me around. It is a stifling thing, war: it is a society drowning.

But the irony, I suppose, is that even my religion has changed. The worship of everybody else seems disjointed and wrongheaded to me nowadays, and increasingly I go to the church at odd times in the day, slipping out of the office to avoid the crowds.

It would be too vigorous a locution to say *I had a realisation*; but perhaps, in a more passive voice, I could say there has come a realisation; it has crept over me in the night. I used to think my vision of God was that of my people, my Leader. But the war has given me the occasion to revise this. I realise that for the enemy, God is nothing but a version of their own egos, a monstrous shadow of desire and appetite sitting on the throne. And of course, as against such blasphemy our cause is just. But the realisation has dawned on me, latterly, that God for the people of Senaar is something collective, like the will that glues together the action of thousands; like the patterns of light cast on a wall, or the scurrying of silver-skinned fish, in the sunlit waters, moving and turning as a single organism. Our Leader sees this pattern in himself, and God is our Leader in another place. God is that into which we all are absorbed. But the longer the war has gone on, the more that has happened to me, the less I think of God in these terms. The *point* of God, if I can say so without overreaching my phrase, is not to dissolve in Him. He is what keeps the others out, he is the membrane that defines me as myself and not as some helpless watery nothing. And the elaborate husbanding of the thing inside me, the constant vigilance, will find its point in God. The thing that it is an unending effort of will not to vomit out, the thing stuck inside me, is a great jewel, the bevelled edges painful, some-

247

times, against my soft internal organs. But a jewel of great price. I see myself clutching my Soul to myself, a case containing an unimaginable treasure, a thing that others would steal. And this guarding of the precious thing is the point: to be able to arrive, and to present the Father with this gift.